The EMPATHS *of* DRAYON

Cheryl Jackson Poules

Library of Congress Control Number: 2011930405

ISBN: 978-0-9836144-0-1

First Edition: July 2011

Printed in the United States of America

Cover Design/Interior Layout: Ronda Taylor, www.taylorbydesign.com
Cover Illustrator: WillowRaven

Drayon Publishing
663 Springvale Road
Castle Rock, CO 80104
www.DrayonPublishing.com

*To my father, who gave me the happiest childhood possible.
He loved who I was, showed me how to laugh, and most of all
allowed my imagination to soar. I miss you, Dad.*

Acknowledgments

I would like to thank my editor, Karen Reddick, for her wonderful suggestions, professional assistance and most of all, for helping to bring the story of Aine and Aiden and all of the empaths to the readers. What a process! I'd never have done it without you.

I'd also like to thank my daughter, Marie, for being the first of my loved ones to read the manuscript and coach Mom on ways to make it better. Thank you for believing in me, dearest.

Finally, to my husband, Jay, for infinite patience in letting me sit eight hours at a time immersed in the world of Drayon and supporting the need to finish just one more chapter.

Contents

THE SEARCH

He slammed his goblet on the table and watched the wine drip like blood onto his hand. Wrapping his cloak around him he rose abruptly from his chair and strode to the ornate mirror obscured in the dark shadows of the corner.

He never glanced at his reflection in the glass as he touched each ornate design in exactly the correct order. The hidden door behind the mirror opened silently and he grabbed the brace of candles from the shelf to better light his way.

With a wave of his hand the lights embedded in the stone along the passage offered pale lighting for the dark stairway leading below. The door closed behind him and he locked the passage even though he knew that no one would ever enter his chambers unless bidden to do so.

The dank air tasted stale, with a faint nausea of death beneath. Spider strands caught his cheeks and lips, and he heard the scurry of rats in the murky alcoves as he passed. Turning the corner at the base of the stairs he startled a large gray cat who stared at him with sinister green eyes. In fury, he tried to kick it, but as if the animal read his thoughts, it hissed and slipped silently away.

Reaching his destination he stood still just to be sure. The deathly silence was punctuated only by the whisper of bat wings and water dripping. Satisfied, he unlocked the door, stepped through, and shoved the bolt to lock it behind him. Lighting the lamps within, he glanced around at the small room cluttered with chests and boxes. To anyone else this would seem a storage room filled with junk from generations past.

Making his way through the clutter he touched his hand to a stone near the floor in the corner. Like the mirror in his chambers keyed only to his touch, the doorway formed and he passed within.

Underneath the bottom shelf in the far corner, the chest he sought laid half hidden. He knelt next to the chest, his dark eyes reflected in the golden latch.

"Ecflon kadis," He murmured and smiled with grim satisfaction as the latch clicked open.

Almost reverently he ran his fingers over the thick leather cover and his heart beat faster in anticipation as he grasped it and lifted it from the chest and held it close, wrapping his cloak around it. He closed his eyes and inhaled, forcing a sense of calm to his angry chaotic thoughts. He was done with waiting, the time was at hand.

Holding the tome close he doused the lights and locked the door behind him again and started back up the steps to his room in the tower above. A fine sheen of sweat beaded his face as he reset the mirror's code and he placed the ancient manuscript on the table dropping his cloak across the chair.

The lights dimmed as he caressed each page and the ancient words danced and faded on the page as he tried to decipher the meaning. For a moment he wondered if he had triggered something dangerous.

At last he found the obscure passage. It had been written in a very old dialect and he was careful to translate every word precisely as he transposed them to a fresh sheet of parchment.

The candles had nearly burned to stubs by the time he finished but as he read the translation, a slow smile of satisfaction grew on his lips.

Gathering the ingredients he knew that it was no surprise that none had ever succeeded the summoning. They had never understood how to make the exact elixir.

He mixed it into his wine and with the elixir singing in his blood he focused intently, grasping his personal crystal. He sensed a throb of power from the pulsing light at the extreme end of the celestial band. It was almost beyond his reach but he thrust his consciousness along the path until her image formed in his mind. The words formed in his mind, filled with menace and control, "Soon enough, dear girl. You will come to me, soon enough."

CHAPTER ONE

The Crystal Ball

Slipping out the front door, Aine rounded the corner of the house and started across the driveway, when Mother's strident voice stopped her.

"Just where are you going, young lady?"

Mother stood in the back doorway; her arms crossed and her infernal radar in full force. Salt and pepper hair and the stern disapproval on her face, made her appear older than her mid-forties.

Aine kept her voice light. "I told Jessie that I would take some things up to the loft in her barn today."

"Why is it that you always find time to help everyone else, but never have time to do what I ask?" Mother glared.

You didn't ask me to do anything, Aine thought. She glanced nervously at the man across the street outside sweeping his porch. There was no doubt that he could hear Mother, in fact probably half of the neighborhood could hear her.

Aine walked toward her mother keeping her voice soft, "What do you need, Mom? I can help Jessie later if you need something now."

Mother's voice dripped with sarcasm, "Never mind, Aine. I can do it myself."

Aine struggled to keep from rolling her eyes. Keeping her face straight she said, "I can come right back, it shouldn't take me long."

Dad came around the back of the house, his jeans stained from working in the garden. He recognized the look of confrontation in his wife's eyes and leaned the rake on the shed wiping the sweat from his face with his bandana. "What's the matter, Nora?"

Mother's lips drew tight, "Oh, it's nothing."

Aine sighed, "Mom..."

"Just go, Aine. Jessie needs your help, and we mustn't keep her waiting," Mother snapped.

"Oh, for Christ's sake, Nora, what is the matter now?" Dad said irritably.

The neighbor put his broom down and sat down on his front step intrigued by the spectacle. Aine, on the other hand, had no desire to witness the inevitable bickering so she walked quickly to her neighbor's barn and picked up the boxes inside the door.

Balancing them carefully she climbed up the steep stairway trying to dismiss her mother from her thoughts. The woman was never satisfied. If they went to a restaurant the food was always bad and had to be sent back; if they visited someone's home they would have to listen for days to criticisms of the décor or the behavior of their children.

Why did Dad put up with it? He was so different from her mother. He never failed to lend a helping hand if someone needed it and with his children, he was fair and open, always a teacher at heart. He taught them to consider their choice of actions. Nothing could be worse, in Aine's mind, than disappointing him. But conversely, Mother was always disappointed with them and with everything else.

Aine surveyed the loft of the barn where the rays of sunlight leaked through the cracks in the walls and ceiling, painting the loft with motes of dusty beams. The dirty window at the apex of the roof shone a brilliant square on the floor of the loft. She sneezed from the dust and musty smell of discarded junk, but could also smell the rich sweetness of honeysuckle from beyond the cracked window. Finding a spot near the corner for the boxes she carefully set them on the floor and sighed. At least today's tantrum had taken her mind off that stupid nightmare.

Aine sat down on an old chair and flipped her long golden-brown hair over her shoulder, *I'm seventeen, only one more year before I'm out of here. I can make it,* she thought.

A clatter of glass startled her out of her musings and Aine chuckled with relief when she saw Jessie's cat, Pin, disappear into the box where she kept her kittens. Curious to see if their eyes were open yet, Aine followed her. The kittens played and tumbled on each other mewing when Pin lay down. They snuggled up to nurse with their tiny paws kneading her belly as muted purrs filled the box.

A stray shaft of sunlight caught her eye and she followed it to a sphere sitting on a low table. She'd been in this loft many times and had never seen anything like it. The globe shimmered as the sunlight refracted along the surface, radiating a rainbow of light throughout the loft. Turning in a slow circle, Aine was enchanted by the sparkling kaleidoscope of colors dancing on the walls and ceiling.

Wanting a closer look, Aine stepped carefully around the clutter on the floor and knelt beside the table. The surface of the globe felt warm to the touch and a strong tingling traveled from her fingertips to her shoulders. Pressing her palms on the surface, Aine felt a sensation of movement as if she were in a speeding car. A wave of dizziness swept over her and her vision faded in and out. She pulled her hands away and the sense of movement and dizziness dissipated. A soft swirling glow shone from within the globe.

She hesitantly reached out to touch it again. Stretching her hands around the sides, she tried to lift it but it was heavy and she feared breaking it. At her touch she heard an insistent mumbling, like that of a distant crowd. The murmur grew into a strong crescendo, filling her mind, like a roaring wave, it threatened to pull her into its undertow. Despite an inexplicable yearning to maintain her hold and go with it, Aine pulled her hands from the surface and sat back.

As quickly as it had begun, the globe's light faded and it was once more an empty orb. Aine felt an unaccountable loss. She lifted her eyes to search in vain for the diamond rainbow of lights, but they were gone.

The light in the window seemed different and Aine heard her mother's faint call to dinner. *Already?* Aine thought. *I just finished lunch before I came to the loft.*

She had to learn more about that globe and she debated trying to take it with her.

Mother's voice, more strident now, called again.

"If I've been here all afternoon she'll be really furious. I have to go!" Aine said aloud.

It was unlikely that anyone else would come to the loft before tomorrow, but she wanted to be sure she could find the crystal ball quickly when she returned. Spotting a dusty red scarf Aine tossed it over the globe, climbed down the ladder and hurried home.

As she set the table, Aine wondered if the nightmare and the globe were linked in some way. She had never experienced two such bizarre events in the same day. She found them both disturbing and intriguing.

Maybe Carolinda would have some idea about the nightmare and the crystal ball. As she finished the dishes she saw her sister grab the keys from the bowl on the table.

"Are you going out?" Aine asked.

"Yeah, Janet and I are working on our project tonight. See ya later, Aine." Carolinda smiled and closed the screen door behind her.

I've got to talk with someone about this or I'll never get to sleep tonight, Aine thought as she walked slowly up the stairs to her room.

Her girlfriends would think she was certifiable, and she certainly couldn't talk about dreams or some weird crystal ball with her parents.

Then it came to her. Lula would be the perfect person to share this with. Lula was a healer who lived on the outskirts of town. Many of the town's people believed Lula was a witch, including Aine's mother, but Aine only saw her as a wise and caring friend. Aine had often spoken with Lula about dreams and she always encouraged Aine's questions without making her feel foolish.

Grabbing a sweater she ran back downstairs and out to where her parents were sitting in the backyard. Her younger sister, Jenna and a neighbor kid were chasing lightning bugs in the yard while her parents chatted over coffee. The citronella candles glittered in the dusk, their sweet scent mingling with Dad's roses.

"I'm going over to Danae's for a while," Aine called.

"Don't go downtown, and be back by ten," Mother instructed.

Aine stifled her sarcastic reply. "Okay," she said, cheerfully.

Aine knew that Danae had gone to the lake with her boyfriend, Johnny but her friend always covered for her with

Mother. If she hurried, she'd have several hours to talk to Lula and Mother would already be in bed by the time she returned home.

Walking briskly up the street Aine crossed the railroad tracks and started up the steep path of the hill. Trees whispered in the gentle breeze and the path opened into a large meadow at the top of the hill. The stars began to appear in the summer sky and fireflies darted through the field and trees, blinking in the long grass. Aine heard the faint tinkling of Lula's harp and picked up her pace so she'd arrive in time to hear Lula play.

A towering evergreen and a handsome weeping willow leaned toward each other in front of the cabin as if they were protecting it with their branched arms. Her nose prickled at the peppery tang of the marigolds edging Lula's garden and in the fading light she could just make out the shed where Lula kept her ancient bicycle.

Lula's nanny goat, Pricilla, bleated in greeting and followed Aine to the porch. Aine chuckled as she fed the turnip she'd brought from home to the greedy animal and imagined her as a grouchy-looking old lady.

Aine knocked and let herself in. Lula always knew who had come before they reached her door but Aine called in greeting, "Hi, Lula."

The rich scent of dried flowers and herbs that hung from crooked hooks on the kitchen ceiling, mingled with the delicious aroma of fresh baked cookies that sat cooling on the table. The kitchen shelves were filled with jars holding Lula's healing herbs and potions. An old-fashioned pump built into the sink supplied sweet pure water. A blackened Franklin stove sat in the far corner of the parlor and it kept the cabin cozy even in the coldest weather.

Lula's skills as a healer brought the Indians from the reservation north of town and some of the older folks to visit her often. Often she was able to cure ailments that stumped the local doctors. She was a mystic of sorts and most people in the village thought she was a little strange.

Aine had known and loved Lula since she had come upon the cabin as a curious eight year old. The older woman had become a mentor of sorts and Aine respected her vast knowledge about everything from music to magic.

The golden glow of the lamps shone on Lula's silver hair and she smiled at Aine in greeting, a gentle touch of love in her eyes. She moved to put the harp away.

"Oh please," Aine pleaded, "Don't stop! Play just one more."

"And I suppose you want *The Gypsy Rover?*" Lula leaned the instrument back against her.

"Oh yes!" Aine said as she pulled one of the cane-back chairs closer. She had always loved that story about a young girl who fell in love with a wild gypsy and ran away with him. The girl's father searched for his daughter far and wide and when he finally found her, he learned that the man was not a gypsy at all, but the lord of a large estate.

Lula tuned a couple of strings and Aine closed her eyes while Lula sang. When the song was done and the harp fell silent, Aine opened her eyes, smiled and sighed. She never tired of the harp or the song.

"So, Aine, what brings you here this evening?" Lula said.

Aine hesitated, still caught in the melody's spell. She met Lula's clear blue gaze, "I found something very unusual in Jessie's barn," she paused, "and I had a nightmare last night that I haven't been able to get out of my mind all day."

Lula put her harp away and poured them both a mug of warm tea. Aine savored the tangy citrus flavor of lemon.

"What did you find in the barn?" Lula asked.

"It was a crystal ball. I thought it was just refraction from the sun coming through the window, but when I went closer to it, I could see that the glow came from within the globe."

Aine described the colorful mist swirling within the ball and how the whole loft had been alight with color. "The sparkles in the air were like the stirred embers from a fire. It was incredible."

Lula nodded. "Did you touch it?"

"Yes. And I had the strangest sensation when I did. The surface was warm, not from the sunlight, and not from the glass either. A tingling feeling traveled up my arms from my fingers and when I pressed my palms against it, I felt like I was moving rapidly. It made me dizzy so I let go.

Then I felt like something was supposed to happen and I got a little scared, but at the same time I didn't want to let go. Even though it made me woozy I wanted to pick it up and take it with me. I didn't want to leave it there. There was a sound … a humming sound, almost like a motor, but different." Aine sighed with frustration. "Oh, I'm not describing this very well."

"You're doing just fine, dear." Lula took a deep breath and a sip of her tea, saying nothing more for a few moments.

Aine continued, "After I removed my hands the colors faded and I felt like I'd lost something…incredible. I don't know why, except it was so beautiful when the whole loft glowed."

Lula nodded and shifted so she could see Aine's face more clearly, noting the mixture of curiosity, skepticism and excitement there. Lula leaned over to raise the wick on the lamp, dismissing the shadows.

"Why do you think it felt like that?" Aine asked.

"It is possible that the globe you found is a crystal of power." Lula smiled at the incredulous look on Aine's face.

"A crystal of power? What do you mean?"

"Crystals of power can be used to communicate or take one to another plane, or even enhance certain abilities. The powers of a crystal can vary as much as their users do. It's hard to know what they can do until they are activated. The only way to know for sure is to try."

Aine's excitement grew. "Is that what the tingling was, its power?"

"Probably. I would need to observe you when you touch it to be sure."

For a fleeting moment something passed through Lula's eyes and a shiver ran down Aine's spine. "If I did activate it, what could it do?"

"That depends on you." Lula replied.

"Is it dangerous?" Aine asked.

"No, if you can activate it, you could never be hurt by it."

Aine was relieved. Lula would never allow Aine to try something that could harm her.

Lula rocked slowly, cupping her hands around the mug of warm tea. "Do you want to try to activate it?"

Without hesitation Aine said, "Yes, yes I would."

"All right then. Ask Jessie if you can bring it here tomorrow night and I'll make dinner and then we can look it over."

Aine smiled, excited by the prospect.

CHAPTER TWO

The Nightmare

"Now, tell me about your dream, Aine." Lula asked.

Aine's exuberance faded. She had discussed what Lula called the "dream eye" with Lula many times in the past. Lula believed that some dreams had a different focus, and could be a premonition or a warning. Nightmares were especially so.

Aine closed her eyes, forcing herself to relive the vivid scene. "The wind was howling like the banshee from Grandma's stories, and I was on my knees, in a place high and exposed. I struggled to my feet and took a tentative step toward the bare outline of a railing. My hair whipped in my eyes blinding me temporarily.

"The gale died enough that I could hear the furious pounding of the sea somewhere far below. It was dark and hard to see but then the crescent moon slipped out from behind a cloud, and shed scanty light. I was standing in the center of a tower that thrust up like an angry finger from the fist of a dark brooding castle beneath me. When I peeked over the edge of the railing, the moonlight shimmered on the frothing waves as they battered the jagged rocks below." Aine hesitated, "It looked like vicious teeth poised to consume me."

She took a swallow of her tea, caught up in the powerful memory of the dream. "A prickle of unease made the hairs on the back of my neck rise and I sensed something, like a malign presence. There was a crash behind me and I raised my hands to shield my eyes from a blinding light that poured from a doorway. There was a tall figure in a swirling cloak that stood in stark outline in the glow of the room behind the door.

"I could see better with the light streaming from the room, but then he closed the door and hung a filigreed lantern on a hook next to it. The lantern's light did little to illuminate him as he turned to face me, but I didn't need to see him to feel the emanations of his power. He opened the cover of the lantern and his face shone red in its glow.

"I stepped away from him and my questions froze in my throat.

"He was older, maybe in his late thirties, and handsome in a dark, dangerous way. But when I looked at his eyes they seemed soulless. I froze, unable to look away or move.

"Then he smiled with lips drawn in cruelty and said, '*So, you are the one?*'

"It took a moment for me to realize that he had not spoken aloud, yet I understood the words clearly. I looked away and stepped back, shaking my head to dislodge the dark demand in his eyes.

"In one swift movement he reached me, and clenched my arms painfully. Thoughts burned like his eyes, '*You are the one, and you are mine.*'"

Aine closed her eyes unable to speak. She wondered if she could continue but Lula patted her hand, "Take your time. There is no hurry. When you are ready tell me the rest."

Aine felt the comfort in Lula's simple touch and took a deep breath and continued, "It was so strange, Lula. His words dominated my mind and my body throbbed with sudden heat but a thrill of fear ran down my spine at the same time. I was repulsed both by his cold lust and my initial response to it."

Aine smiled just slightly. "I realized that I had to get away from him and I tried to kick him. Failing that, I threw my head forward and hit his nose with a solid thunk.

"Free of him, I bolted to the edge of the turret but his laughter rang in my mind. *I love your spirit, my beauty, but you cannot escape.*'

"I refused to look directly at him and sidled along the stone railing.

"The wind whipped his dark cloak as he rubbed his nose and spoke, aloud this time. 'There is no escape, surely you see that.'"

Aine's eyes filled with remembered terror as she met Lula's eyes, "Oh, Lula, he was so powerful and his words tugged at me compellingly. I could feel the power emanating from him and he seemed to sense that I was trying to escape. He started toward me.

"There was no more time. I screamed, 'No!' and vaulted to the railing. He snatched my ankle and I shook myself free. The cold wind battered me and I plummeted toward the hungry sea."

Both Aine and Lula were silent for several minutes. Then Aine continued, "I awoke gulping the air of my darkened bedroom. My oversized t-shirt twisted around my sweating body and my heart was still racing.

"I tiptoed to the bathroom, turned on the light over the sink, and splashed warm water on my face washing the tracks of tears away. When I reached up to turn off the light, I saw dark bruises on my upper arms exactly where the man in my nightmare had squeezed them! I leaned forward to look in the mirror, rolling the sleeve of my t-shirt up to my shoulders. My stomach lurched. There was no mistaking the shape of a man's large fingers on my arms.

"No one gets bruises from a dream, Lula," Aine finished, with a hard swallow.

She pulled up the sleeve of her sweater, but the bruises she'd seen that afternoon were gone! "There were bruises there, really! I saw them…in the bathroom!"

"I believe you, Aine. Tell me about the man. What did he look like?"

"He was tall with shoulder length hair, and his eyes…" Aine swallowed. "His eyes were dark and I couldn't seem to look away from them."

"Have you ever seen him before?"

"No, that's just it, but he was familiar."

Aine saw the shadow of concern in Lula's eyes. Lula put her cup down, "Powerful dreams, can be memories of the future or of the past."

Memories of the future, Aine had always been intrigued by that idea but now it frightened her. Lula believed that life was infinite, and unusual dreams or feelings of déjà vu were simply the mind recalling something one experienced before or would experience in the future.

"Well, I sure hope that this particular dream was neither in the future nor the past. I was afraid of him, Lula, but in some eerie way I was also drawn to him." She shivered, "I'm really glad I woke up when I did."

Lula smiled again, "I am too, Aine. Now, do you remember how to remove this painful memory from your conscious and unconscious thoughts?"

Aine nodded, "Yes, you mentally put them in a drawer and don't open it until you feel strong enough to deal with them. I remember."

"Then that is what you should do now." Lula rose from her chair.

"You don't think I'll dream about him again?" Aine asked as she helped Lula take the cups back to the kitchen.

"I'll give you something to mix in a drink before you go to bed. It will help you sleep, but not to dream. Before you sleep, refocus your thoughts on what you might learn from the crystal ball instead."

Aine didn't want to think about the dream anymore anyway, but she felt better having at least told someone about it. Somehow, sharing her fears had diminished them.

Lula tipped Aine's chin with her finger tips and looked directly into her eyes. "We can never know what life has in store for us until we take the steps to live it, and we must never be afraid to live our lives to the fullest."

CHAPTER THREE

The Traveler

The next day Carolinda waited in the car in the driveway of Mr. Miller's piano studio. Aine ran down the steps and jumped into the front seat, relieved that the lesson was over. A grin lit Carolinda's pretty freckled face as Aine closed the door.

Noting the stern look on Mr. Miller's face as he watched Aine leave, Carolinda's smirk faded, "Wow, he looks grouchy. Did you forget to practice?"

"No, I practiced as much as always. I should have played much better, but I just can't seem to concentrate today."

Carolinda chuckled as she tried to cheer her sibling. "Don't worry about it, Aine. He'll get over it and so will you. Actually, I'm really glad I don't have to take piano lessons anymore. If I ever hear *To a Wild Rose* again, I'll probably vomit!"

"I feel the same way about *Fur Elise*," Aine replied, and both sisters laughed.

Carolinda chatted on the drive home about her secret meeting with her boyfriend Richard, but Aine was only half listening.

When they got home, Aine hurried from the car dropping her books on the piano and she bolted upstairs to her room. Mother was waiting for her in the hallway. "Aine, you were supposed to do the dishes before your lesson, how many times must I remind you?"

Aine faced her mother and gritted her teeth. "I'll do them. I just didn't have time before we left because Mr. Miller had to schedule me a half hour earlier today."

Icy eyes bored into Aine's, "You always have an excuse don't you, Aine."

A sudden fury at her mother's relentless disapproval brought bright color to Aine's face. "Yeah, I sure do. I lay around all of the time just dreaming up excuses."

Mother's eyes narrowed and a quick sting slapped across Aine's face, bringing tears to her eyes. "Don't you dare talk back to me!"

Aine's hand covered her stinging cheek. She had never been struck in her life and her heart raced with the shock. Numbly, she stumbled into her room.

Seconds later she heard Carolinda trying to diffuse the situation. "I'll do the dishes, Mother. It was my turn anyway, Aine did them last night. I just need to call Janet about Friday's reading."

Their voices faded as they went downstairs and Aine sat on her bed clenching her fists. More shocking than the slap was the overwhelming fury she'd felt at her mother.

"I wish I could just disappear," she murmured.

She glanced out the window when she heard the car door slam and Mother drive off. Moving to the other window she saw Dad working in the garden. *I've got to get out of here... now. Maybe Lula won't mind if I come a little early.*

Dad looked up smiling at her as she walked across the lawn to the garden. He leaned the hoe against the bushel basket filled with weeds and removed his gloves and wiped his face with his handkerchief, "Hi, how was your lesson?"

"It could have been better," Aine answered honestly.

"Hmmm, it didn't sound bad to me when you were practicing, but then I usually think *Chopsticks* is an outstanding musical accomplishment. You look a little pale, are you okay?"

"I'm okay, Dad. Mr. Miller says I just need to focus more. I think if I practice more this week, I will be better next time." Aine tried to keep the haste out of her voice.

"I'm sure it will. Sometimes we learn even more when we make mistakes."

Dad always did that. Without scolding his children, he encouraged them to do their best, and as a result they usually did. For Aine, there was nothing worse than disappointing her father.

Aine nibbled her thumb, nervously trying to think how to ask him.

He saw it and picked up the basket of weeds and started for the compost pile. He didn't ask but just waited to see if she'd share what was bothering her.

Aine loved that about him and she trailed along and finally blurted, "Dad, would it be okay if I went to Lula's for supper? I could take some of the sweet William seeds that you promised her."

"Have you got your homework done?"

"Yes."

"And what about practicing?"

"I practiced my band music already and I think I'll do better on the piano if I wait until tomorrow, if that's ok." Aine tried to breathe slowly and keep a smile on her face.

The look in Dad's eyes showed that he knew very well that she was evading him, but he didn't push her. He smiled,

"All right, I'll put a bottle of the wine I decanted last night on the porch and you can take that too."

Aine avoided his eyes. "Could you tell Mother that I won't be here for dinner?"

"Afraid to ask, huh?" His brilliant blue eyes twinkled and he put the basket down and tilted her chin so she had to look at him.

How could she tell him that he was exactly right?

"Don't worry about it. I'll tell her something, but you make sure that you are home by ten." He reached over and mussed her hair, just as he had done when she was little.

"Finish your chores before you go or we'll both pay."

"Thanks!" Aine hugged him impulsively. He enfolded her in his arms and kissed her forehead. She inhaled, smelling the warm sunlight on his skin and the slight acrid scent of honest sweat mingled with his Old Spice after shave. She sighed, feeling safe and loved once more. "You're the best, Dad!"

"Of course I am," he grinned. "And don't you forget it!"

With the warm afternoon sunlight lighting the garden she took a mental snapshot of her father. He always knew how to make things better, but he never pushed. That was the difference between her parents. Dad expected the best of his children while Mother expected the worst. For a second she wondered if she should share what had happened with him, but she dismissed the idea immediately. As kind and understanding as Dad was, he would not approve of her talking back to Mother. In some ways her heart hurt more than her face, and she wanted just to get away, at least for a while.

She finished her chores and stuck the envelope of herbs that Lula had sent for Jessie in her pocket, relieved that Dad would deal with Mother. She wanted to get the crystal ball and be on her way to Lula's before Mother got home.

She heard Jessie call her to enter when she knocked. Jessie was older than her parents, a lively woman who had been widowed several years ago. A sports fanatic, she was in the living room watching a baseball game on TV.

"Hello, Aine." Jessie smiled as Aine sat on the chair near her. "Are you running away from your mother again?"

Aine blushed. Jessie had an uncanny knack of knowing what was going on, especially where Mother was concerned.

"Lula asked me to bring you these herbs. She said it would help with the pain in your knees."

Jessie took the packet and grinned. "And she's right. These herbs are great! I could probably beat the boys on the track team if I wanted to after I've taken it."

Aine laughed.

"Thanks for taking all of those boxes up to the loft."

Aine nodded, "You're welcome. I wanted to ask you about the crystal ball I saw when I was up there. What is it?"

Jessie looked confused for a moment as though she was trying to remember something, then she snapped her fingers. "Oh, that's right, now I remember. It belonged to Hy's mother. I think she brought it from Russia. I didn't even know it was up there."

"Could I borrow it and take it up to Lula's to show it to her?"

"Sure, go ahead." Jessie refocused on the TV. "Tell Lula to keep it as long as she likes. There's a canvas bag on the back porch you can use to carry it."

Aine found the satchel and climbed up to the loft. It was cloudy and darker in the loft today and it took her a moment to find the red scarf. As she took a step toward it she almost tripped as Pin weaved and purred between her ankles. That was so strange. The mother cat was wild and had never let Aine touch her before.

Pin's bright green eyes were wide and the pupils very dark and Aine could have sworn that the animal was trying to tell her something. Aine knelt and stroked the cat's soft fur and felt the purring vibrations in Pin's throat. Seemingly satisfied, the cat wended her way back to the box where her kittens slept.

Aine knelt next to the crystal ball touching it and felt the same warm tingling sensation travel up her arms. She wrapped it with the scarf and placed it carefully in Jessie's bag.

Lula had prepared a wonderful garden-fresh vegetable stew and molasses cookies for dessert. The sun had almost set by the time they finished the dishes and Lula lit some of the lamps and candles in the parlor. A mourning dove called forlornly from the trees outside and Aine remembered her grandmother saying that the call of the mourning dove brought peace and good luck. She hoped it was true tonight.

A stunning three-pronged pewter holder sat on the low table in front of them. Each prong was in the shape of a fairy with upraised arms and all three were connected with a circle of flowers.

Aine's fingers tingled again as she set the crystal ball in the holder. "The stand is beautiful, Lula. Do the fairies have any special significance?"

Lula sat down opposite Aine and nodded, "Yes, since they are reaching out, the power of the ball will extend outward."

Lula ran her hands over the crystal but did not pick it up, and the ball remained clear. "Responsive crystals like this one were created by craftsman who infused special powers into their making. That is what allows the user to activate the crystal so that it will do whatever it was designed to do.

"When a person bonded to a crystal of power dies, the power of that crystal is transferred, along with their spirit or essence to a new incarnation." She smiled at Aine, "Or at least that is one premise. I suspect that is why the crystals of power will only work for one individual at a time."

Lula sat back, "Do you understand what could happen if you activate it?"

"You said it could tell the past or the future, or it might take me somewhere."

"If it is a traveling crystal, you could find yourself in a very different place, perhaps even in another world and you might not be able to sense this world at all. If that happens, you will be able to return, but only when you are ready and perhaps not right away."

Lula looked away briefly and Aine wondered if she had been about to say something else. A different world? It would be amazing to experience something like that, and she could barely wait to try. "You'll be right here won't you?" Aine asked.

Lula nodded, "Of course, I will always be here for you, Aine."

"Okay then, I'm ready." Aine sat down on the chair and shifted so that she could reach the ball easily.

Lula's voice was low and calm, "Be sure that you are comfortable and then empty your mind of any extraneous thoughts." Lula snuffed all but one candle, creating a soft singular radiance. "Once your mind is clear, place your fingers on the globe."

Aine reached out and touched the surface. It was warm and as soon as her fingertips contacted it, the colors began to swirl within. Thoughts crowded Aine's mind like the image of Dad in the garden, Jessie's loft and the strange way Pin had behaved. She couldn't stay focused and looked at Lula with dismay, "It's not working, I can't seem to empty my mind long enough."

Lula smiled, "Hasn't Mr. Miller taught you a special way to focus on your music?"

Aine nodded enthusiastically, "Yes he has! I'll try that." Aine blocked everything from her thoughts and once again placed her fingers lightly on the surface of the crystal. The flame of the candle bobbed and shivered as a reflection on the glass and her mind focused suddenly and intently. The ball began to glow and hum just as it had in the loft. There was a sense of movement and she stared at the candle's reflection and let herself go with the movement.

Lula's voice was soft as if she was very far away. "Now, Aine, reach for what you see within the crystal and let your consciousness delve into it. Don't resist, let it do what it will. Remember, it is yours, and you are safe within it."

Lula's voice faded and very faintly Aine heard another voice whisper, *"She is the one."*

Lula's reply was almost lost in the vortex that surrounded Aine. *"Yes, Priscilla, she is."*

CHAPTER FOUR

Zephyr

The interior of the globe brightened with colors changing from gold to brilliant blue, and finally a soft green. A warm tingling sensation rode up her arms like an electric shock and she felt as if she were being pulled at a dizzying speed toward the vortex forming in the center of her vision. This was just as it had been in Jessie's barn, only much stronger. She held on stubbornly though she could no longer feel her hands touching the heated surface. The colors churned wildly, growing smaller and smaller like the diminishing lens of a camera, until a laser-white light stabbed her eyes. Aine traversed a barrier and was buffeted violently, caught in a raging stream of movement. The initial hum of the crystal ball expanded to a deafening roar and she screamed, thinking herself lost forever in the maelstrom. She drew a breath to shriek again but the cacophony stopped abruptly.

From what seemed a dizzying height she tumbled down a sword of light surrounded by a vortex of shadows. Her ears rang with the throbbing of her heart and her ragged breathing.

Sharp stones bit into her hands and knees and cool rain caressed her shoulders. She was kneeling on a stony path next to a small stream. Aine stumbled to her feet brushing the pebbles from her jeans and hands, then inhaled the rich loamy freshness of the water. A teardrop of rain fell from the long needles of a pungent dark pine and hit the water below with a musical ping. Turning in a slow circle she closed her eyes and forced her mind away from the sense of unreality that lingered from the turbulent passage.

A robin sang his rain song from the tree and she rejoiced in recognition. Lula had been right; the crystal ball had taken her somewhere. She recognized the shape of the canyon and the path of the streambed. This was the glen, a lovely tree-filled ravine not far from Lula's cabin. She would have no trouble finding her way home from here.

Yet, there was something subtle in the scene around her. Despite the coolness of the glen, she felt a strange sense of urgency to move quickly. As she started toward the stream Aine felt a stab of unease and realized what was wrong. It had been dark when she and Lula finished dinner and when she had first touched the globe. Though the light now was subdued from the misty rain, it was definitely daylight.

There had to be a logical explanation. Perhaps the crystal had moved her backward or forward in time. It had been rainy yesterday, maybe she had simply regressed a day.

As she continued toward the water, Aine perceived subtle differences in the landscape as well. Unfamiliar trees and rock formations were interspersed with familiar ones.

She sat down and removed her shoes and socks and rolled her pants up picking her way barefooted from rock to rock. Occasionally she stepped into the water still frigid from what she assumed was spring runoff and allowed the stream to chuckle over her feet. Ancient trees leaned toward the stream with long beards of moss glistening diamonds of moisture. The subdued light made them seem larger than she remembered.

Rounding a bend, a waterfall with steep shale sides spilled into a whirlpool and she nearly laughed aloud with relief. She knew this place. Scuttling over the slippery rocks that led to the whirlpool, Aine found a long branch and pushed it down into the center of the vortex, just as she had a hundred times before.

She frowned. The depth was well over her head. She had never seen the pool this deep, even in early spring and the sense of unease returned. Her eyes fixated on a stick that floated on the surface of the pool below. Caught in the flow of the water it was never quite released into the downstream flow. It was trapped, never sinking, always moving, but trapped.

Then she realized what was bothering her. She clearly remembered this whirlpool from many visits in her childhood but now the whirlpool's flow was backwards, counter clockwise. For a second she envisioned herself as the stick caught in the flow, trapped by a strange current.

Feeling a sense of urgency to move on, she donned her socks and shoes and seized the roots of a tree to pull herself up the steep shale bank. Somewhere above her was a shortcut out of the glen, if only she could remember where it was.

The bank was much steeper than she remembered, but she dismissed that because she had not come this way for a long time. She hunched low as she pushed through the heavy underbrush feeling an intense desire to be free of it.

After struggling to a more gradual slope she realized with dismay, that there was no path. The bushes pulled at her hair and clothes and she had to crawl on her hands and knees just to get through. Finally, she saw a patch of light ahead and came to a level open space.

"Where am I?" she mumbled looking around as she picked the leaves from her hair. Still breathing heavily from the effort of climbing, she didn't register the muffled sounds at first.

"Please, help me."

Aine froze at the sound. The sense of urgency she'd felt earlier returned only stronger.

"Where are you?" She whispered.

"Over here, behind the bushes. Please help me!" The tone was different now, not as forlorn but nearly frantic.

"I'm coming, hold on!" Aine cried as she ran toward the bushes. Squeezing into the narrow space behind them she found a flat platform of rock with a wall of stone abutting it. In the center of the wall was a hinged door of thick bars and she heard something moving behind the door.

There was another muffled cry and sounds of struggling from behind the bars. *"Help me…please!"*

"I'm here, hang on!" Aine called. "Let me get this door open."

She grasped the metal bars of the door and pulled but she couldn't budge it. She looked around for a branch that was thick enough to use as a lever but the bushes were too small. Finally she braced her foot on the wall and it shifted just enough for her to squeeze past it into a dim, musty cave. Water dripped somewhere nearby and the smell of dank leaves and earth assaulted her nose. Her eyes were slow to adjust and she felt her way slowly along the wall toward the sounds of movement deeper in the cavern.

A joyful shout startled her, *"I thought you'd never come! I am so glad that you are here! I've waited for you for so long!"*

Aine froze with her hand still flat against the cold stone of the wall. She had not actually heard the words aloud, but she had heard them in her mind, just as she had heard that man in her nightmare.

"Who are you?" Aine gasped.

The voice didn't sound like the man from her nightmare at all. In fact, it had a feminine timbre to it and there was no sense of menace in the voice.

"I am your friend. I need your help, please." It was almost as if the voice belonged to someone she knew.

Excitement battled wariness, but curiosity won out. Placing her palm on the wall as she moved forward, her eyes had finally adjusted enough to see more clearly.

A light dappled silver horse with a long snowy mane and tail stood tethered to the wall. When it moved Aine was stunned to see two wings folded across its back. Rich brown eyes regarded her and the animal shifted nervously and nickered, *"Please help me, we must get away before he comes back."*

Aine didn't know why or how the horse was talking to her in her mind, but she felt the animal's emotions as if they were her own. The strong current of fear and the need to flee, made her want to run as well.

She rested her palm on the neck of the lovely creature. At the touch she was immersed in an incredible rush of emotion, like stepping into a warm shower of feeling. The shout in her mind was filled with joy. *"It is you...Oh, I am so glad you found me!"*

Shocked by the sensation, it took a moment before Aine untied the knot that held the animal captive. The horse pushed past her toward the entrance of the cave. *"Come now my mistress, we must hurry!"*

The space between the door and the wall was too small for such a large animal, and it tossed its head and pawed at the hard rock by the door.

Aine touched the horse's side feeling the connection between them once more. "Back up, let me push it open further so you can get out." The animal did as Aine requested and finally, with her back on the wall she pushed with her legs. A loud screech sounded as the gate grated open. The horse pushed its way outside and Aine followed.

Aine stared at the animal in amazement. It was the most beautiful creature she had ever seen. The size of a large horse, with a dappled silver coat, snowy white wings, mane, and tail it had a deep and strongly muscled chest and it flipped its white wings nervously. Aine laid her hand on the animal's neck amazed to feel the incredible sense of warmth and caring again.

"It's okay, you're free now," Aine comforted.

The animal flipped its wings rapidly and looked from side to side. *"I thank you for freeing me but we must flee, it is not safe here. We must be gone before he returns."*

"Before who returns?" Aine looked quickly around.

The horse's mental response was shaky. *"I have been trapped here for two suns. There is no time to explain. We cannot remain, if they return neither of us will ever be free of him. I will take you to safety. But, please believe me, we must fly!"* The wings flicked in agitation.

Aine felt the rising panic as if it were her own. "I can't go with you. I don't know where I am but I know I don't belong here." She was interrupted by a sudden cacophony of yips and snarls from the forest beyond.

Her companion bolted briefly to the air and then landed again. *"They are coming! They will find us, you must listen to me! It is dangerous, please come!"*

For a split second Aine wavered. She stumbled past the horse trying to see through the dense bushes. The yapping and growling were much closer now, coming from the bank below them, beyond the clearing.

Aine felt a tangible menace from the creatures racing toward her and she was at last convinced they must flee. "Let's go!"

She grasped the mane and pulled herself up to the animal's back. The winged horse took two steps and jumped to the air. The strong white wings lifted them at dizzying speed and the sounds of pursuit faded as they rose to the sky high above.

Aine's heart beat with exhilaration and she threaded her fingers into the snowy mane, holding on tightly with her legs, it was as if she were one with this amazing creature. They sped through the sky like a falcon on the wind.

Aine sat up straighter to see the land that blurred rapidly past as they soared. There was no evidence of civilization, only a deep forest of trees with an occasional clearing.

Where was Taylor's maple farm just outside the glen? In fact from this height she should have been able to see the whole town of Riverdale but there was nothing but forest beneath them.

Until she had seen the cave and the creature within, Aine had refused to admit that the crystal ball had really taken her anywhere but the glen she knew. Now she knew it wasn't just a different place but another world, just as Lula had suggested. A world where horses could fly and talk, and where evil was tangible, and a world far from the one she knew.

CHAPTER FIVE

Mabon

They flew at a steady pace and Aine hugged the animal closely, feeling exhilarated, curious, anxious and quite close to panic.

Mother had always accused her of being impulsive, convinced it would bring trouble. If Mother could see her now, flying around on a horse that talked to her, well she knew what Mother would say.

"We're almost there," she heard the creature's thoughts. The tenderness in those words as they brushed Aine's mind calmed her fears. She made the effort to open her thoughts and felt her consciousness merge with the animal. The strong wings soaring through the air seemed as much a part of her as her hands entwined in the pure white mane. The joy of it bubbled up, and Aine laughed aloud sharing a thrill of elation from the animal.

As promised, the filly soon banked her wings and circled to land in a clearing surrounded by a ring of tall pines. The air was cool despite the bright sunlight and a faint path led to the forest beyond. The horse folded her wings along her back as Aine jumped to the ground and moved around in front of the horse. When Aine gazed into the animal's rich brown eyes she saw an intelligence and depth much beyond that of an ordinary horse.

"I hear your thoughts and feel your emotions as if they are my own. Why is that?" Aine asked. "Horses don't fly where I come from, they don't even have wings, and they most certainly don't talk to people!"

The animal shook its head as if disagreeing. *"Of course horses do not talk. Personally, I think that's because they are not nearly as smart as we are,"* the slight arrogance in tone made Aine smile.

"My name is Zephyr, and I am a pegasite filly. You hear me in your mind and feel what I feel because we are empaths and bond mates. When empathic partners find one another and acknowledge their partner's thoughts, they are joined this way forever."

Zephyr nudged Aine with her nose as if to emphasize her point. *"You are mine and I am yours, nothing will ever change that."*

Aine's knees felt suddenly weak and Zephyr moved closer seeming to sense her confusion. The filly's telepathic tone softened as if she were whispering. *"I am very glad you found me."*

Caressing Zephyr's neck with her hand, Aine was amazed at the warm shower of emotions cascading over her; the joy of belonging, fierce protection and a sense of love even stronger than what she felt for her family. It was amazing and overwhelming.

Aine stepped back, "Zephyr is a good name for you. You fly like the wind."

"Thank you, my mistress."

Aine tilted her head and asked, "Did you call me somehow? I had the sense that something was drawing me to you from the moment I arrived."

"I felt you coming when I was still in the cave. I called you and you came." Zephyr's tone sounded shy and wondering. *"We will never be alone again."*

So simple, so logical. Aine rested her cheek against the filly's neck. She had never felt anything like these feelings before. Certainly she loved her family, but this connection was something different. It made her feel less alien in this strange place. With Zephyr, she belonged. As they stood in the sunlit field, she allowed the peace and comfort of the new bond between them to succor her.

Zephyr nudged Aine, *"Mabon has come, Mistress."* The pegasite seemed excited to see the man walking toward them. She flipped her wings several times with her ears pointed forward.

Aine stood quietly at Zephyr's side, unsure what to do.

The man had dark hair tied back with a cord and strands of silver at his temples. His short trimmed beard gave him a dapper look, like a college professor. His eyes were a piercing slate-blue and he regarded her evenly, neither staring nor looking away. Dressed in a long brown woolen vest with pants in shades of gray and brown he blended well with the woods behind him.

When he reached them he nodded to Aine and reached up to scratch Zephyr where her wings met her shoulder. "Hello, Zephyr, I'm glad to see you again, we have missed you."

"And, I am very glad to see you as well, Mabon." Aine heard Zephyr reply as she raised her wings high and flapped them causing Aine's hair to blow wildly.

When Mabon smiled at the filly's antics, Aine saw that he was younger than she originally thought, maybe in his early forties.

Zephyr brazenly nuzzled in his cloak until he pulled a root from his pocket then chuckled as she rumbled low in her throat and devoured it.

Mabon stepped back and met Aine's eyes, touching his heart and lips and bowing slightly. "My name is Mabon, and I think that Zephyr is very happy to have found her bond mate at last."

Remembering her manners, Aine said, "I'm glad I found her too. I found her tied in a cave so I helped her to get free. We heard something pursuing us so Zephyr brought me here."

"Ah, that explains why we have not seen Zephyr for the last few days. Please, be welcome, young…"

"Oh, Aine, my name is Aine." Aine blushed having forgotten her manners.

His eyes took in her clothing, pink sweater, blue jeans and tennis shoes. "I see that you have come from afar."

Still unsure of herself she nodded, "Yes I have."

He glanced back in the direction he had come. "We probably shouldn't remain here just in case you have been pursued. If you will come with me I can offer safety and shelter."

Aine hesitated. "I'm not sure if I should."

Mabon gestured to Zephyr. "Zephyr brought you here so that I could help you. She will tell you that I mean you no harm."

The bond with Zephyr radiated trust for Mabon, but Aine definitely caught a sense of urgency too. Zephyr felt Aine's hesitation. *"Mabon is my friend. I called him as we left the cave so that he could help us and keep us safe. He is called the First Protector and you can trust him as you would me, my mistress. He is correct, it is not wise to remain in the open if the Wuenta pursue us."*

Wondering who the Wuenta were, Aine regarded Mabon, "I sense Zephyr's trust of you, Mabon. If I come with you, will you answer some of my questions once we are safe?"

"I will do my best."

She thought, *"Well this is probably the only way I will learn where I am so I suppose I have to go with him."*

"That is wise, my mistress."

Having forgotten that the pretty filly could hear her thoughts, Aine nodded slightly at Mabon and they moved quickly along the path into the trees. She glanced behind them, dismayed to see that the evidence of their passage through the tall grass of the clearing had vanished.

Sensing her mistress's alarm Zephyr explained, *"Mabon obscures our tracks so that no one can follow."*

Aine followed along. Soon they came to a small fenced clearing where bushes ran tightly together on both ends. Mabon moved in close to the screen of bushes murmuring softly as a silvery-blue hue surrounded him. The bushes parted, revealing a solid rock wall with a stout wooden door in the center. Metal bands braced the thick wood like ribbons on a package. Next to the door, a row of diamond-shaped windows spilled a glow from within. Bowing slightly, he opened the door, "Please come in."

Thinking it was a small building built into a hillside, Aine was surprised to find that she was in a large cavern once she stepped through the door. Lamps hung from notches in the walls and from the high ceiling, creating a comforting blush of light. Several other rooms adjoined the main room and two passages led deeper into the cave.

Mabon removed his thick vest and hung it on a hook by the door. A fire crackled in the fireplace built into the corner and Mabon used a thick cloth to lift the steaming kettle from the hook where it had been warming.

Gesturing for her to sit on one of two wooden benches by the fireplace Mabon gathered cups and sprinkled something from a small canister into them. The thick citrus tang of the tea gave Aine a twinge of homesickness for Lula's lemon tea.

Mabon settled himself on the bench opposite her and sipped his drink. "Now, I believe you had some questions," Mabon said.

"Yes, I do. But I'm not sure where to start," Aine admitted.

Mabon nodded as if he understood her confusion. "Why don't you tell me how you found Zephyr?"

Aine realized that he was as curious about her, as she was about him. She shared how she had found the crystal ball and how Lula had shown her how to use it. "After I activated it, I was suddenly in the glen, only it wasn't my glen from home." She frowned and murmured, "I don't think I am anywhere near home anymore."

Mabon leaned forward. "Ah, then as I suspected, you are not from Drayon."

"Drayon?"

Mabon gestured with his arm, "Drayon is the name of this world." He fished out a small pipe and a leather packet from his pocket and took his time filling the pipe with a crumpled plant that looked like tobacco leaves. Lighting it with a twig from the fire, Mabon drew on the pipe and the sweet smelling smoke obscured him for a moment. He waved the smoke away and cleared his throat. "If you have traveled to us from somewhere else, your glen would likely be similar to ours. When you arrived did you see a rock or tree or special formation that seemed common to both places?"

"Yes I did, there is a whirlpool." Aine paused, unsure how to describe the subtle differences.

Mabon drew on his pipe, "I suspect that the whirlpool is the portal between our worlds. It may not be the only passage to the celestial band."

"Celestial band?" Aine cocked her head and leaned forward trying to understand.

"Each world in the universe exists in its own unique space. Between those worlds is a celestial band that functions as a conduit or passageway. Not all worlds are connected this way, but there are a remarkable number that are. Any life form that can traverse that pathway is a traveler.

"Within the band there are gateways, or portals, that open to each world sometimes connecting them with other worlds. The gateways can be accessed in any number of ways. Some with crystals, bodies of water, fire, stone formations, jewels and probably things we have never even imagined."

Aine realized that her crystal ball was not only a source of power, but a tool that had brought her from her world to this one. She had not considered that there could be other ways to travel between worlds but she immediately saw the possibilities.

"Then why can't I just go back to the whirlpool and use something else to return home?"

He nodded, "You probably could. Do you have another crystal of power with you?"

Aine's elation faded. "No."

"You would need a similar device to return, just as you needed yours to come to us." Mabon explained.

Aine's hope was crushed. She had hoped that Mabon could help her return home. Now, she was fearful that she might be stuck here for a very long time. She couldn't stay here, this had all been very exciting and interesting, but there just had to be another way.

Zephyr sounded anxious, *"Please do not leave, my mistress!"*

Aine had forgotten Zephyr's ability to hear her thoughts and she quickly tried to comfort the filly, *"I'm sorry, Zephyr. I didn't mean to upset you. But don't worry, I'm not going anywhere. I don't know how."*

Aine's dismay clearly showed on her face, but Mabon waited politely. She sipped her tea trying to organize her thoughts.

"Lula did say I could return when I was ready. But I upset Zephyr when I thought about leaving to go home."

His kind gray eyes met hers, "That is understandable, new bonds are fragile. It will take some time for you both to become accustomed to each other. And the love between bond mates is often overwhelming at the beginning."

This whole experience was so strange; conduits between worlds, empathic animals and partners, crystal balls and travelers. One part of Aine's mind wanted to reject it all and pretend it wasn't happening. "Is a crystal ball the only means to travel this celestial band?"

"No, I believe that there are many tools for traveling."

Aine's eyes brightened with hope.

Mabon smiled, "I might have just the thing you need although it might take some time for you to learn how to use it effectively."

He rose and tapped the dottle from his pipe into the fireplace and gestured toward one of the passages leading deeper into the cave. "This has been quite an adventure for you, hasn't it? It has probably been a shock to be unexpectedly thrust across the universe into a whole new world."

Aine nodded and blinked rapidly at the tears forming in her eyes and bit her lip.

Mabon pretended not to see her struggle and smiled again, "Well then, you must come with me. Let me show you something wonderful."

Hoping that he had not noticed her tears, Aine followed as they walked through a passage perfectly delved and smooth as glass to her touch. Recessed lighting brightened as they approached and returned to a soft barely discernable light once they passed by.

The tunnel inclined downward turning gradually to the left and they came to a doorway with bright light leaking around the edges. When they were in front of it the door slid silently to the side and disappeared into a finely delved opening like the glass doors of supermarkets at home.

Aine followed Mabon into a room with walls and ceiling alight with color. Thousands of multi-colored crystal icicles hung suspended from the high ceiling and tinkled musically as she and Mabon passed beneath. She was unable to discern a specific source of the rosy radiance of light in the room but it was a beautiful rainbow of warmth.

Shelves made of a clear glass-like substance were suspended throughout the room and arranged upon each shelf were statues of people paired with animals.

One statue was bathed in bright golden light and she was shocked to see that it was a perfect replica of Zephyr and herself. A long golden chain with a teardrop-shaped crystal hung above it.

"It's Zephyr and me." She turned in amazement to Mabon. "How could that be?"

Mabon swept his arm wide, indicating the entire room. "This, my dear, is a small portion of the empathic repository of Drayon. Each statue that you see here represents a pair of empathic partners. There are hundreds more in the adjoining chambers. They simply appear when a new pair is partnered, no one quite knows how."

She looked slowly around the room and reached out to touch the statue. "This is so beautiful; it should be shared by all of your people. Why is it here, hidden away?"

Mabon's eyes widened, *"She will light our world and way. Without her, darkness has its sway."*

Those were the words from one of Drayon's oldest songs. Turning his face to hide a surge of excitement, he kept his tone even, "Unfortunately, it must remain hidden because there are those who would destroy this place if they could. Only a few trusted souls know where it is and you are now one of them."

"Why would anyone want to destroy this?"

A flash of anger crossed Mabon's eyes and then he visibly controlled himself. "There are some who seek power by controlling others and some of these artifacts would be distorted in the wrong hands."

"Oh," Aine said softly. "Do you have a statue, Mabon?"

He showed her his statue and there was a huge wolf lying at his feet. As they moved around looking at the various figures Mabon explained, "Some people are full empaths and others recessives. Those that are not full empaths may carry recessive empathic traits but they can bear fully empathic offspring. And of course there are people and animals with no empathic traits at all."

He smiled, "No one knows why the animals choose their bond partners. One of my good friends is partnered with an owl." Mabon pointed to the statue of a slender woman with an owl on her shoulder. "Of course she is wise, as is he, so it makes sense."

Aine tried to imagine which of her parents may have passed that trait on to her. Somehow the idea of her mother being the least bit empathic seemed impossible. Dad would be the more likely candidate.

Mabon touched the statue of Aine and Zephyr. "By far the most common empathic animals are pegasites and wolves." Moving the statue back to its place on the shelf he unhooked the pendant from its hook above it.

Dangling the pendant from his fingertips he held it out to Aine. "This is why I brought you to see this room. Let me help you put it on, you should wear it always. It is a key to returning to your world."

Mabon noted the excitement in her eyes. "Each of us wears a talisman like this. Like your crystal ball, it is tuned only to you and will only respond to you." Mabon slipped the necklace over Aine's head. "It looks like crystal, but it is actually a dense structure not unlike a diamond."

"Tuned to me? What do you mean?" Aine held the stone in front of her and examined it.

Mabon smiled, "A talisman can be used in many ways, but primarily, it enhances your empathic gifts."

"Can you teach me how to use it?"

"I could, but a much better place for you to learn is at the School for Empathic Discovery. We call it the S.E.D."

Aine looked toward the door not hiding her disappointment, "I don't really think I have time to go to a school. I should probably try to get back as soon as I can. My family will be frantic if they discover I'm missing."

Mabon patted her arm gently. "Time passes differently between the worlds along the Celestial Band. Only a second or two will have passed in your world, yet hours and even days or weeks can pass here. Occasionally, time is even reversed, or so I've been told."

"Reversed time?" Aine was skeptical about that. Having activated the crystal ball at home relatively quickly, she wanted to see if she could do the same now. "Can I see if I can activate it?"

The corner of Mabon's mouth quirked and he nodded. "Certainly, go ahead." He crossed his arms and watched her.

Aine wrapped the crystal necklace in her right hand and closed her eyes. She concentrated on clearing her mind as she had done with the crystal ball, but nothing happened.

Thinking that she might need to touch it with both hands, she clasped it and tried again with no response. She opened her eyes once more.

"Do I need to return to the whirlpool, to the portal, to make it work?" Aine asked anxiously, struggling to control her frustration and disappointment.

"Not necessarily," Mabon replied evenly.

Aine tried again for several minutes without success. Finally, she met Mabon's gaze. "It's not going to work is it?"

Mabon shook his head. "Probably not now, but once you are trained it will. I have no doubt of that. You have a very strong empathic signature after all."

Failure was not something Aine had ever accepted easily. Carolinda would have teased her about it. Not sure what an empathic signature was she asked impatiently, "When will that be?"

"You will learn at your own pace. Like any skill, managing your empathic gifts takes time and practice."

Aine took a deep breath to calm down. "What has happened to me back home?"

"Since you cannot be conscious in two places at once, you will remain quiescent there and cognizant here. It is normal for first time travelers to leave an unconscious self behind the first few times that they travel. While you are here, you will appear to be in a trance there. But I believe your friend, Lula will watch over you until you can return."

Aine realized that he was probably right. One thing she'd learned with her music studies was that the only way to truly master a difficult passage was to isolate it and practice small sections until she'd accomplished her goal. Since there was nothing she could do immediately to facilitate her return to her home, she'd have to approach the problem differently. Perhaps she would learn more quickly at the school.

Mabon started toward the door. "It is late and past the time to settle for the evening. Come with me if you will, there is someone I would like you to meet."

Curious about who it could be, she followed Mabon back to the main room where she heard scuffling and growling from outside the door. They stepped out to see Zephyr flying up and down just a bit above the ground while an enormous wolf raced past her leaping and snapping at her hooves.

Zephyr's tone was light and playful, *"He can never catch me, the silly thing, but he loves to try."*

"Now that's enough of that you two," Mabon chuckled. "Come here and meet Aine." The wolf bounded to Mabon and stood on his back feet with his front paws on his master's shoulders and proceeded to lick Mabon's face.

Aine took a step back never having been this close to such a large wild animal.

Mabon grumbled and pushed the wolf down. The wolf then trotted to Aine sitting in front of her exhibiting perfect behavior. Mabon smiled as he joined them patting the canine's head. "This character is Phelan, and as you probably suspected, he's my empathic partner."

The wolf regarded Aine for a moment before he bumped his head against her hand. Aine scratched behind his ears and Phelan literally smiled at her, his long tongue lolling out the side of his grinning mouth.

"Don't stop, that feels so good!" The thought entered her mind.

"He's telling me not to stop, it feels good." She laughed.

Mabon gasped and Aine saw the look of shock on his face. "What's wrong?" she asked looking around quickly.

He looked in disbelief at the young woman and then at the wolf. "I know that's what he said. But you heard him?"

"Yes I did, is that bad?" Aine worried.

"No, no, not at all. It is just that most of us can only hear our own partners." For a moment, a yearning sadness shone on his face but Mabon controlled it quickly. "It has been a very long time since we've had a multi-lingual among us, it should make your education very interesting."

"So hearing more than one empathic animal is unusual?"

"Yes, it is quite rare; in fact, you are only the second person I've ever known with that ability." The look of deep sadness was in his eyes again. He cleared his throat, "Here, I'll show you the stable and you can feed and water Zephyr."

A small donkey brayed loudly when Mabon opened the door and Aine helped Mabon feed him and Zephyr. It was nearly dark when they returned to the cave for a simple meal. Afterwards they sat quietly watching the shadows from the fire play hide and seek on the walls.

"Tell me more about the school, Mabon. Is it the only way I can learn to use my talisman?"

"It is not the only way, but it is the best way. The students there are all new empaths and you will learn more quickly in a group with others. The senior trainers are experts in training and I think you would enjoy meeting some of them."

Since her earlier failure to use the talisman, it was obvious that she needed instruction. Aine considered Mabon's premise that time was different between worlds. Perhaps she could learn quickly enough at the school to return home before anyone missed her.

She made her decision, "Well, I need to learn, and if going to the school is the quickest way to learn what I need to, I will go to the school."

Mabon stood and stretched. "Impeccable logic, my dear. We'll start early tomorrow. It's a long way to the school so we'd best get to bed early."

He showed her to a bedroom and she yawned twice as she removed her clothes and donned a long nightshirt she found folded on the dresser. Mabon spoke from outside her door, "Do you need anything, Aine?"

"No, thanks, Mabon." She yawned again, feeling exhausted.

"I'll wake you bright and early." He hesitated and then added, "I'm glad you are here, Aine. Sleep well."

As she pulled up the covers Phelan came in to the room and touched her hand with his cold nose. His voice was a faint whisper, *"Yes, we are glad you are here, we have been waiting a long time for you, little sister."* The wolf moved to the doorway and curled up on the floor, his eyes glowing in the faint light.

Too tired to wonder what he meant, Aine gave in to her fatigue and dropped off to sleep.

CHAPTER SIX

Visions

The gray light of dawn filtered into Aine's room from the tiny windows built high in the wall and the faint chatter of birds offering welcome to the day penetrated her sleepy mind. She snuggled into the warmth of the covers trying to go back to sleep but a cold nose nuzzled her hand and she heard the wild thrumming of a wagging tail. Thinking it was Penny, she pushed him away, but Phelan continued to nip up and down her arm with tiny wolf bites, something Penny had never done. She opened one eye to see his wolfish grin and her heart raced as she flung off the covers and rose from the bed. So, it wasn't a dream! She was still here on Drayon.

Zephyr's gentle thoughts brushed her mind and Aine sighed, momentarily longing to bury herself in the covers and hide from this strange world.

"All is well this morning, little sister. My master says that breakfast is almost ready." Phelan seemed to sense her reluctance to face the day.

Wrapping herself in a dark blue robe she opened the door and forgot her reluctance to awaken when she smelled freshly baked bread. The front door stood open and the light from the early sun spilled across the threshold giving the room a cheery brightness.

Mabon's smile crinkled the corners of his eyes as he looked up from pouring tea into two mugs. "Good morning, Aine. Come and enjoy some breakfast. We have fruit, cheese and my specialty, fresh bread."

Aine's stomach grumbled loudly. The bread was soft and warm nearly melting in her mouth and she smiled at Phelan begging mournfully from his place near the fireplace.

Mabon tossed him some dried meat from a pouch on the shelf behind him. "He is perfectly capable of feeding himself, but he's still a persistent beggar."

She started to help Mabon with the dishes but he fore-stalled her. "I can take care of these." He pointed to the left passage that led from the room. "Follow that passage to the end and you will find a pool for bathing. By the time you are finished, I should have everything ready for our trip to the school."

Aine hesitated looking at the dishes. "My mother would never approve, are you sure I can't help you?"

"Not at all, there are only a few dishes and it will only take me a minute. You will find soap and towels in a basket by the pool." Mabon turned to his task.

Aine gathered her jeans and sweater from her room. Searching the drawers of the dresser she found clean socks and underclothes, she tried them on, not entirely surprised that they fit her exactly.

Following the smooth walls of the passage she again noted the lights that brightened as she passed and wondered at the level of technology that could delve such smooth walls and embed the unusual lighting.

The bathing pool was not at all what she expected. The room was huge and the pool itself much larger than two swimming pools at home. The ceiling was so high that she couldn't really see it clearly and the water shone like a silky black mirror with wisps of steam rising from its surface.

Aine removed her robe and laid it across the stone bench by the door and took the soap and towels from the basket. Closing her eyes she inhaled the scent of fresh daffodils in the bottle of soap. Making her way to the edge of the pool she stepped down on to the first step. The water was warm, just shy of being hot and she moved to the center of the pool. There was a slight underwater current and she immersed herself enjoying the water's warm caress, as she lathered her hair.

After she rinsed the soap from her hair she moved back to the lowest step and sat so that the water lapped about her shoulders. The soap bubbles floated away in the current until the pool ran clear again and she pulled her fingers through her wet hair. Climbing out of the pool, she wrapped her wet hair in a towel and put on the robe.

As she bent down to pick up the shampoo she saw an image on the surface of the water. Stepping forward to get a closer look she saw her own towel-wrapped head in the reflection. She started to turn away when another face appeared next to her own. She spun around to look behind her, but no one was there.

She turned back to study the face. It was a handsome boy about her age with black hair and dark blue eyes that sparkled with humor. His full lips parted with a slight smile and he was looking directly at her. He seemed familiar, yet she had never seen him before. He smiled as if he was looking directly at her and she wondered who he could be. She felt strangely attracted to him.

A sudden ring of fire surfaced on the pool surrounding the image of the young man and then another face rose like steam from the water.

Aine gasped. It was the man from her nightmare. Her heart raced at the demand in his eyes. His mouth smiled sardonically, mocking her. She felt her throat close in fear and she could not look away. A low humming sound filled her mind and she swayed with a tinge of dizziness.

His voice caressed her mind just as it had in her dream. *"So you have come at last. You have come to my world, and you will be mine. You must find your way to me, my bride. I need you. Come to me!"*

Aine watched helplessly as the vision drifted closer. She gasped at the burning touch of his fingers on her cheek and she felt a hot knife of desire scorch her body. It was unlike anything she had ever imagined. In some strange way she craved for him to touch her again. And if he did, she would do anything he asked.

Then, as if from far away, she heard Zephyr's scream. *"No! Do not let him touch your mind. No, my mistress, use your talisman, you must grasp it. Quickly!"*

Aine felt the urge to bat away Zephyr's intrusion as one would a pesky fly, but she found herself shrinking back as he reached for her again.

Zephyr's shout, louder now, filled her mind. *"No! My mistress, fight him. Do not let him touch you. He is evil; you must not let him touch you. Use your talisman."*

Mabon was filling the water jugs at the spring when he saw Zephyr fly to the entrance of the cave beat her wings against the door to get inside. Phelan crashed through the underbrush at the edge of the clearing and raced past the filly. *"Come quickly master, little sister is in danger!"*

The jars fell to the ground and Mabon raced after the wolf into the cave. They sped down the hall to the pool and skidded inside.

Phelan growled and snapped but Aine didn't seem to hear either of them. She stood on the steps of the pool, one hand reaching for her talisman and the other toward the shimmering image in front of her. Mabon could see the look of longing on her face, and the hesitation in her eyes. He pulled a crystal the size of an orange from his pocket and held it in front of him. A dazzling blue light filled the air and he shouted his telepathic command, *"Leave this place and do not return or I will follow you and destroy you, Takkar!"*

A look of surprise and frustration changed Takkar's face as he pulled his gaze away from Aine and regarded Mabon. *"She is mine, Mabon. I will have her! She will come to me when you and that sniveling cur of yours cannot protect her. She is mine!"*

Mabon kept the blue light focused on the vision. *"Be gone!"*

Fury filled Takkar's face and the image wavered.

"Mistress, use your talisman. Now, please," Zephyr pleaded.

Dazed, Aine slowly reached up and grasped the pulsing light of her pendant and the image of the cruel face dissolved.

Aine turned and stumbled toward Mabon. He helped her to sit on the bench.

"It is over, Aine, the vision is gone." Mabon handed her a small flask that had been attached to his belt and her hands trembled as she reached for it. The towel fell from her wet hair and she shuddered as the strong spirit burned her throat, but it did warm and calm her.

Mabon clasped her cold hands in his own. "Are you all right now, child?"

Aine face was ghostly, "Yes, I think so."

They walked together back to the main cave and Mabon brought her a brush from her room. She moved close to the fire to brush her damp hair until it started to dry.

Mabon's eyes were kind, "Tell me."

Haltingly, Aine described her vision to Mabon. "Who is he, Mabon? What does he want?"

Mabon closed his eyes as if in prayer. He drew in another deep breath and opened his eyes to meet hers.

Aine watched the struggle on his face. "You know him, don't you?"

"Yes," Mabon said. "And you have seen him before as well haven't you?"

Tears stung her eyes at the memory and Aine dashed them away. "Yes, in a nightmare when I was still at home."

Mabon sighed and nodded. "His name is Takkar. It is troubling that he has found a way to project a summoning through the celestial band. He was probably responsible for Zephyr's capture as well."

"How could he possibly have been in my dream at home? And why would he want to capture Zephyr?"

"Takkar is an empath too, though to my knowledge he has never bonded with an empathic animal. It appears that he has discovered how to reach beyond our world, and enter yours, even if only in a dream. The reason he wants you is a long, complicated story."

Aine's voice rose, "It makes no sense. He says that I am his, but he doesn't even know me."

"Aine, the reason why Takkar seeks you may be difficult for you to understand while you are so new to us, but if you will listen to me, I will tell you."

The memory of Takkar's compelling demands lingered in her mind and brought a taste of fear to her throat, yet she had to know why he sought her. She nodded. "I want to know."

Mabon looked away gazing into the dying fire. "There is an ancient prophecy on Drayon. A woman will come to us, from afar, perhaps even from another world. The fate of

Drayon's future will be determined by her choices. She must face a man called the malevolent one. It is said that he desires ultimate dominion over all of Drayon. Some of the legends associated with the prophecy hint that the woman will be bonded to a light colored pegasite."

Aine crossed her arms, holding herself tightly, unconsciously rejecting Mabon's words. "Is that why Zephyr was captured?"

Mabon nodded, "I believe so."

Brushing his hand on Phelan's coat he murmured, "I wondered if you were aware of the prophecy before you came to Drayon, but that is impossible. Just knowing of the prophecy, might have affected your choice to come to our world."

Aine interrupted, "What choice? I didn't choose to come here!"

Then she hesitated and bowed her head. Of course she had chosen to come. Hadn't Lula asked her several times if she wanted to try? No one had forced her. She'd made a conscious choice to touch that crystal ball and she had wanted to come. In fact she had felt compelled by the strange crystal.

Aine sighed. What had first seemed like an exciting adventure was rapidly becoming something strange and sinister.

Mabon cleared his throat. "The people of Drayon believe that the young woman will be either the catalyst into total dominion, or ultimate freedom." He sat straighter, a look of steely determination in his eyes, "I think you may be that young woman, Aine. I believe that you have come to us for a reason and that reason is the prophecy."

Aine bit her lip and looked down at her clenched hands. Every fiber of her being wanted to reject his premise, but when she met his gaze again, she saw the truth of his belief in his eyes.

He reached over to take her hand. "Aine, there are three things you must understand. First, and most important, it is not yet time for the prophecy to be fulfilled. The ultimate confrontation between the evil one and the young woman is still in the future. There are many things that must occur before that time.

"Secondly, despite Takkar's attempts to reach you, he cannot force you to do anything. The principle premise is that the woman of the prophecy must be free to choose that destiny and neither he, nor anyone else can force that choice.

"Finally, you are not alone in this. You have a wonderful partner who will always defend and protect you, as will Phelan and I. And I know there are others who will help us keep you safe, until you have made your choice."

Phelan moved in next to her putting his head in her lap as Mabon continued. "Though he may try to compel you to follow him, Takkar can never force you to do so. If you are the young woman, and you choose to return to your own world, and leave Drayon to its fate, that is what will happen."

"I get that you think I'm this woman," Aine said. "But what makes Takkar want me badly enough to intrude in my world and into my dream?"

Mabon looked away for a moment obviously trying to think how to answer her. His evasive look bothered her.

Finally, he squared his shoulders and made sure that he was looking directly into her eyes. "You need time to adapt to being here. You need…" Mabon stopped and looked away.

"What is it, Mabon? What do I need?"

Mabon took a deep breath, "If the malevolent one of the prophecy gains dominion over our world, there is also the possibility that he can do so in other worlds as well."

Aine shook her head denying Mabon's words. Takkar had said that she would join him and they would possess the universe. That must mean that he needed her, or someone to help him achieve that. Mabon's next words confirmed her suspicion.

"Even though he is an empath like you and me, he is warped and uses his gifts as compulsions, to manipulate others. Yet despite that, there is also the potential for his defeat. The woman of the prophecy has it within her to save our world too. Evidently Takkar believes that the woman of the prophecy can give him access to other worlds." Mabon's eyes were intense. "You are a traveler, Aine. You could well be able to do that."

Aine scoffed in disbelief, "I can't even get myself home. How could he expect me to take him anywhere?"

"You will learn, eventually. Of that I am absolutely sure."

The momentary pleasure Aine felt at Mabon's confidence in her dissipated when she noted the worry on his face.

"If he could gain access to your world or other worlds, the results could be devastating."

She was momentarily relieved that she didn't know how to get home. At least, for the time being, her family and friends were safe.

Mabon's eyes cleared and she saw the resolve in them. "Listen to me Aine. He will not find you again easily. I can, and will, keep you safe and hidden now that I know he seeks you. Phelan and I know many ways to stay hidden from him and I will teach you some of them. This has been a shock to you, and much too sudden, but I think you should try not to think about it for a while. Keep your focus on what you will learn at the school."

Aine burst out, "But, he made me want to give in to him Mabon. I couldn't seem to resist. If Zephyr hadn't…"

Mabon interrupted, "Zephyr sensed you were in trouble and she did exactly the right thing by warning you."

"Phelan's partner used his powers to drive the evil image away as well," Zephyr explained.

Aine felt a surge of relief. "Zephyr says that you drove him away too."

Mabon smiled, "That is why you must not be afraid anymore. I will protect you until you can learn how to protect yourself. Now, if you are all right, we really should be on our way."

Aine dressed and met Mabon outside. As they packed the baskets tied to the donkey's back Aine asked, "Who was the young man that I saw in the vision, before I saw Takkar. He seemed familiar and not dangerous at all."

"Others have seen images in that pool before you, Aine. Usually it means the vision has a special meaning to the viewer. From your description, I think you saw the image of Aiden. He is one of the senior trainers at the school. He is a fine young man, although a bit cocky. I think you will like him though."

After balancing the load, Mabon raised his hands and the trees and brush once more disguised the face of his cave.

They started along a path and Zephyr settled behind Aine nudging her shoulder as Phelan loped ahead. *"I will never allow anyone to hurt you, my mistress, I am glad that you took your talisman when you did."*

"Thank you, Zephyr. I am so glad that you were there for me." Firmly pushing her thoughts and fears regarding Takkar from her mind, she followed Mabon.

"How long will it take to get to the school, Mabon?"

Mabon spoke over his shoulder. "We should arrive tomorrow afternoon. We need to make some preparations first to diffuse our empathic signatures. It's not far, but we don't want to dally along the way."

The trail became harder to navigate with rocks and brush obscuring the way. Initially the forest was hardwoods like maple and oak gradually changing to densely crowded pines and grew as dim as twilight beneath them. At times the trail disappeared completely but Mabon never faltered.

Aine mulled the events of the past two days. She wondered if Mabon's belief in the prophecy meant it was possible. It would certainly explain why she had felt such a powerful need to activate the crystal ball. Yet the idea of her being some sort of hero was ludicrous. She was a girl from a small town whose only possible skill was in music. There was no way she was any kind of a hero. In truth she had no desire to be. She just wanted to go home.

Then she recalled the vision of the younger man with the black hair and startling blue eyes. There was something about him that intrigued her and if he was at the school, she'd meet him. She looked forward to that.

They continued on their way, the forest growing denser. Phelan ran ahead fading in and out, using his excellent vision and sense of smell to guide them. The wolf was not laughing or playful today, he was all business.

Aine wondered if Lula had known about the prophecy and where the crystal ball would take her. There had been something evasive in Lula's eyes when they had been talking about the crystal ball. Aine remembered it now clearly.

Was it possible that Lula had known what might happen to Aine? Aine had chosen to come, although now she wished she hadn't. Well, what had happened already could not be changed so she turned her musings away from why things had happened and changed her focus to what she would do about it.

They stopped several times to rest the donkey and once to eat. The sun sat low in the sky when they finally reached a small meadow with a babbling brook surrounded by tall pines with a deep carpet of needles beneath. Aine helped Mabon unload the donkey and she watched as the donkey ambled off to join Zephyr to feed on the long grasses at the edge of the woods.

Mabon warmed ingredients for soup over a small fire and Aine filled the water skin and the kettle for tea. After they had eaten and hobbled the donkey, they sat quietly for a while, watching the fire as the stars began to appear. The forest smelled of wet leaves and pine, and the cool night air caressed them with a soft breeze. If she weren't so far from home, she could almost look upon this as a fun camping adventure. But the disturbing memory of Takkar's demanding eyes was never far from her thoughts.

"Mabon, why did the vision of Takkar disappear when I touched the pendant?"

Mabon stoked the fire with a branch causing the embers to shoot brilliant bursts of fireworks. "One of its functions of your talisman is to protect you from harm, and that my dear, is exactly what it did."

"Do you have a talisman?" Aine asked.

"Yes, mine was made long ago and I received it when I became competent at some basic empathic skills." He pulled a dark stone that looked like onyx from under his shirt. It hung on a leather cord and was shaped like a wolf's head.

"To answer your question; when you grasped your talisman, it broke his summoning so he could not sense your empathic signature anymore."

"How does it work?" Aine asked.

"Let me show you." He pulled an orange-sized crystal from the deep pocket in his cloak. "Can you feel the fact that I'm an empath right now, Aine?"

"I'm not sure if I know what you mean, but I have a sense about you, I feel your bond with Phelan strongly and I can certainly hear his thoughts."

Mabon chuckled, "Yes, he is hungry isn't he."

Mabon bribed Phelan with a promise. *"Stay with us for a moment while I show her how to hide herself, then you can go."*

Phelan pulled his lips back in a wolfy grin just as they heard a howl in the distance. *"My brothers call me. I will wait but not for long."*

"You can probably sense me because we are so close together. It would be more difficult with distance. But every empath can expand their protective aura if they know how. Now, I am going to touch the talisman, and then I will speak to Phelan, when I do, tell me if you can hear us."

Mabon held the crystal in one hand and touched it to his pendant and Aine saw a bluish aura around both objects.

"I think little sister can hear me even if you try and hide, my master."

"Did you hear him?"

"It was faint and sounded far away, but I could hear him. It was different from the way I've heard him before."

"You have great talents, my dear. Rose will be delighted to have you as her student."

"Now, touch your pendant. Think of speaking telepathically only to Phelan but no one else, like a whisper. Let's see if I can hear his response."

Aine held her talisman and thought for a moment, finally speaking in a mental whisper. *"Phelan, you are the most beautiful wolf I have ever seen. Not that I've seen many."*

"Thank you, little sister. Can I go soon? I hunger for the hunt with my brothers."

Mabon shook his head. "Nothing. I could tell you were communicating, but I wouldn't have even noticed if I hadn't been focused on you." Mabon chuckled and waved dismissal to Phelan, "The lesson is over my friend, run along and hunt well." Phelan leapt up and disappeared into the woods.

"I'm not sure I really understand. What did the crystal do?"

Mabon held the crystal out to her. "This is my personal crystal ball. It works in conjunction with my talisman to enhance my empathic abilities."

Handing his crystal to her, he had her touch her own talisman with it. When she did, he spoke some words she didn't understand. "I have created a shield around your talisman. It will mute your empathic signature even more so that you will be nearly impossible to sense. It only lasts about a day, then it will dissipate, but that should get us to the school safely. Now you should sleep and when Phelan returns I will rest as well."

Aine spread the bedroll and settled next to the fire. She was grateful that the night passed quietly, and they awoke and started on their way just as the sun's first rays touched the tops of the trees.

CHAPTER SEVEN

Memories of Evil

Lula moved around the room relighting the candles and lamps. Aine remained in her trance sitting at the table with her hands resting lightly on the crystal ball.

Priscilla butted the screen door on the porch and came through it, flowing into the form of a woman who could pass for Lula's sister. Tall and gangly with short white hair the exact shade of her coat when she was a goat, her dark brown eyes met Lula's.

"Is she all right?"

"Yes, although I was surprised to see her make the transition so quickly. I wish I could have explained more to her."

Lula had accepted her role as Aine's guardian with the knowledge that Aine must choose to follow her destiny with no coercion from anyone, not even Lula who loved her dearly.

Lula said, "*Aine's empathic gifts are exceptionally strong, but she has grown up in a predictable and sheltered environment and knows nothing of them. Traveling to Drayon will be a shock to her.*"

Priscilla crossed her arms, regarding her friend. *"She is more than ready to fledge from the nest of her childhood. It is time and you know it."*

"I suppose you are right," Lula sighed.

"What about her dream, was it a summoning?" Priscilla asked.

Lula sat down on the couch. "Perhaps. It was Takkar, I am sure of that. If he has found a way to travel the celestial band and attempt a summoning, his powers are considerable."

"What will you do?"

"I must know more about him and why he seeks her. We must know if he is the evil one of the prophecy so that we can protect Aine. The only way to learn the truth is to travel back through the timeline and observe him."

Lula was a traveler as well as a powerful empath. She and Priscilla were alien entities as were many of the guardians of the paired worlds within the celestial band. Others on Aine's world were called angels and Lula supposed that was an apt description. In their native form Priscilla and Lula were an essence of energy rather than corporal one. Both could transmutate to any life form they chose. It was as simple as breathing for them but assuredly not something the people of this world could comprehend. Lula had taken her human form upon becoming the guardian of Aine's home world, long before the girl had been born.

When Aine described her nightmare, Lula had concealed her concerns not wanting to frighten the girl. She suspected that the man Aine described was Takkar and when Aine left that night, Lula created a block so that he would be unable to summon her again. The block prevented Lula from communicating with her old friend Mabon to warn him that the time was at hand. Now that Aine had traveled to Drayon, the block was gone. She hoped that Aine would find Mabon quickly so that he could help to protect her.

Today, Lula would return to the Drayon of the past. Like transmutation, it was something she did easily, yet she configured the timeline carefully. She decided to focus on the time when Takkar was a young man to learn more of what motivated him.

First, she wove a forgetting barrier around the cabin that would cause anyone who ventured near to forget why they had come. The barrier would also slow time for Aine in this world so both she and Aine would have the time they needed to accomplish what they must. Then she and Priscilla made their way to the closet portal in her bedroom.

"Are you sure you must do this?" Priscilla said.

"You know I must."

She unlocked her closet door and touched the hidden switch that moved the panel. A cool, earthy smell flowed up the stairway as they moved silently down the stairs into the subterranean transfer chamber. Priscilla retreated to the doorway while Lula touched the pendant around her neck. She shimmered and disappeared.

Having prepared her timeline precisely, she met the first thread of time she sought exactly as intended. She had changed into an unremarkable bird, a sparrow. As she focused on the time and Takkar's empathic aura, she was drawn to the dim recesses of a cottage high in the mountains. Takkar would be about twenty years old, already possessing dangerous skills if she wasn't wrong. She flittered through the open window and hid quickly in a shadowy corner.

Takkar was face to face with a bent, irate old man and they were arguing. "I am going to learn what you know, Okat. I will never allow anyone to control or compel me again and you will see that I master it!"

Despite the fact that Takkar towered over the old man, he ignored the threats and limped to a pile of scrolls to sort through them. He found what he sought and squinted up at Takkar, "Your impatience is a waste of energy and you do not frighten me, so sit down and stop making a fool of yourself."

Surprisingly Takkar did as he was told. Okat shuffled to a table near the window where the light was better. Pouring a flagon of ale from the pitcher he drank deeply, wiping his mouth with the back of his hand. "Learning how to compel others is relatively easy. Controlling your desire to demand more and more from the power you gain, is not. Your empathic gift is among the strongest I have felt, but you will be warped and hated if you use only the dark side of it. She's made you want it too much. You must understand the limitations as well as the power."

Takkar laughed, "What Ravyn taught me has nothing to do with this. Are you jealous old man? Are you angry that she took what she could from you and then left you alone?"

Okat drank again deeply and gazed at the younger man, shaking his head slowly. "I always knew her for what she was. Do you?"

Takkar laughed, "She has only started me in this quest, but she knew what I could become. I got what I wanted from her, as did she. Now, you will teach me the rest."

Taking a long swallow of his drink Takkar added, "Warped and hated? What would you know of it? I've lived with hatred my entire life."

Okat was silent as Takkar continued, "That's why I finally killed him and when I did, they were all grateful." His eyes burned into the older man's. "That is why they serve me still."

Okat regarded Takkar without surprise. "It was rumored that you murdered your father."

Takkar raised his brows, incredulous. "Of course I killed him, what else would I have done?" He stretched his long legs beneath the table and twirled the glass in his fingers.

"Do you know how he used to entertain himself?" Takkar didn't wait for an answer. "When I was no more than five or six he would tell me, in lurid detail, everything he had done to hurt my mother. He told me how he drugged her so that she wouldn't fight him. He knew I was the only thing she had in the world to love, and he tortured her, threatening to hurt me if she didn't do everything he told her to. He was obsessed with controlling her. His warped, drunken mind could not conceive of how repulsed she must have been. He delighted in regaling me with stories of his brutality."

A look of disgust and hatred passed over Takkar's face, distorting his handsome features. "When I was just a toddler, he began to hit or burn me and she would do anything he said to prevent it." Takkar sighed, and his voice calmed a bit. He poured another drink and downed it. "He knew about compulsion and never hesitated to use it to make everyone in that castle do his bidding. He especially liked to humiliate her, usually in front of others. Once when the other men in the ruling council came he took me to her room and bound me to the bed. He told her that if she refused to obey him, he would kill me. Just to prove that he meant it he sliced my palm and refused to let her bandage it." At this Takkar held out his hand and Lula could see the white line of a scar on his palm.

"I remember how beautiful she was with her rich dark eyes and ebony hair. She was pale and warm and always loving to me, the only person who ever really loved me." Takkar's voice softened and tears glistened in his eyes.

He was silent then, and Lula wondered if he was done. When he raised his eyes to regard Okat, they were dead and dark like those of a shark. "When I was about four, she discovered that she was pregnant again."

Takkar rose and paced back and forth as he talked, his voice tight and grating. "She could not bear the thought of bringing another child into that den of evil and she begged the old nurse to take me and escape. Nurse thought that my mother would come to meet us, or she never would have agreed. There was a secret passage that led from the tower where my mother's room was. I remember what she said to me, 'I love you, my little man, and I will always love you.'"

He shuddered. "I remember the long spiral stairway. It was dark and I was frightened. The nurse held my hand the whole way down and we ran to the woods beyond the castle. We were running through the woods when I heard her voice calling him as he rode into the courtyard with his men. She laughed at him and she almost seemed happy. She was dressed in a deep crimson gown with her long black hair blowing around her like a dark halo in the dying sunset.

"I tried to run back to the castle but the nurse held me tight and covered my mouth. He threatened her, he threatened to burn me alive and force her to watch unless she did as he bid. But she laughed at him again, 'He is safe from you, Runik. My son is safe and you cannot hurt either of us anymore."

A fine sweat beaded Takkar's brow and a look of profound sorrow crossed his features. "She cursed him and she told him that he would die a terrible death, in unbearable pain, begging for release. Then, silently, she held her arms to the sky and the wind whipped the sleeves of her dress back. She was so beautiful in that dark red dress with her ebony hair flying out behind her like a cape. She told my father that she would never rest until her curse came true."

Takkar bowed his head, his voice so soft that Lula had to strain to hear him. "Then she dropped her arms and fell without a sound. Her body made a horrible sound as it broke on the rocks below."

Takkar was silent for a long time, staring at the glass in front of him.

"When she jumped, he became frantic, so maddened that he fell to the ground foaming at the mouth. The nurse and the man who was helping us took me away, but I was not to be free of him."

Takkar raised his dark eyes to gaze at Okat. Lula shuddered at the look on his face. His eyes were glazed and empty and she wondered about his sanity. "When he learned that I was missing, he threatened to lock all of the servants in the barn and burn them alive if they didn't find us. Of course they did find us, eventually.

"For years afterwards he swore that he could see her cursing him from that turret. He locked her rooms only opening them once a week to be cleaned. He tried to fool himself into believing that she had died some other way, but he never set foot in those chambers again."

Takkar regarded the other man, "She's still there, I have seen her."

Taking seat by the window, close to Lula, Takkar said, "I'm only sorry it took me so long to oblige him and see him dead. It was my duty to fulfill her curse when the opportunity arose. I had to avenge her. I had to be free of him as well."

Takkar continued. "I lived my entire childhood in fear. He threatened and beat me every day. It's a wonder I didn't suffer any lasting damage. I was nearly fourteen when he abused one of the young serving girls until she was almost dead. She was a lovely girl with long dark hair and dark eyes, eerily familiar to me. Someone took her back to the village where her family could care for her. The girl had a younger brother who came to work for us shortly afterward. Of course my father didn't know he was her brother. One night my father was in the stables after another girl and the brother saw them and hit my father from behind with a shovel. Thinking that he had killed my father, he and the girl fled. But my father wasn't dead."

There was a look of demented pleasure in Takkar's eyes and Lula flipped her wings shuddering.

Takkar looked up at Okat and smiled. "He was paralyzed, unable to move anything below his neck."

"I saw him every day, drooling and filthy in his bed. It was remarkable how quickly his body decayed. His mind was there, but his body was useless. He was covered in waste and boils and in terrible pain."

Takkar smiled with true delight. "He would beg me to help him. And I reminded him of my mother's curse and reminded him that he took her from me. I looked at the stinking slime that had fathered me, and I laughed. Then I picked up the candle and set the sheets by his legs afire. He screamed long before the flames reached him. I tired of his ragged pleading and the stench of his burning flesh so I stood at the edge of the room by the window.

"The sound of his screams filled me with gratification. And then she was there. My mother was there. If I had reached out I could have touched her. Her long black hair danced lightly around her head and her dark red gown clung tightly. She stared at him and smiled as he screamed her name. The flames engulfed him and he died with her name on his lips. When he was finally dead she turned to me and smiled, just as she had when I was little, and then she faded away. A fitting end, don't you think?"

Takkar finished his wine as Okat faced him shaking his head slowly, "You are as hopeless as he was and more a fool." Okat's eyes darkened. "You will end as he did unless you change your ways."

For just a fleeting moment a flash of fear crossed Takkar's dead eyes. Then he shrugged. "Perhaps I am a fool, but once I have mastered all of your dirty little tricks, there is nothing I can't have or become. And once I have that power I will find the woman of the prophecy and she will be mine. The world will be mine and no one will stop me from taking anything that I want." Takkar chuckled again with that evil laugh chillingly reminiscent of a mad man.

Lula had heard enough. She flew out the window and winged her way to the forest and then shimmered to transfer back to her home. She was exhausted and distraught as she merged into her human form.

Lula fell into Priscilla's arms and they shimmered to the pure pulsing light of their native forms. Pricilla murmured, "Do not worry. All will be well, my dearest friend." Gradually the glow melded and they were once again two human women.

CHAPTER EIGHT

The School for Empathic Discovery

It was mid-afternoon when Mabon and Aine passed under an arch of reddish stones that stood twice the height of a man. The arch marked the northern boundary of the school's property. Beyond it climbed a series of steep hills. The crest of the final hill before reaching the school was treeless affording a breathtaking view of the vista beyond. A narrow valley cradled a crystal clear lake and a group of buildings were nearly obscured under their canopy of pines. The soft breeze brought the scent of water and evergreen and the faint sound of laughter.

As they came closer Aine saw that the roof of the expansive log building was blanketed in the iridescent rainbow of moss. Behind the building a graceful slope led to the lake and the deep blue waves skipped into whitecaps. A group of young people shouted and whistled while two boys swung another between them and threw him into the lake. He burst from the water roaring with laughter.

Mabon chuckled at the revelry. "Ah, initiation for the red pod, spirited as usual."

A tall young man, his hair glinting like a sunset of red and amber, strode to the group from behind the building. His dark crimson tunic was impeccable a sharp contrast to the dripping red garbed group that scrambled into line in front of him. His gestures marked his displeasure, and when he finished speaking the group quickly dispersed. As he turned to follow, Aine saw a smile tug the corner of his mouth. Realizing that she had stopped in her tracks to watch, Aine hurried to catch up with Mabon.

The door at the main entrance to the building was deep chestnut wood richly decorated with elaborate scrollwork. As Mabon lifted his hand to knock at the door it swung open and a tiny being with bright clothing, silvery curls and gossamer wings, hovered in front of him. In a pert musical voice she sang, "I'm so happy to see you, Lord Mabon. I will tell Lady Rose that you are here." She spun a somersault before dashing out of sight down the hallway.

Mabon turned to Phelan, "Show Zephyr to the stables and see if someone can come up and unload the donkey for us."

Aine followed Mabon into the hall, "Who was that?"

"Oh, that was Faye, she's a pixie," Mabon answered.

As if on cue, Faye returned and led them through a long hallway. The ceiling beams of dark black wood were a stark contrast to the pure white walls and they passed a number of ornately carved doors. When they reached their destination Faye hovered for a moment and then dashed through the open door.

Crystal latticed windows lined one wall spilling a rainbow of colors on the rich wooden floor beneath. An ornate desk in mahogany stood near the center of the room on a forest green carpet. Aine saw an owl perched on a T-shaped stand behind the desk and thought it was a statue until he turned his head to regard her intently with his unblinking yellow eyes.

A beautiful woman entered from a smaller room beyond the desk. She smiled as she held her hands out to Mabon. The woman's amber eyes lit with pleasure as she grasped Mabon's hands and then hugged him, kissing both cheeks. "It is so good to see you again, my dear friend."

Dressed in a silky dress the color of new spring leaves her long hair, too dark to be blond too light to be red, shone as the sunlight from the window touched it.

"It is wonderful to see you too, Rose." Mabon's voice was husky for a moment and then he cleared his throat and gestured to Aine. "I have brought a new student for you, Rose, this is Aine."

Rose smiled and reached for Aine's hands. When they touched Aine's nervousness dissolved. Just like Mabon, this woman inspired trust and welcome with a simple touch.

"I am Rose, the director of the School for Empathic Discovery, and I am very pleased to meet you, Aine." Rose's smile made her seem even younger, and there was kindness and welcome in her golden eyes. "So you have come to learn your art with us."

"Yes, I hope so."

Mabon grinned, "You will be delighted to know that Aine is a multi-lingual, and she has bonded with the silver pegasite filly, Zephyr."

Rose stepped back, releasing Aine's hands. "Mabon has told me of Phelan's friend, Zephyr. I am thrilled that she has found you at last. You are very lucky."

Aine smiled, unsure what to say, but Rose continued blithely, "How exciting for you to have the gifts of a multi-lingual, I shall look forward to teaching you." At Rose's invitation, they moved to three chairs in front of the desk. "Now, tell me all about yourself. How did Zephyr find you, or was it the other way around?"

Rose's friendliness was infectious and before long Aine found herself telling Rose how she had found the crystal ball and how Lula had helped her come to Drayon. She shared the wonders of her bond with Zephyr and even told about her family. Realizing that she had been talking too much she paused, and then blurted, "I don't mean to be rude, but I really must return home as soon as I can. How soon can I start to learn about my talisman?"

Rose showed no overt reaction to Aine's story. "I think we can begin your instruction tomorrow. It seems that you have already had some impressive adventures, and it would be good for you to be settled first." Rose's amber eyes met Aine's, "Mabon will have explained how time passes differently between the worlds in the celestial band, is that not correct?"

Aine nodded but her face was skeptical.

Rose saw it immediately. "The ability to travel is a remarkable one. I am sure that your friend Lula would not have encouraged you to do so, if you would be unable to return."

Aine shook her head trying to stifle her impatience. "She did tell me that I would return when I was ready."

"So you shall." Rose said. "You must understand that it will take time to master your talents. Even our most gifted students have discovered that they sometimes learn more slowly than they wish."

Aine bowed her head hiding the disappointment in her eyes.

Rose tilted her head to the side and tapped her lips with one finger. "I must consider which training group, or pod as we call them would be most appropriate for you.

"You will have seen the Red Pod group as you arrived." A slight smile tugged at Rose's mouth. She was obviously well aware of the antics by the lake. "The reds are natural leaders but can be a bit stubborn." Rose smiled at Mabon, "Although I'm sure Peter would dispute that.

"There are seven different training groups at this school. Each one has unique characteristics and we like to place our new students in the group that will best align with their innate abilities."

She ticked her second finger, "The Orange Pod members are brave but impulsive. They tend to act first think later. They are born risk takers and often quite blunt, but also fiercely loyal to their partners and friends. They are probably our most noncompetitive pod.

"The Yellow Pod is probably our most amiable group tending to be mediators who get along with everyone. They are good at sensing other's feelings and are steady and predictable.

"The Greens are known for their calmness in an emergency and are also our best healers." Rose tapped her lip again. "That might be the group for you. I sense a strong ability to heal within your signature and I think you and Jill, their senior trainer, would get on very well. Greens can be independent but few are partnered with pegasites, so they may not be the perfect match for you."

Mabon said, "Many of the Indigo Pod members are partnered with wolves. Their senior trainer, Lara, is partner to one of Phelan's first litter. Indigos are researchers and love to solve mysteries. Of course, I'm a bit prejudiced toward them, having been an Indigo member myself."

Remembering the variety of books and gadgets in Mabon's cave, it was easy for Aine to see why.

Rose continued, "The Violet Pod members are inventive, always looking for ways to improve things. They are often perceived as cool and logical, but I think it's more that they have their mind on their next innovation. While I sense that you can be persistent, I don't see that as being a strong match for you."

Rose smiled, "I think the best group for you would be the Blue Pod. Like the reds, they are natural leaders although they can be a bit showy at times. Many have musical gifts and that is an extremely strong facet of your empathic signature. Most Blues are partnered to pegasites, and they are intensely loyal with strong character and equally strong passions. What do you think, Mabon?"

"I agree. The blend of musicianship as well as the strength of character in the Blue Pod is perfect for Aine."

"Then it's settled."

Aine felt a slight nervousness, wondering if she would indeed fit in with the group chosen for her.

Rose pushed a button in the wall beside the door and a few minutes later a young woman Aine's age entered. Tall with what Aine's cousin Mike would call "an incredible bod," her short brown hair stood out in wild curls. Her dark eyes snapped to Aine and Aine felt a chill in her glance. Her bright red vest molded to her body. Her lips were tight and to Aine she almost looked angry.

Rose's amber eyes intensified as she regarded the student, "Rika, this is, Aine. Please show her to the novice rooms in the Blue Pod and I will inform Aiden that he has a new student."

"Certainly, mistress," the girl's reply was clipped as if the task was beneath her. There was a touch of insolence in her tone.

Rose's eyes narrowed. "May I remind you, Rika that you are the greeter today and you will do as you are told—in a pleasant manner?"

Rika dropped her eyes and a red flush suffused her neck and face. "Yes, mistress." With her back to Rose and Mabon, she narrowed her eyes at Aine her voice controlled and even. "This way, please."

Rose sighed as Rika left the room, "Go with Rika, Aine, she will show you to your room and then to the dining area. We'll make further arrangements for your orientation after Mabon and I have had a chance to chat."

Aine's pack was outside the door and she lifted it quickly struggling to catch up with Rika. Trying to keep pace, Aine had no time to view her surroundings or get her bearings. She was relieved when Rika finally reached the third doorway in one of the many hallways. Aine lowered her bag to the blue-tiled floor and rubbed her aching shoulders.

Rika opened the door and stood cross-armed while Aine struggled to pick up and carry the heavy pack into her room. Then staring up and down at Aine's jeans and sweater, she said, "Someone will be along with blue pod clothing so you can change out of those clothes as soon as possible."

Aine was just about to ask her what her problem was when they heard some other students calling, "Hey, Aiden, wait up."

Rika's eyes lit immediately and she glanced at the door. Without a word she spun and marched through the door slamming it behind her.

Aine stared at the closed door and a flush of anger heated her face, "Nice to meet you, too!"

Aine dragged her pack to her bed wondering why Rika had been so rude. Her stomach growled loudly reminding her that she had not eaten since early morning. "Looks like I'll have to find the cafeteria on my own."

When she passed the entrance to the blue pod the third time, she realized that she was lost and going in circles. "It can't be that hard," she mumbled as she spotted a door leading to a verdant garden outside. "Maybe there is a shortcut through here, or I can find someone to direct me."

The bright garden flowers bobbed their heads like cheerful children, and Aine followed the pathway past several tinkling fountains. She had almost despaired of ever finding her way through the jumbled maze when she heard voices. Relieved to find someone to help her, she started toward the voices but froze when she was close enough to hear their words.

"You are always too busy to ride with me, yet you seem to have time for your friends, Aiden. Sadid and I can keep pace with you and Dark Fire. Take me with you, just once, please. I want to go faster, let me show you what we can do. Peter goes too slowly."

Aine peeked through the thick bushes. Rika's back faced Aine and her blood red vest and snug riding skirt, showed every facet of her long legs and voluptuous figure. Aine started to back away hoping to quietly retrace her steps when she got a clearer look at who Rika was talking to.

Aine stifled a gasp. It was the young man from her vision in Mabon's pool!

He brushed his black hair back with one hand, his voice exasperated, "Rika, second year students train only with their pods. There are no exceptions to that rule. I will not change it, nor would I expect Peter to. And frankly, it is none of your business how I spend my time. Sadid could certainly keep up with the other stallions, but no matter how good you think you are, you are not ready for advanced training."

"But, Aiden," Rika interrupted moving closer to him.

"And, if you don't change your attitude," he interrupted, "you won't be here long enough to be eligible for advanced training." His face darkened and his dark blue eyes snapped with anger and Aine noticed a muscle twitch in his jaw. "I was told that there is a new student assigned to my pod and I'm on my way to meet her. You are the greeter today, aren't you?" He folded his arms across his chest looking stern.

Aine remembered Mabon saying that Aiden was a senior trainer in the blue pod. He wore a long royal blue tunic like the one she had seen on the man from the red pod earlier. Aine was pleased to hear that Rika was not in his pod but her musings were cut short when Rika stepped even closer to Aiden.

"Yes, there's a new student. I did what I was supposed to and took her to her room and I hope she stays there!" Rika's chest heaved, almost touching Aiden's folded arms.

A look of irritation crossed his face and he dropped his arms. "And you were supposed to help her get settled and show her to the dining room, weren't you?"

"I don't like giving tours to dumb newbies." The defiance in her voice changed from snappish to sultry, she reached out and grasped his arm. "You know, Aiden, if you'll just…"

He shook free of her as if her touch burned him. Aine could see the repugnance on his face clearly now and his eyes became blue ice with his tone just as frigid. "If you cannot manage a simple orientation, perhaps you could benefit from additional training with your pod. Afterwards you can muck out the stalls since you seem to need something to do." Aiden stepped forward forcing Rika to step back. "You will train with your pod or not at all. I saw Peter leading a group toward the stables. Join them, now."

Rika stiffened and when she didn't respond immediately he spoke low and sharply, "That's an order from a senior trainer and I expect it to be followed." He bushed past her leaving Rika frozen for a moment. She glared after him and then stomped off muttering under her breath.

Aine backed away from the scene watching Rika's retreating back. Stepping backwards onto the path again, she was suddenly knocked off her feet. She landed in a painful thump on her bottom and her hair fell in front of her face. Frantically, she pushed it away.

The look of shock on Aiden's face matched her own. "I am so sorry. I wasn't watching where I was going. Here let me help you."

He reached to help her up but she stumbled to her feet without touching him and straightened her clothing and hair, her face a brilliant red.

Sensing her embarrassment Aiden waited patiently, adjusting his tunic to give her time. Then he bowed slightly and his lips held the slight glint of a smile. "You must be the new girl in my pod."

She looked intently at his shoes for a moment before mustering the courage to look up into his amazing blue eyes.

"So are you?" Aiden crossed his arms and cocked his head to the side, the corner of his mouth twitching with amusement.

"Am I what?"

"Are you the new girl in the blue pod?"

"Oh, yes, I'm sorry. I'm Aine." Her stomach chose that moment to growl loudly and she wished she could just disappear into a hole in the ground.

His quirk blossomed into a grin. "I am Aiden. And I'll bet you were trying to find the dining area?"

Handsome enough without the smile, with it he was magnetic.

"Yes, I was." She stuttered looking away shyly.

"Come on," he said. "I'll take you there myself. I'll also show you around the school if you'd like." Aiden motioned to indicate which path to follow and stepped aside so that she could walk next to him.

"I suppose you heard the little exchange with Rika?"

Aine's reply was so soft that he barely heard her. "I really didn't mean to, I was trying to find my way and when I heard you talking I thought I'd ask for directions. Then when—" Aine paused, "I didn't mean to stay but I was afraid that you would hear me if I tried to leave."

Aiden studied her from the corner of his eye, just as she tried unobtrusively to observe him. They came to a patio with tables and chairs and large glass doors leading inside. As he held the door for her he said, "Don't worry about what you overheard, Aine, I'm sure half of the school heard that conversation. Rika is a real pain sometimes."

Significantly taller than she, he moved with a lithe grace. The deep blue tunic of his pod affiliation offset his midnight blue eyes perfectly and he wore tight black pants with high boots. She stifled a smile thinking that Aiden had a really nice "bod" too and was glad that he couldn't read her thoughts as Zephyr could.

He showed her to a large dining area where they found fresh fruits, vegetables and a variety of breads and cheese. She took a plateful and followed him to a table by the windows overlooking the garden.

Aiden quartered an apple and popped a piece into his mouth offering the rest to her. "I was told that you came with Mabon, and have bonded a pegasite filly. Where are you from?"

Aine couldn't imagine how to tell him that she was not even from this world? Stalling for time she took a bite of the apple and chewed it slowly. "I'm from a place far away. Mabon brought me to the school and Zephyr, the silver pegasite with the white mane and tail is my bond mate."

"Ah, so that's how it is." Aiden leaned back in his chair, stretched his long legs out in front of him. The sunlight from the window painted his hair blue-black, and his eyes sparkled with mischief.

"What?" Aine asked finally meeting his gaze.

His voice was soft with a hint of flirtation, "Well a beautiful new student from far away? It sounds quite mysterious."

Aine smiled deciding to give as good as she got. "Well, a girl has to have some secrets."

"And nothing is more interesting than a mysterious woman." Aiden grinned.

He leaned forward. "I have to admit, though, I feel like we've met before."

Aine noted the furrow marking his brow and she swallowed. She didn't want to spoil the ease between them but she had to tell him the truth. "I have seen you before, but we've never met," she said, looking away from his interested gaze.

"Hmmm, even more mystery?" He smiled, "Have we met in your dreams then?" He was definitely flirting now.

Aine took a deep breath. "Not exactly, I saw your reflection in the pool in Mabon's cave."

Aiden dropped his feet to the floor his attention completely on her and his interest palpable. "Well, that explains it then," he said. "The reflections in that pool are portents of the future."

Regret filled her eyes and the light humor on his face faded when he noted it. "What's wrong Aine, you've gone very pale?"

"It's not what you think. Almost immediately after I saw your reflection, it was eclipsed by another image." Aine forced herself to continue unable to meet his eyes, "Mabon says that the image I saw was that of Takkar."

Aine was shocked his reaction. His eyes grew dark and piercing and he seemed almost angry, with no hint of flirtation or humor in his tone now. "You might want to rethink your secrets, Aine, if Takkar is involved."

"I really don't know anything more about him—" she started to explain.

"Oh I can tell you all about him. Takkar attacked my family once and they barely escaped with their lives."

Aine blanched at the cold fury in his voice and unconsciously moved further back in her seat.

His once gentle gaze pierced her and his voice grew hard. "How do you know Takkar, Aine? Who is he to you?"

Shocked and confused by his questions, Aine could only think of getting away from him. She stood and walked quickly to the door and outside into the courtyard struggling to keep the tears from flowing.

"What is it, Mistress?" Zephyr's voice carried her alarm.

Realizing his mistake Aiden rose so fast to follow her that his chair crashed to the floor. Ignoring the interested stares of the others in the dining area, he ran after her. "Wait, Aine! I'm sorry."

Aine walked away as quickly as she could but Aiden caught up and grasped her arm. "Please, Aine. I didn't mean to—"

She jerked her arm free and stopped. Her hands fisted tight at her sides.

"Are you in danger, where are you? Do you need me?" Zephyr implored.

"No, Zephyr. I'm all right."

Aine took another step back and noting the earnest apology in Aiden's expression. "I am so sorry, Aine. Dark Fire says that I have upset your partner and that is inexcusable. Please forgive me, I know better. Please tell her that I mean you no harm."

Aine blinked quickly and turned her back to him, dashing the tears away. Finally she said, "I've told her."

Then she took a shaky breath and confronted him. "Look, I don't know Takkar and I certainly don't know why

I saw him in that vision. I don't know why you got angry when I told you about him." She felt the heat on her neck as her frustration grew, "I do know that I want to go home and I need some time to think! So right now, I'm going for a walk. Alone!"

She stalked off not seeing Aiden staring helplessly after her.

CHAPTER NINE

At the Lake

Aine walked briskly to the shore of the lake, oblivious to the beauty of the water and the sky. Her thoughts swirled, and a huge lump in her throat cut off the air to her windpipe.

She fisted her hands in her pockets and continued slowly along the shore. Zephyr landed with a flourish in front of her, tossing her head. *"I am here, mistress. You are upset, let me take you away. You will feel better if we fly. We won't go far, just to the end of the lake."*

Thinking that was exactly what she needed Aine jumped to Zephyr's back and in moments they were aloft, sailing over the lake. Neither the pegasite nor the girl saw Phelan running along the shore of the lake behind them. Nor did Aine realize that she had effectively blocked his call to stop her.

As they flew, Aine felt the strength of the bond with Zephyr calm her jumbled emotions. They flew to a waterfall that danced and sparkled as it fed into the far end of the lake and Zephyr landed next to it on a small beach of rocks surrounded by thick bushes.

The filly stood very still as Aine touched her forelock. *"Your thoughts are troubled, mistress, what is wrong?"*

"Oh, Zephyr, I need to go home. I shouldn't be here."

"But you can't leave, I just found you! I have waited for you for so long. It is wonderful to be with you at last. You can't know how frightened I was before you found me. Please do not leave!"

Aine was instantly contrite. "Oh Zephyr, I'm sorry!" She pressed her face against Zephyr's neck needing the touch that strengthened them both. "I want to be with you, too, but I feel like I'm being torn apart."

The lump in Aine's throat returned. "I wish I knew how to explain it to you so that you could really understand." Aine sighed, "I don't belong here. I'm in way over my head, and I just don't know what to do." Aine stepped back so that she could see Zephyr's intelligent eyes. "Does that make any sense?"

Zephyr's dark eyes met Aine's. *"I think I understand. It is just as it was when I first left the herd. I was alone as you were, but even then I think I was waiting for you...to bond with you. I knew that I did not belong with the herd, but I did not belong anywhere else. Phelan found me soon after and we became friends but I was not complete until I found you.*

"But you must understand. You are not alone, my mistress, you will never be alone. I will always be yours, and you do belong. You belong to me as I belong to you. Nothing can ever change that as long as we both live." Zephyr answered. *"Yet, I can sense that you are very unhappy and I do not want you to be unhappy."*

Aine rested her head against Zephyr's and gave in to the surge of emotions, finally allowing the tears to stream down her face. "I am not unhappy with you, dear one. You are the most wonderful thing that has ever happened to me. But, I'm so far from my home. I just feel lost."

She continued to stroke the filly's neck sensing the warmth of Zephyr's caring through the bond.

"What will happen to you if I do return home?"

Aine clearly felt the profound sadness of Zephyr's response through their bond. *"I do not know. I might return to the herd, or stay here at the school. I do not know."*

"Would you take me back to where I found you, to the whirlpool? Mabon thinks it is a portal between our worlds. Maybe if I go back there and try really hard, I can find a way to return."

Zephyr was quiet for several minutes shifting her feet and flipping her wings nervously. Aine watched her, knowing how difficult this must be for the pegasite as well. The prophecy that Mabon had told her about worried her. The idea of her being some kind of hero, or demon—she wasn't sure which, seemed unreal. The threats from Takkar, Aiden's sudden anger, and Rika's animosity was just icing on the cake.

Finally Zephyr said, *"I do not know if you could go back even if you went to the whirlpool. It certainly will be dangerous, and I am afraid we could be captured again. But I will take you if you must go."*

Zephyr's mental voice was filled with longing. Aine's need to return home would leave Zephyr bereft, but Aine reasoned if she returned soon, it might be easier for Zephyr in the long run. Perhaps a quick, clean break would be less painful.

Neither of them saw the man who crept from the bushes lining the edge of the waterfall. Zephyr spotted him first and fluttered in the air for a moment and then landed between Aine and the man. Beating her wings rapidly she rose up on her back feet and whinnied loudly.

The man scurried away from her hooves but threw a rope over Zephyr's neck and pulled it taut. Zephyr thrashed, literally pulling him off his feet, but he retained his grip.

Aine felt a sudden rage at seeing the rope around Zephyr's neck and she ran to him and shoved him hard to the ground. Yanking the rope from his grip she loosened it and pulled it from Zephyr's neck and threw it as far as she could out into the water.

Zephyr moved between the man, who scrambled to his feet, and Aine. He started to move toward the filly again, his face intent on his goal.

Aine shouted, "Leave her alone! Get away from us."

"Oh no missy, I want the reward," he whined in a squeaky voice. His lank, greasy hair fell into his eyes and his clothes hung worn and dirty. He smelled as if he had not bathed in a month and Aine swallowed with revulsion at the glance from his furtive, rat-like eyes. He couldn't meet her gaze for long, but when he did, there was a sly, scheming glint there.

"What reward? What are you talking about?" She backed up a step moving closer to Zephyr. *I'll keep him talking until I can get to your back, then we'll fly away.*"

"I am ready," Zephyr replied.

"He gives us money and women, if we catch your kind." The man scratched his armpit.

"Who gives you money?" Aine took one more step toward Zephyr, almost in position now.

The man squealed and a look of utter terror crossed his face and he fell backwards to the ground, covering his face with his arms screaming.

Aine heard a ringing whinny and turned to see Aiden atop a powerful black winged stallion. They landed next to Zephyr.

Aine and Zephyr backed away as the stallion moved in. He reared up and his front hooves pounded the ground on both sides of the man's head. "Don't move a muscle, Turat, or I'll see that he doesn't miss next time!" Aiden commanded.

The sniveling man drew up into a ball and moaned, "Get him off me, please, don't let him trample me."

Aiden glanced at Aine, his voice sharp, "Get on Zephyr, Aine and wait for me by the waterfall."

It was not a request but a demand and Aine complied immediately. Maybe the man was more dangerous than she thought. She leapt on Zephyr's back and they hovered above the waterfall.

The stallion backed up a couple of steps and Aiden jumped off stalking menacingly toward the man who scuttled backwards like a crab. Aiden towered over him and reached down with one hand and pulled him to his feet. His hand tightened on Turat's shirt and he shook him as if he were a small child.

"Get off our land, Turat. There are no second chances; if I ever find you or any of your slimy cohorts here again you won't live to regret it!" Aiden shoved him hard and Turat stumbled and then bolted into the bushes and disappeared.

Aiden jumped to the stallion's back, "Follow me," he yelled to Aine and Zephyr. And they soared to the edge of the lake about halfway to the school. Aiden's blue eyes were still sparking with anger as he dismounted his stallion.

Zephyr trembled beneath Aine sending strong emanations of chagrin through their bond. Once landed the black stallion bumped Zephyr with his shoulder. *"It is forbidden to be alone and away from the school in your first year of bonding. Do you want the evil one to find you again? Why would you take such a risk and endanger your mistress? You are a foolish young pegasite!"*

Aine dropped from Zephyr's back and strode boldly between the filly and the stallion. "Stop it!"

The stallion towered over her, surely big enough to crush her in seconds, but she held her ground. "Back off and leave her alone! Zephyr was trying to help me."

The stallion took a step back and a look of surprised astonishment replaced the anger on Aiden's face.

With her eyes flashing green sparks, her chest heaving, and her hair bristling, she faced both Aiden, and his partner, without fear or apology.

Aiden realized that he was staring and he forced himself to relax his features. Then her words dawned on him. "You heard Dark Fire?"

Aine glared at him, "Yes I heard him. I hear all of them. I will not allow you or anyone to bully Zephyr."

Aiden's mouth quirked and he spoke to Dark Fire. *"She is magnificent and no shy child. She is a woman defending herself and her partner, and what a woman!"*

Aine crossed her arms in front of her, defiance raging in her eyes as she moved a step closer toward him.

Dark Fire rumbled in his throat, *"She is also very angry, I think you might want to remember that."*

Aine spat, "We didn't do anything wrong. Zephyr was just trying to comfort me. She only did what I asked her to do." With her last words her voice shook and tears formed in her eyes. Angrily she dashed them away with the back of her hand turned her back on him and moved to Zephyr.

He patted Dark Fire and spoke to his partner. *"She may be brave, but she is also afraid. They had no idea that they needed permission to leave the school grounds. We have not handled this very well, see if you can calm the filly and I'll try to apologize to the girl."*

Dark Fire spoke with a strange whispering tone and Aiden realized that he was speaking privately to him so that Aine could not hear the stallion's words. *"You'd better stop thinking how exciting she is if you want her to listen to you."*

Aiden patted Dark Fire in silent agreement and said, "I'm sorry, Aine. We didn't mean to make things any harder for you, or threaten either of you. We didn't want to impose on your privacy, but Dark Fire is right, it is not safe to be here alone. Neither you nor Zephyr could have known that, and it is my fault as your trainer for not making that clear. But we must go back now."

Aine was silent and stood watching him.

Aiden stepped past her to the filly and patted her neck. He offered Zephyr a root from his pocket and she gobbled it. "All right now, my pretty filly?"

Zephyr tossed her head and whinnied loudly in his face scolding him just as her mistress had and Aiden laughed. Aine looked away quickly, struggling not to laugh too. It broke the intensity of the moment.

"Will you come now?"

Aine nodded and jumped to Zephyr's back. *"They really were just looking out for us you know,"* Zephyr told Aine as they flew. *"Dark Fire was right. We should not have come here alone. I have put you in danger and I am a foolish young pegasite."*

Aine wrapped her arms around Zephyr's neck, "Perhaps we just both have a lot to learn. I'm sorry Zephyr. It wasn't your fault, I overreacted and I feel like a fool!"

Zephyr tossed her head and nickered at Aine. *"You were very brave and I was proud of the way that you defended me. We may both have taken an unnecessary risk, but we are just inexperienced. It will not happen again."*

Aine sat up, cheered by Zephyr's confidence and praise.

"I am sorry to have frightened or angered you, young mistress," a baritone voice interrupted Aine's thoughts. Aine realized that it was the stallion, Dark Fire apologizing. She glimpsed a ghost of a smile on Aiden's face.

"Thank you for your concern for both of us, Dark Fire. We have much to learn."

When they reached the beach behind the school, Mabon and Phelan hurried to greet them. "Are you all right, Aine?"

Mabon's brow was furrowed with worry.

"We are fine, Mabon. I am sorry to worry you. Zephyr and I needed a little time to think, and I didn't know that it could be dangerous to go off on our own. It won't happen again."

Mabon nodded and turned to Aiden. "What happened? Phelan says something about the smelly one."

"It was Turat," said Aiden. "He was trying to collect a bounty, but I think we convinced him that he is not welcome here." There was a slight emphasis on the word convinced, but Aiden showed no other emotion.

"Well then, since Aine still needs an orientation to the school, perhaps you could take care of that." He held out a bag. "I went back to the dining room and got some food for you, I thought you might be hungry."

"Thank you, Mabon." Aiden took the sack, still carefully neutral.

"I'll meet you both in the stables in a couple of hours." Mabon and Phelan started back up the path toward the school.

As they walked away, Aine realized how rash her adventure with Zephyr had been. She had run away like a little child and worried Mabon unnecessarily.

She called him, "Mabon?"

Mabon stopped and she ran to him and grasped his arm. "We really didn't mean to worry anyone."

Mabon's eyes shone with kindness, "Of course you didn't." Mabon enfolded Aine in a warm hug. Phelan brushed against Aine's hand and she knelt to pat him. *No one was harmed, little sister, all is well. You must listen to Dark Fire's partner now, he and my master will keep you safe, but you must give credence to their words.*

"I will, Phelan. It won't happen again."

Aiden gave Dark Fire a slap on the rump commanding him back to the stables and Zephyr followed. Aine watched the two magical creatures lift from the ground with ease and glide silently out of sight.

CHAPTER TEN

Aiden

"Why don't we eat on that bench by the garden?" Aiden asked pointing to a wooden bench with twisted iron legs sitting alone in a field surrounded by a colorful bounty of wild flowers. Aine nodded and they strolled to the bench.

"New students normally have a group orientation," Aiden said, keeping it all business. But when someone arrives mid-term the senior trainers give a private orientation."

Aine tucked her feet under her and asked, "How long does it take to complete the training?"

"Well, that depends on the student and their partner." Aiden said, handing her an apple.

"Is all of the training done here at the school?"

"Yes, although Rose plans to develop a more advanced training facility in the future. This whole complex used to be a hunting lodge belonging to one of the barristers in Kierst, our largest city. His daughter was an empath partnered to a hawk so when he died, he donated the facility and the grounds to us."

The sun had moved higher in the sky crowning Aine with a halo of brilliance. He smiled, "It's getting warm, would you like a drink?"

"Yes, thank you."

Aiden held the water skin up above his mouth and sprayed a steady stream of cool water into his mouth. He made it look simple and he handed it to her. Following his lead, Aine held the skin up and squeezed. Cold water sprayed all over her chin and chest, missing her mouth completely. She quickly gave it back; her face flushed with embarrassment.

"Well that's one way to cool down," Aiden grinned, "Here let me help you. Put your hands here and just squeeze harder." This time it worked, and Aine swallowed the cool sweet water.

"Enough?"

"Yes, thanks." Aine met his eyes, smiling ruefully. "You must think I'm an absolute idiot. First I fall at your feet, and then I explode and lose my temper, and finally I drench myself."

"Actually, you're the first girl to fall at my feet. I found it rather flattering." He grinned, pleased to see her roll her eyes in response. Leaning forward he said, "And you are actually quite impressive when you are angry."

She made a move to punch him and he held his hands up in defense laughing. Aiden put his hands down, "Actually, after our inauspicious start, I'm glad to see you smile."

Aine's cheeks colored but she did not reply.

"What did Mabon tell you about me?"

"He told me that you're from a distant village and you bonded with Zephyr just before he met you."

A look of relief crossed her face and then she changed the subject. "How are the students chosen for the school?"

Aiden placed the water skin on the bench between them. He spoke softly to Dark Fire. *"I wonder if she'll tell me more about herself? Maybe I can get her to relax a bit. It's pretty normal for new students to be homesick and confused and I sure blew it back in the dining room."*

Dark Fire replied, *"I don't think the filly trusts us either, but that is usual for those new from the herd. I will keep my eye on her."*

Aiden smiled mentally, *"I bet you will."* Then he added, *"There is something different about this pair though. It's not just the way she talks or dresses. She is fascinating, sometimes shy and also vivid, like when her temper flared. I don't think I'd want to be on the wrong side of that very often."*

"Just keep it friendly, master." Dark Fire advised. *"These two have been through much in a very short time."*

"I will, my friend." Aiden replied hoping he could find a way to gain Aine's trust.

He kept his comments light and friendly. "Students are not chosen to come to the S.E.D. It is simply the best place to learn empathic skills. Every student here is an empath, though some have not bonded yet. There are a variety of empathic animals such as pegasites, wolves, birds of prey, large cats, and even some exotics like elephants and zebras."

Aine liked how his eyes sparkled when he spoke of the school. She asked, "How did you learn you were an empath? Did you find Dark Fire, or did he find you?"

"It was a little different for me. Most empaths have at least one parent with the gift, or someone closely related to them. If they learn about empathic abilities while they are young, they are less likely to be fearful of their gift. Empaths who find their partners when both are young grow up together." Aiden shifted to face her.

"My family is called the West Wind Tribe and some people call us gypsies. We live an unfettered life compared to farmers, shop keepers, and city folk, and we have traveled throughout Drayon for generations."

Aiden smiled at Aine and chuckled. "In fact, you'd be surprised to know that my family was once considered royalty, the first house of Drayon. My great-great grandfather was a prince and he fell in love with a gypsy girl and gave up his kingdom to marry her."

"Oh, I see," Aine said a bit confused. "Mabon told me that Takkar's family was the first house of Drayon?"

Aiden's face sobered at the mention of Takkar, but he controlled his response quickly. "Takkar and I are distantly related on his mother's side, very distant, thankfully. Takkar's family became the first house when his father married her."

Aiden stood up and stretched pointedly dismissing Takkar from his thoughts. "You asked how I learned that I was an empath. In truth, I had no idea that I was one until I found Dark Fire."

He began to pace back and forth. "I was twelve years old, off alone hunting when my family was attacked by Takkar's bandits and thugs. No one was seriously hurt and the men of the tribe drove them off, but when I returned and found a burned wagon I panicked, fearing that everyone I loved was dead." His memory of loss and fear was clearly on his face. "Of course if I'd thought of it logically, I would have followed their tracks and found them, but twelve-year-old boys are not very logical. I searched for my family for a couple of days and eventually I became lost near the Sperrenial swamps. Even though there are obscure trails leading through them, they can be quite deadly as they are filled with bogs and quicksand. I was trying to retrace my tracks and find my way out when I heard frantic splashing in the distance. I followed the sounds thinking it might be someone from my tribe."

Aiden sat back down on the bench next to Aine, his eyes focused on the lake. "A pegasite mare was caught in quicksand and her tiny colt ran back and forth along the edge of the pit. She made things worse as she struggled to get out and she kept whinnying to her baby, as if to tell him not to come near. I used a long vine and tried to pull her out, but she was too big and I couldn't manage it. Gradually the mare stopped fighting but continued to sink slowly. All I could do was stand and watch."

Running his hand through his hair he took a sip of water. "At the end, she looked at me with eyes filled with sorrow and meaning. The colt ran shivering back and forth on the bank, crying for his mother and unable to understand what was happening. I realized what she wanted and I caught him and wrapped him in my cloak and took him away so he would not have to watch his mother die."

Aiden's hands clenched in his lap, "He knew it anyway. Moments later, I felt the anguish of his soul, as he cried out for her. I held him for a long time talking to him trying to comfort him."

Aiden waited a few minutes and his calm eyes met Aine's. "While I sat there with him, I got the strangest sensation of hunger, yet I knew that I wasn't hungry since I had eaten the last of my food just before I found them. Then it dawned on me that it was the colt that was hungry. I didn't think to wonder why or how he communicated that to me. I plucked some grain from the grasses nearby and ground it up and mixed it into a mash. I put it on my fingers for him to suck."

Aiden smiled. "He was a greedy little thing and he ate all of it. I didn't want him to wander off into the swamp, so I braided some grasses to make a rope and tied it loosely around his neck. I laid my cloak over some pine needles and lay down with him, stroking and easing him until he slept. In the morning, when we awoke his first word to me was

'*Hungry*!'" Aiden grinned. "I heard it in my mind just as you hear Zephyr, and we've been partners ever since."

Aine wiped her eyes, totally moved by the story.

Aiden continued, "After a few days I found my family and it wasn't long before Dark Fire was eating more than any three of the other horses. He was already much bigger than colts of the same age and while I could communicate with Dark Fire, I knew nothing about training a pegasite or being an empath, so my father brought us to the school. I was twelve, and Dark Fire was the equivalent of a six year old, so we both had a lot to learn."

Aiden smiled at Aine, allowing that spark of mischief in his eyes again. "I think it will be easier for you because both you and Zephyr are older. Zephyr will be paired with other more experienced pegasites, and you will learn what you need to know just as we did."

He shifted to look directly into her eyes. "In fact I think Dark Fire is interested in becoming Zephyr's mentor, just as I am in becoming yours."

His eyes were intense and unconsciously Aine leaned toward him.

"I am here to help you learn," Aiden said, "but I would like to be more than your senior trainer. I want to be your friend, too, if you'll let me. I know what it's like to be new and lost and feel like everything that's familiar is a million miles away."

Aiden reached for her hand and they were both surprised by the surge of electricity that passed between them at his touch. He caressed the backs of her hands gently with his thumbs. "I am a good listener and I never repeat a confidence."

Aine lost herself in his eyes for a moment and then she pulled her hands from his and stood up thinking, *I need to slow this down a bit.*

"Could we walk for a while?"

Aiden rose. "Sure, let's take this path by the lake and I'll show you some of the other buildings."

As they walked along the shore Aine asked, "Who was that man back by the waterfall, and what did he mean by a reward?"

Aiden picked up a stone and skipped it on the surface of the water. "Turat has been in and out of prison for years, but I haven't seen him in this area for a long time. In fact I didn't think Turat knew where the school was. For some reason Takkar must be offering rewards to capture empaths. I'm not sure what he wants but we're not going to let him get away with it."

"Who's we?" she asked.

"We..." He spread his arm indicating the school, "...are the empaths who want Takkar removed from power so that he is no longer a threat to us."

Aine said, "Mabon told me that he had a disagreement with Takkar years ago too."

Aiden nodded. "That's true, they've been rivals ever since they were in school together. But that's a long story and one I think would be better heard from Mabon."

Aine smiled glancing at him, "You really do know how to keep a confidence don't you?"

"Of course." He grinned and winked at her.

Aine rolled her eyes and laughed as she bent down to pick a bright daffodil. Holding the flower she inhaled the delicate scent. "Daffy's are my favorites. Near my home there is a hillside covered with them and every spring I pick a big bouquet for my mother. I'm not sure she's all that crazy about them but I just love their happy faces and cheery yellow trumpets."

"Tell me about your family, Aine." Aiden kept his eyes on the lake as they traversed the shore and started back up the path toward the buildings.

Aine told him more about her family, her face and eyes grew animated as she spoke. Then she stopped and met his eyes directly, "Do you think I will be able to learn how to use my talisman so that I can go home again?"

Her pendant had slipped out of her sweater when she picked the flower. "Did Mabon give that pendant to you?"

"Yes, he did. He said that travelers can use several different kinds of portals to go between worlds, and he thinks the pendant will help me."

For a split second Aiden looked shocked but he covered it quickly. "I would imagine it will help you. Using your talisman is one of the first things you will learn. Sometimes it takes a while, especially the more complex skills, but you'll learn it, I'm sure of that. The talisman is structured to protect us, but it also enhances our innate abilities. If Mabon thinks it can take you home, it will."

Aine twirled in a circle. "That's wonderful! I can't wait to get started."

Aiden laughed and picked another daffodil, offering it to her as he flourished a fancy bow, his eyes dancing with humor. "The fairest flower, for the fairest maiden."

Aine shook her head at his antics and accepted the daffodil as they started back toward the stables.

He grinned, "Tell you what. I'll race you back to the stables. See that building over there?"

"I see it. You're in trouble, I'm a good runner. If only I didn't have this stone in my shoe." Aine knelt pretending to pick the pebble from her shoe and Aiden stopped waiting for her. Then she jumped up and sprinted off just barely beating him to the door of the stable. She bent over with her hands on her knees gasping for breath.

"So you want to win but you don't play fair." Aiden laughed as he caught up with her. They stood quite close. Her hair cascaded in a brown-gold mantle around her shoulders and her cheeks were touched with pink from running.

She noted the feeling in his eyes and stepped back. Aiden cleared his throat and led her into the stable. "Let me show you where to find Zephyr's food and water. Everyone is required to care for their partners and feed, water and exercise them daily in addition to the training."

After they fed both pegasites he touched her cheek gently and looked down into her eyes. "I'm looking forward to tomorrow." Crimson crawled from Aine's neck to her forehead. They stood frozen in time and she became lost in his sapphire eyes.

They were interrupted by a shuffling sound from behind them as a female voice challenged. "It seems like some people get special privileges and few chores, even as first year students." Rika stepped out of a stall of a powerful brown pegasite stallion. She shot a venomous glare at Aine her knuckles white as she gripped the pitchfork she'd been using.

"Well, I guess that just wouldn't be any of your business would it?" Aiden drawled as he purposely put his arm around Aine's waist drawing her closer to him.

Aiden's movement was not lost on Rika and her face filled with fury. She stuck the pitchfork in a bale of hay and shot Aine another burning look as she stalked past them out of the stable.

"Ignore her, Aine. She's just pissy because she was told to muck out the stable because of her bad attitude." Aiden's arm stayed on her waist and Aine found she didn't want to move away.

When Mabon and Phelan came through the doors, they moved apart quickly. "Ah, there you are, Aine. If you'll come with me, I'll show you how to find your rooms without getting lost this time," Mabon offered.

"I'll see you tomorrow, Aiden, thanks for showing me the stables and telling me about the training," Aine murmured.

"You certainly will see me tomorrow, and you are most welcome." Aiden bowed, flourishing an elaborate gesture.

Aine's face tinged with color as they walked back to the school.

Mabon showed her how to read the tiles in the building. "There are seven different wings in the building, each laid out in the colors of the rainbow. The corridor nearest the main entrance is the red pod rooms and they progress in a circle around the building."

Remembering her high school science class, Aine recalled the order of the colors of the rainbow spelling Roy G. Biv, (red, orange, yellow, green, blue, indigo and violet.) Knowing now, that her pod was between green and indigo halls, it would be easier to find.

In her room a large box of clothing had been left on her bed. "Ah, they have brought your blue pod clothing. You can catch up with Jill tomorrow and she'll help you adjust them to fit better. "Is there anything else you need?"

"I don't think so," Aine replied.

"Why don't you rest and relax? I'll have someone meet you for dinner. Just have Zephyr call Phelan if you need me?"

"Thanks, Mabon, I will."

Aine sorted through the box of clothing and the things she'd brought from Mabon's cave, placing things in the closet and drawers. Then she took a warm shower and sat down on the bed to brush her hair. From the time that she'd arrived on Drayon there had been almost no time to really reflect on all that had happened.

Remembering the conflict with mother and her intense desire to escape her, Aine wondered if that might have been a reason why she had been so eager to uncover the secrets of the crystal ball. She shook her head, it was more than that. From the first touch the crystal ball had been something she felt driven to explore, just as the unconscious drive to find Zephyr had led her to the cave.

Looking back, things seemed to have followed a logical progression; the nightmare, the crystal ball, travelling here, finding Zephyr, meeting Mabon, and coming to the school. It felt almost pre-ordained.

Then there was Aiden. Closing her eyes she recalled the electricity she'd felt when they touched. She wanted very much to trust him. He'd said he wanted to be her friend, but she knew he was attracted to her, as she was to him. His midnight blue eyes had been intense as he'd said, "I think Dark Fire is interested in becoming Zephyr's mentor, just as I am in becoming yours."

Aine smiled as she laid the brush on the table thinking, *That's just fine with me.*

CHAPTER ELEVEN

Thwarted

Pacing back and forth like a predator, Takkar glared at the groveling wretch before him. Not bothering to control his fury he leveled a solid kick to the man huddled before him, and Turat sprawled on the floor moaning in pain.

"Get out! Get out of my sight you sniveling idiot."

Turat scrambled to his feet and bolted through the door. Takkar strode to it and slammed it leaning against it with his hand on his forehead. "Such incompetence!"

He straightened and walked slowly to the table by the fire. Pouring a goblet of wine from the intricate crystal carafe, he sipped silently as he brooded. His dark maroon pants clung to his powerful thighs and he moved to the chair by the fire. Long booted legs stretched out in front of him while the dancing flames reflected in his ebony eyes.

Takkar twirled the goblet idly, remembering the first time he touched the young woman through her dream. That first touch of her mind was enough to convince him that she was the one. He had never tried summoning along the celestial band before and he had nearly given up before finally sensing her powerful signature, so very far away.

Only a dream touch, it had been a pale imitation of a true summoning, but it was enough to make his empathic senses sing. Her empathic signature was unique, unlike anything he had ever experienced before, and he would have her even if he had to capture and torture every slippery wretch in the land to find her.

She was unconsciously powerful and adept at managing to escape him. The dream touch had been pure chance, but now, she'd been well hidden by his arch rival, Mabon, after he'd summoned her from that pool. Now he'd lost the element of surprise because of Turat's bungling attempt by the lake. No matter. He would find her. She was an empath and Mabon had obviously taken her to the school. The fools didn't think he knew where the school was, but of course he did. He had to come up with a plan to capture her.

The woman of the prophecy was the vital link to his future, yet a trickle of unease passed his mind. Takkar remembered very well what it was like to be on the receiving end of mind control. He must find her and win her to him before she learned how to resist. She had to make the choice to be his consort freely, or so the prophecy said.

He looked down to see his white knuckles grasping the wash stand. Taking several deep breaths to calm his mind, he threw open the door and the men outside of it snapped to attention.

He took the stairs to the tower two at a time, enjoying the feel of his blood pounding. The crisp salt breeze whipped his cloak back as stepped out to the balcony on the tower. The raucous calls of ravens echoed off the stark walls of the castle from the dark pines beyond.

Their cries reminded him of the woman, Ravyn from whom he had first learned the art of compulsion. How like her namesake Ravyn had been, quick, intelligent, wild, and completely centered on her own desires. He had learned the physical arts of compulsion from her and mastered the other types of mind control with Okat, her former master. Now that he had stolen and copied Okat's precious book, he was the master.

The use of compulsion and the resulting mind control were as natural to him as breathing. A thought or even a glance could make those who were susceptible grovel to please him. All of them, his men, his servants and the people of the lands he controlled, lived in terror of angering him.

Takkar leaned over the stone railing letting the surge of retained anger drain from him. Turat said that his young cousin Aiden had called the girl Aine and had protected her from Turat's bungled attempt. To know someone's name made it easier to visualize them and would make a summoning stronger. That boy was no match for one such as he.

Takkar returned to the tower room leaving the doors open to the warm scents of the sunny afternoon. He poured another glass of wine, and settled in to think.

The woman had responded to him when he touched her mind at the pool. The power of that connection even as brief as it was had been incredibly potent. He closed his eyes, allowing himself at last, to imagine what it would be like to have her as his consort. She was quite lovely, this Aine and still malleable, which was very good, and he found he desired her more than he had desired anyone since Deidre.

Legends foretold that the woman would partner a light-colored pegasite, and indeed she had. They had found the silver filly surprisingly alone and kept her in the cave for several days hoping to draw her partner. Takkar wondered how Aine had found the filly, especially since he now knew she was not of his world. He rose and placed the empty wine glass on the table. How she had found the filly was irrelevant now. What was important was how he would get her away from the school.

Takkar was shaken from his musings by a loud clamor from the courtyard below. An angry female voice screamed, "Let me go you stinking old goat! Don't you dare touch us! Get your hands off me you fatherless toad!"

Takkar smiled, and rose from his chair. Whoever this was, she certainly had a colorful vocabulary. From the balcony he watched several men struggle to hold a flailing young woman, and a flighty brown pegasite stallion.

"What have you, Makor?" He called to the man holding the girl.

Holding her arms tightly behind her the man looked up at Takkar. "She's from the school. We found them up near the high mountain lake."

The girl twisted and kicked hard and Makor jumped away, but not fast enough. Her boot caught him in the groin and he screamed and dropped to the ground. The brown pegasite stallion, kicked madly and bolted from the men, knocking several over as he flapped his powerful wings. The girl sprinted toward her partner.

"Stop!" Takkar bellowed and she skidded to a halt. Breathing heavily she looked up at him in confusion. The tight red blouse hid nothing of her voluptuous body and Takkar's interest grew. Perhaps his luck had changed. She was too young to be on her own with a pegasite stallion so she must have run away from the school. Her clothing was torn and dirty but it looked to be a red pod uniform. If he could compel her to his demands, she could be exactly what he needed.

Never breaking eye contact, he spoke in a normal voice, yet dripping with the dark coercion of compulsion. "Bring her."

The pegasite had stopped just as the girl did and two of Takkar's men threw ropes around his neck. He fought them, beating his wings furiously almost lifting them to the air as he tried to flee.

"You idiots! Throw something over the stallion's head and take him to the stables. If you damage him, you will wish you were never born." Takkar glared at the men. "Get the girl away from him and bring her to me. Now!"

One man threw his cloak over the stallion's head and the animal continued to fight, but finally with a few more ropes they had him. A flying hoof hit another man in the temple and he fell limp to the stones. The others ignored the fallen man and dragged the pegasite toward the stables.

Takkar looked back at the girl to see if she'd noted her partner's efforts. Still gazing at him, she had not moved, never once looking for her partner.

Interesting, he thought. Empaths were usually resistant to the voice, but she seemed quite within his power. He smiled, "Now come to me." His eyes locked with hers.

One of his men grabbed her arm. "Don't touch me!" She spit and shook him off. She looked at Takkar once more and started for the door, the men following behind. Takkar tapped his lips with his finger as he considered how to best use the girl.

"Leave us." Takkar dismissed them from the room as she entered, noting the dampness on her brow, and her heaving chest as she caught her breath.

Controlling her with his voice he had her stand in the sunlight near the window. Without a word he looked her up and down. Sticks and leaves poked out of her dark curly hair. She rubbed the raw marks on her wrists wincing a bit. There was a calculating hardness behind her dark brown eyes, but her lips were full and red, and he savored the thought of tasting her charms. She had either put up a good fight or his men had played with her a bit. He couldn't blame them; it had been a very long time since he'd had one this delectable.

Takkar knew from the lingering touch of her mind, that she was confused and ready to bolt, but she had surprised him with her immediate response to his command in the courtyard. In fact, she seemed to have forgotten her partner completely, and that boded well for his eventual control.

He stood silently in front of her. The thought of "convincing" her to do as he desired, stimulated him to test his control. "Come to me."

She hesitated. *Good,* Takkar thought, she is capable of resistance after all. He commanded her again intensifying his control and this time she wavered only a second before complying.

He touched her face lightly never breaking eye contact using one of the more complex weavings of the power of compulsion. Most subjects reacted first to voice commands and only later to visual ones, yet this girl responded to both. It was interesting and rather stimulating and he decided to measure her capacity for resistance.

He pinched her cheek enjoying her gasp of pain. She stepped back, tears springing to her eyes. Ah, so she could oppose his demands. That was good; he was easily bored with women who capitulated too readily.

She managed to take her eyes from his and looked toward the balcony. He sensed her trying to call to her partner and he blocked her easily. Her brow knit with confusion and she took another step away from him.

"Do not move!"

She froze at the sound of his voice. He grasped her arm and clenched it, enjoying the fear and pain that filled her eyes. She bit her lip trying in vain to resist the intensity of his eyes.

Takkar spoke to her telepathically, *"That's right, my dear. I am here to help you and you really do want me to talk to you.*

Don't try to resist. I want to make you feel welcome, pretty one."

Rika had never heard a person speak telepathically with her as Sadid did. It confused her, yet she strained to listen to his words in her mind.

Takkar smiled with anticipation, pleased to see that she relaxed slightly as he touched her mind. Releasing some of his control of her, Takkar picked up a packet and sprinkled the contents into a glass of wine. He held it out to her and smiled graciously, "You must be tired and thirsty, my dear. Please, come and sit with me and have a drink. I've added something that will relax and refresh you."

Rika took the glass and took a tiny sip. She was obviously afraid to drink, and fearful of what he would do if she didn't.

Takkar saw the reluctance in her eyes and cocked his head to the side. His voice dripped with concern, "This is only wine, with a small additive to refresh you." He poured himself a goblet, adding the same amount of powder to his own drink. "I'll join you, and then we can get to know one another better."

Rika relaxed as he downed the entire goblet.

"Now, come and sit with me and tell me what happened." Takkar's tone was calm and he kept his power to coerce her subtle.

Takkar took the carafe of wine to a pair of chairs set in an alcove. The sun shone in on the rich tapestry of the fabric of the chair and Rika closed her eyes momentarily, enjoying the warmth on her face. The split at the side of her skirt opened to show her leg to the hip and when Rika opened her eyes she saw that Takkar's eyes lingered as he openly appraised her.

Leaning forward he enhanced his control over her and was thrilled to see her breathe faster and her lips open slightly. "Would you like some more wine?"

Rika looked down at her wine goblet surprised to find it empty. She nodded absently realizing how thirsty she was.

Adding another packet to her drink, Takkar waited for the stimulant to do its work. Beads of sweat broke out on Rika's brow and he smiled as he handed her the second glass of wine. It had been easy to convince her to drink the wine by drinking it himself. He had taken an antidote to the effects of the stimulant for years. He'd convinced many young women before this way by persuading them that the additive was harmless. It was anything but harmless. After only a few infusions she would become addicted to its effects. He smiled to put her at ease. This girl would be no different; she was already his.

He modulated his voice allowing her to respond normally. "So, you are from the school? I assume that the stallion is your partner?"

"Yes he is," she replied breathlessly, a slight confusion in her eyes as if she had forgotten her partner.

Takkar watched her carefully, trying to ascertain how well the stimulant was working. She sat erect in the chair.

Feigning polite interest he said, "What is your name?"

"Rika," she whispered.

Takkar leaned and touched her lips with the tip of his finger. Rika raised her chin, almost begging for a kiss. Keeping control of her mind he asked, "Where did the men find you?"

His question jolted her thoughts and she shook herself, breaking free of his gaze. Her face burned with anger. "I go to that lake sometimes when I'm..." She hesitated.

"Go on." Takkar commanded easily.

"I go when I'm troubled. I had fallen asleep and was awakened by Sadid's mental screams." Her eyes burned with fury. "They tied us both up. I'll kill them if I ever get a chance. Truly I will!"

Takkar pretended sympathy. "Tell me why you want to kill them, Rika?"

"They tied me to a tree and…" Her eyes grew dark and her mouth was hard with fury.

Compelling her more strongly, Takkar frowned. "Go on, Rika."

Breathless with rage she rasped, "They held me and had their filthy hands all over me and kissed me with their stinking mouths."

Rika gulped more of her drink and Takkar sat in silence willing her to continue. "Sadid was tied somewhere behind me and I could hear him screaming in a fury to match my own. They told me that they would kill him if I didn't cooperate. I was so afraid they would hurt him, so I had to tell him not to fight them. Then they left me alone saying they must keep me pure for their master. They kept drinking until they were too drunk to stand and they left me tied to that tree, freezing and alone."

Rika drew in a ragged breath her eyes dark with memory. "I swear I will kill them, I will kill them all!"

Takkar touched her cheek gently, pretending solace. "I am sorry that they frightened you that way. They will be punished, dear Rika, I will see to it." Takkar noted the satisfaction in her eyes. "In fact, I may even allow you to watch while they are punished, would you like that, Rika?"

Her eyes darkened with the desire for revenge. "Yes, oh yes!"

Takkar knew that he had her now, and he took his time to savor the moment. Two glasses of wine and additive would do their work for him. He held her hands lightly, stroking and caressing hers and finally pulled her to her feet. He pulled Rika into his embrace and kissed her, feeling her instant response. He talked to her, bringing her deeper and further into his control until any sense of her own will was nearly gone.

When she was completely in his thrall he pulled his knife from his belt and yanked her hand, opening the palm to slash the knife across it. Rika swayed but he held her tightly. Takkar knew that he must bind her now, before she could think of escape. Still holding her eyes with his, he watched the blood well up from the wound.

She was caught between wanting to flee and fascination. She moaned as he lifted her hand to his lips and sucked her blood, still piercing her with his mesmerizing gaze.

Turning his knife to his own hand, he drew the sharp blade across the thick part of his palm, enjoying the painful lust it caused. "Now you," he demanded, lifting his hand to her mouth.

She took his hand almost eagerly, tasting the hot bitterness in his blood. They were bound by blood now. She did not know it, but she would never be free of him again.

He leaned down licked a drop of his blood from her lip finding that intensely erotic. Then he surprised her and stepped back.

"Now, my dear Rika, you have been through an ordeal and I will see to your comfort. We can talk later and find a way to return you to the school if you like." His eyes held hers, the compulsion strong.

He poured a brandy noting the confusion on her face. "Now, drink this, and do so quickly."

She grabbed the glass and downed it. He rang a bell and a middle aged woman in a black dress and starched white apron entered and bowed low.

"Take Rika to the south tower, please and see to her comfort. I will see her again at dinner." Takkar tapped his finger lightly against his lips, "The green dress I think and the appropriate jewels. See that she is given some more of our special restorative for she has had a difficult time on her way to us. Also, see to the comfort of her stallion."

He brushed Rika's cheek with the back of his hand. "We certainly wouldn't want your partner to be hungry or uncomfortable, would we, my dear?"

Rika looked confused as if she had no idea what Takkar meant. Then she looked down and murmured, "No."

The woman bowed and motioned to the door, and Rika stumbled after her.

After they left, Takkar sipped his brandy. Rika would be an easy conquest, too easy, most likely. He would tantalize her and win her over and once he had bound her to him, in every way, he would enlist her to capture the real prize. Yes this would be enjoyable after all and he looked forward to the evening ahead.

As Rika dizzily followed the woman, her head cleared slightly. What had just happened to her? How could she have completely forgotten Sadid, and why had she let that man kiss her and hurt her that way? She shook her head trying to clear it thinking about his voice and his eyes. There was something about him, especially when he spoke with her telepathically. It was like the empathic bond she shared with Sadid but even more potent and she had no idea why. She could not understand why she had been so eager to please him, and even worse how she had forgotten Sadid.

The woman led her to a seat outside a set of doors and told her to stay there. Rika closed her eyes and rested her head against the back of the chair, praying that the confusion and dizziness would abate.

She remembered how her uncle and brother had forced her older sister finally driving her to run away. She also remembered her brother's attempts to do the same to her. If one of the other women hadn't shown her how to use a knife, she may have ended up just as her sister had. Yet now she had just let this total stranger hurt her, and she had been a willing participant.

Sudden hot tears flowed down her cheeks and she dashed them away with shaking hands when the woman returned to lead her up a dark steep stairway. She was breathless and exhausted when the woman unlocked the door to a tower room.

Three women stood in the center of the room and the servant who had brought her busied herself lighting candles and lamps until the room was bright. Dark red drapes covered a window and there were chairs, tables and a couch covered in the same red material. Steam rose from a beautiful golden tub by the window and Rika smelled the flowery scent of herbs.

There was a knock at the door and a servant girl entered carrying a jeweled golden wine goblet and some fruit and cheese. The girl placed the tray on the table and Rika noted her blank face. Her long black hair was lusterless and Rika shivered remembering the same dull dead look in her sister's eyes just before she ran off. Without acknowledging any of them, the girl went to the door and waited while the woman with the key let her out.

After the girl left, one of the women picked up a sharpened knife, her eyes glittering and an evil grin grew across her face. Afraid, Rika tried to step back toward the door but the other two women grasped her arms. She heard the door lock behind her.

"Don't even think about it, missy." The knife woman growled. The knife woman picked her nails with the sharpened point and gestured with her chin at the food. "That's for you. After your bath, you will eat and drink all of it before you go back to the master. Make it easy on yourself and do it, missy, we can make you, if you won't."

A surge of hopelessness slithered down Rika's spine. She looked down at the cut on her hand and she clenched her fist using the pain to help her focus her thoughts. She closed her eyes a moment remembering the demand in the man's eyes and voice and then shook her head violently. She could not let this continue, she had to find a way out.

"Sadid! Sadid, are you all right?"

His empathic voice answered, filled with love and worry. *"I am well. What of you, my mistress? You sound strange and far off. I am not bound, I can take you away."*

Rika sighed and ran her fingers through her hair. She had to get away, but she couldn't risk them hurting him until she could escape without being caught. She tried to keep her fears from her thoughts. *"I think it will be all right Sadid. I will find a way for us to leave. Please, try and rest my love, I will come to you soon."*

Sadid didn't like the way she sounded, she was hiding something, and it frightened him. But he loved her and would never disobey her. *"As you wish, my mistress."*

CHAPTER TWELVE

Deception

One of the women ordered her to discard her filthy clothing and get in the steaming tub of water. The mirror next to her showed knots in her hair and dirt on her face and arms, and the thought of being clean sounded wonderful, despite her dizziness and confusion.

Eyeing the woman with the knife, Rika undressed and bit her lip to keep silent while the women scrubbed her vigorously. She stepped from the tub and they rubbed her skin with towels until it glowed. One of the women rubbed a cool tingling ointment into her skin. The second woman covered the cut on her hand with ointment and wrapped it with a clean linen bandage. They dried her hair with towels and helped her into a green satin gown that fit her like a second skin. The dress was beautifully made but cut very low. Rika often wore revealing clothing but this dress made her own clothing look modest. She was almost relieved when one of the women gave her a beautiful shawl.

They combed and dressed her hair and gave her a blood red pendant with matching earrings. They stood her in front of the tall mirror and Rika admitted to herself that the overall effect of the dress and the jewels was striking.

Realizing how hungry she was, Rika moved to the table and ate the food under the gaze of one of the women. It filled and calmed her, but it had also brought clarity back to her thoughts. She had to find a way to get out of this place. If she could get to Sadid, he could take her back to the school. She'd rather face Peter's anger at her for leaving without permission than the strange feelings and loss of control that she'd experienced with Takkar.

Rika watched while the knife woman mixed the packet into her wine and ordered her to drink it. Knowing that there was no choice in the matter, she drained the goblet.

The women left and Rika heard their laughter diminish as they left her alone, locking the door behind them.

The wine grew warm in her belly and spread like fire to the rest of her body. Her thoughts became hazy again.

Looking at her reflection in the mirror, she actually liked what she saw and it occurred to her that there might be another way out of this situation. If she could get Takkar to trust her, she might be able to escape. Rika tried not to think about how readily she had already responded to his eyes and his demands. It was a dangerous game for sure and she had no doubt she could end up a zombie like that servant girl if she wasn't careful.

If she did escape and went back to the school, there was a strong possibility that they would expel her for this latest transgression. She couldn't go home and she had nowhere else to go.

She had to think of something different. Walking around the room she touched the vibrant tapestries and rich furniture.

Everything she had seen in this castle was opulent and beautiful. She'd never seen its like. She found herself wondering what it would be like to become Takkar's consort. He was a very powerful man, a member of the ruling first house of Drayon. It might not be so bad at all. She would have much more freedom here than she had ever had at home or at the school. The women had told her that things might go well if she kept his interest.

If she did what he wanted he might even keep his promise to let her punish the men who had captured her. She and Sadid would be free to do as they wished. She smiled seductively in the mirror the deep red of the necklace matching the crimson smile on her lips.

Not long after a key turned in the lock and the woman in the black and white maid's uniform entered and took her to dine with Takkar. She followed the maid into a beautiful dining room lit by crystal chandeliers and soft golden light. Takkar stood at one corner near a massive black marble fireplace. He was dressed formally, his dark coat contrasting with the snowy white shirt and tie and he looked very handsome.

Rika's smile faded when she met his eyes. They devoured her and for a moment she saw the coldness of a predator hovering over his prey. Rika hesitated, suddenly fearful and confused. *What am I doing?*

Without looking away from her, he dismissed the servant. "Come Rika, into the light. Let me see you."

There was a hot hunger in his eyes and he smiled slightly.

She moved closer standing as still as a statue.

His voice caressed, "You are quite lovely, Rika."

Rika was thrilled. Suddenly there was no thought of anything but pleasing him. With no further thought of resistance she walked to him.

His grin brightened his face but never reached his eyes. He raised his hand to touch her lips and Rika leaned forward.

He smiled again and backed away to pour them both a glass of wine.

As Takkar sipped his wine he remained cool and distant and Rika felt confused and fearful that she had somehow displeased him.

"So tell me, Rika. How long have you been at the school?"

Disoriented for a moment, Rika couldn't think how to answer him.

Takkar chuckled, "Oh come now, my lovely girl, I want to learn so much more about you."

The words seemed to magnify in her mind and she answered him quickly. "This is my second year."

"And you have been bonded how long?" He asked.

"About nine months."

Takkar nodded and led her to the table. Soon after the servants brought the food and drink and as they ate he compelled Rika with words, soft touches and his eyes. He learned all about her family, the drunken father and abusive uncle and brother. Takkar commiserated with her and laughed when she told him how she'd learned to use a knife and convinced her brother not to bother her again. Rika freely told him of her bonding with Sadid and her respect for Peter and unrequited passion for Aiden. She finished telling him how she'd fled the school when she had seen Aiden caressing the new girl, Aine.

Takkar's gaze was suddenly that of a raptor ready to devour its quarry. "Are they lovers?"

Rika looked away, afraid of the intensity in his eyes and not wanting to think of Aiden and Aine together.

"Look at me, Rika!" Takkar ordered, grabbing her arms hard. "You must never lie to me. Do you understand?"

Staring into his fathomless eyes, she stuttered, "I…I don't know if they were lovers, but I don't think so."

Takkar smiled and led her politely to the fire to share an after dinner drink. Once again she felt dizzy and confused, as if her thoughts were not her own.

Takkar had seen that more of the drug was in her food and she was almost pathetic now to please him and do his bidding.

"Do you still want him?"

In her confusion, Rika couldn't remember who they spoke of.

Filling his words with contempt he grated, "It matters not what you want. The only thing that matters is what I want. You are mine and your only wish will be to please me. Do you understand?" Without waiting for an answer he grabbed her arm and yanked her to her feet.

Rika swayed with dizziness. Tears filled her eyes, and she prayed that she would not anger him further. The drugs Takkar had given her enhanced his control of her mind. Soon her need of the restorative would become her only reason for life. The only escape from the need would be to have more, and the only way she would get more, would be if he gave it to her. She was helpless to resist him.

Afterward his outrage had ceased, Takkar feigned concern. "You look chilled; I will build up the fire." Rika huddled numbly and he brought her a drink of cool water. After she had taken a few sips he sat next to her. "Better now?"

Rika nodded.

"So you believe that Aiden and the new girl, what is her name?"

Rika sighed, "Aine, her name is Aine."

"You say they are not lovers?" Takkar mused absently, releasing his control of Rika so that she could speak more easily.

Rika felt the release, took a deep breath. She thought back to what she had seen of Aine and Aiden eager to answer

Takkar as completely as she could. "She was only at the school for a day when I left. I don't think she had met Aiden before, so they hardly had the time to become lovers."

Takkar focused intently. "Where is she now?"

Rika took a quick breath trying to control her thoughts, wondering why he wanted to know about Aine. "I don't know." Then she remembered something. "I took her to her room when she arrived, but I heard later that she is a multi-lingual. They say she is just like Deidre."

A sudden onrush of blood filled Takkar's face, and then he turned his fury on Rika. He struck her hard with his closed fist, knocking her to the floor the chair clattering. She cried out and cringed, scurrying under the table to keep him from hitting her again. Dizzy with pain, her ears ringing she could just barely make out his words.

"You will never say that name to me again!" He shrieked, "You are filth, not worthy to wipe the sweat from her brow, much less speak her name!"

Takkar looked down at his hands wrapped around Rika's neck. She was turning blue and had almost stopped resisting. He thrust her away from him with such force that her head slammed into the floor. She gasped and choked trying desperately to fill her lungs. Her dress was torn in the front and she tried to hold it together as she crept to the corner by the fireplace. Shaking and dizzy she vomited. Trying to sit up she leaned awkwardly against the wall as tears streamed down her face.

Fighting to contain his rage, Takkar poured a brandy and tossed it down. He refilled the glass and took it to Rika.

"Drink it," he said wearily. "It will ease the pain."

With a shaking hand, Rika lifted the glass and sipped. Her neck throbbed, adorned with purple bruises. The brandy burned all the way down but it warmed her. Takkar tossed her shawl to her, still shaking, she wrapped it around her shoulders covering her ruined dress. Gradually her breathing steadied. Her eyes cleared enough to see through the haze of pain. The obsession to please him had disappeared abruptly when he struck her and she was aghast at what he had done and terrified that he would hurt her again. She bit her lip to keep from sobbing although hot tears rolled down her face.

Takkar stared into the fire, in a dull voice he whispered, "You must never say her name to me, Rika. I cannot be accountable for what happens if you do so again."

Rika nodded her understanding.

Takkar looked at Rika's swollen neck and tear-stained face and suddenly felt an intense tenderness toward her. He was shocked, not having felt that way in years. He examined the feeling as he would a new bauble. *How interesting?*

He needed to know what Rika knew, and he must enlist her as his ally. He would never gain her trust by brutalizing her so he helped her up, kissing her gently on her brow. "I am sorry, Rika. I didn't mean to hurt you. Sometimes I cannot control my anger when I think of her, and how she betrayed me." He picked up a napkin from the table and wrapped some ice in it, holding it gently against her head where he had pounded her into the floor.

He kissed her gently on the forehead, "You are tired and hurting. Can you ever forgive me?"

Mute, Rika nodded.

He smiled; his eyes dark and lustrous and kissed her again and rang the bell to call the maid. "Take her to her rooms and see to her needs."

"Yes, master." The woman murmured.

Numbly Rika followed. When they reached her rooms the maid helped her into a sleeping gown and gave her a glass of clear water.

"I don't understand," Rika murmured.

For a long while the woman was silent as she helped Rika prepare for bed, giving her some pain medication. Finally she relented, "What don't you understand?"

"Why he tried to kill me when I spoke of Deidre."

The woman continued, emotionless, lighting the candles in her room and turned down the bed. "I shouldn't tell you this, but it might just save your life someday." She stood by the edge of the bed. "Deidre was the only person, besides his mother, that Takkar ever cared for. His mother died tragically when he was very young, and though they claimed it was an accident, I've heard that he killed his father. The lady Deidre was his passion, but she had eyes only for her husband, Mabon. Even after Takkar took her from Mabon, Deidre could never be coerced."

The woman tucked the blankets up around Rika. "I didn't know she was Mabon's wife. What happened to her? I thought she died?"

"Maybe she did, maybe she didn't, but she escaped from this castle and from Takkar, and she was never seen again. It nearly drove him mad."

The maid sighed, a heavy sorrowful sigh and blew out most of the candles, carrying one to the door as she opened it to depart. "Sleep as long as you can, miss. He'll want to see you again tomorrow, he always does." She closed the door and her footsteps faded away.

CHAPTER THIRTEEN

Attack

The sun streamed through the high window, its bright light on her face jolted Aine awake. Exhausted by the events of her transition to Drayon, she had slept deeply but knew she should have awakened and joined the other students for early classes. Washing quickly, she chose a dress of deep blue and rushed through the doorway to find Phelan waiting for her grinning happily, his long tongue lolling from his mouth. *"I told my master that you had awakened. He wishes to meet you for breakfast."*

Aine patted the wolf's huge head and thanked him. Mabon smiled as she joined him in the cafeteria. "That color becomes you, Aine, and you look well rested."

A blush of embarrassment grew on Aine's cheeks. She cut a piece of bread from the fresh loaf and sipped the tangy tea. "I hadn't planned on sleeping this late, especially on my first day."

"Nonsense, you needed your rest, dear. And now that you are refreshed it is time for you to begin your studies."

Mabon's beard had been trimmed to a fashionable goatee and his hair was pulled back in a pony tail. The black vest accented with indigo trim fit him well and he reminded Aine once again of a professor she knew from Carolinda's college.

They passed the training grounds on their way to class where squads of students dressed in the rainbow vestments of every pod, worked at various paces. Young students shouted encouragement to their equally young pegasite partners who were clumsy in their efforts to take off and land properly.

"Somehow they seem younger every year," Mabon noted as they entered a building and walked down the hall.

"Rose wanted you to join this class today. While most of these students have been here two or three years I think it will be a good place to begin. I am confident you will catch up quickly."

Aine looked uneasy as they entered the classroom of twelve students. As she found a seat near the front she saw two senior trainers, one of whom was Aiden. He grinned at her, his sparkling eyes matching his rich blue tunic.

Rose was explaining the properties of the pendant hanging on the neck of a young man standing in the front of the room. He fidgeted nervously, shifting from one foot to the other and pulled at his bright red vest to straighten it several times. That awkward age between adolescence and manhood, a sprinkle of freckles covered his nose where the slight down of facial hair sprouted on his lip. His dark curls made him appear young but his tall lanky body was that of a young man.

"Each talisman responds only to its bearer. Most of you have experienced the muted light or humming sound that indicates activation," Rose explained as she demonstrated the process by grasping her talisman, which took on a golden glow. The book in front of a pretty blond girl wearing a green tunic, rose from the desk and then down again.

"Once you have mastered the key to activating your own talisman it will respond as soon as you touch it. More experienced empaths can translocate or utilize their talisman without even touching it." She smiled as a long braid of a girl in light yellow colors lifted high off her back. The girl shivered and the braid fell to her back once again.

A beautiful hawk flew through the window to land on a perch next to Rose's owl. The young man standing next to Rose glanced at the hawk and straightened, his nervousness forgotten. The bird cocked his head, his piercing eyes intent on the student.

Aine heard the bird clearly, *"You have learned this task well, master. It will please Merlin's partner for you to demonstrate your skill."*

Rose continued her instruction. "Andy discovered how to use a 'trigger' to activate his talisman, although he also has learned some of his skills without that aid." Rose's golden eyes, so similar to those of her owl, rested on the student. "Will you explain how you use your trigger, Andy?"

Andy nodded and cupped a peculiar looking stone in one hand and his pendant in the other. Both the pendant and the stone glowed with an orange aura, and in a blink, Andy was standing in the back of the room.

"I have to hold the stone before I touch the pendant, or I don't go anywhere." Andy smiled shyly. "The farthest I've been able to translocate has been from the courtyard to the training field." His voice cracked in a high falsetto and he reddened and lowered his gaze.

"Thank you, Andy, nicely done," Rose added. Andy made his way back to his seat.

"Now, everyone choose a partner. Those of you, who are proficient in translocating objects, should work with someone who is not."

Andy introduced himself to Aine and they worked for a while, but she was unsuccessful. "Don't worry about it," Andy encouraged. "It took me three weeks before I could move anything, and then it was only when I discovered my trigger by mistake. Sometime's I think we try too hard and then when we relax, all of a sudden, it happens."

A shadow crossed Aine's face when she remembered using her talisman to dispel the image of Takkar in the pool. Yet even having done so then, she had no idea how to do it again. Pushing the memory away she focused on Andy's instructions.

The other senior trainer was a pretty girl with short dark hair in a deep indigo tunic. Rose said to her, "Lara, you and Aiden can demonstrate personal translocation. Let us reconvene at the rock arch."

Aiden caught up with Aine as they left the building. "You look nice today, Aine. Our pod color becomes you."

"Thank you, Aiden, you look quite dashing yourself." The men who were senior trainers wore longer tunics in their pod color over white shirts with black pants and boots.

"What did she mean by personal translocation?" Aine asked.

"Well, basically it is when you move yourself from one place to another like Andy did," Aiden explained. "Everyone starts with objects and once they are able to move objects easily, they learn to move themselves."

Everyone gathered beneath the rock arch. Rose nodded to Aiden and he grabbed Aine's hand with one hand and his talisman with the other, and in a blink they were standing on the top of the stone arch.

"That was a bit theatrical, Aiden." Rose turned to Mabon and said, "Blue pod trainers are always so flashy, aren't they?"

Aiden grinned, "I wanted to demonstrate that more than one person can translocate at the same time."

"You could have given me a little warning, you know." Aine whispered as she caught her breath.

He motioned to the base of the arch, a smirk on his face, "Shall we?" He returned them to the ground and Aine was relieved that she was assigned to work with Lara. She had no doubts that Aiden was showing off.

None of the students in Lara's group were able to translocate and Lara winked at Aine, "You'll figure it out, I'm sure of that, if only to keep certain people on their toes." Lara nodded meaningfully toward Aiden who was working with two younger students.

"I sure hope so." Aine smiled, acknowledging Lara's hint.

Suddenly they heard shouts and whinnies and a cacophony of snarls and chaos from the direction of the training field. A huge wolf, the size of Phelan streaked to Lara and she sprinted off after him. Rose's owl flew to her arm and she and Mabon hurried the other students to the safety of the building.

Grabbing Aine's hand, Aiden took them to the top of the arch again just as Dark Fire, followed quickly by Zephyr appeared. From that vantage they saw twenty large reptilian creatures racing toward the training field from the forest. Aiden jumped to Dark Fire's back and shouted, "Follow me, Aine!"

Hiking up her skirt she jumped to Zephyr and they sped toward the training field. Some of the older students and trainers swooped in to pull the younger students to safety. But more inexperienced students struggled with partners who were panicked or out of control.

Peter, the red pod senior trainer, astride a white stallion only slightly smaller than Dark Fire joined Aiden in incredible acrobatics that drew the attackers away from the frightened youngsters. The white stallion shouted to Zephyr who had just helped Aine pull a young boy and his wolf puppy to her back, *"Take them to the stables!"*

Before she left, she saw more reptilian-looking beasts the size of small horses, pour from the distant woods. They attacked with lightning speed and sharp fangs and teeth. Some of them were ridden by scruffy looking men who seemed to be searching for someone.

Other senior trainers joined Aiden and Peter throwing knives with remarkable accuracy to strike them down. Rose's owl raked an attacker's face with his razor talons and the man fell shrieking to the dust.

Aine spotted a younger student who was trapped at the far end of the training field. She was still struggling to get her terrified pegasite off the ground and the ugly beasts were almost upon them. Zephyr turned on a wing tip and dove at the beasts driving them away from the young girl. She shot straight up just as the creature jumped for her and Aine gasped with fear and pride holding tightly with both arms.

Phelan and the other wolves shot between the attackers and the girl and drove them back so that the girl's filly finally leapt to the air and flew off toward the stables.

As Zephyr turned to follow them, Aine gasped. One of the men riding the vicious beasts was Turat. He saw her at the same time and pointed, shouting, "There she is! That's the one he wants. Kill the filly but take the woman alive!"

Aine felt a great surge of fear for Zephyr as some of the men had bows and arrows. Suddenly Aiden and Dark Fire were there diving between Zephyr and the beasts, perilously close to the ugly creatures. "Get out of here, Aine!" Aiden motioned to the group of creatures racing for her and shouted, "Take the other side, Peter!"

Turat and the others tried in vain to redirect their beasts to follow Aine, but they could not control them. The two stallions tantalized them keeping just out of reach and the ugly creatures could not resist the chase. They worked in tandem to draw the reptilian beasts and their frustrated riders further and further away.

One of the creatures jumped wildly, unencumbered by a rider. Its vicious claws caught the white stallion's front hoof and Peter leaned sideways holding on with only his legs as he stabbed the creature in the eye. It fell howling to the ground and was obliterated by Phelan and the other wolves. The strong white wings took the pegasite and his rider high to the sky and safety.

A lion joined by a midnight black panther and more wolves streaked across the field attacked the remaining beasts and the men riding them. Soon the vicious reptiles were fighting for their lives and ran desperately for the cover of the thick forest. In moments they were gone, pursued by the wolves and other large empathic predators.

Aine's heart was racing as she and Zephyr landed in front of the stable. At the front of the stable the healers were busy bandaging scratches and cuts on both students and their partners

Rose tapped her staff on the ground and everyone quieted. Her voice was calm and deliberate. "Trainees, return to your rooms after you have stabled your partners. Security detail will take the dead to the far end of the lake for burning. John, please have the stable lads pull some wagons out to help."

"Senior trainers please assess injuries in your pod and report any needing attention to the chief medic."

Everyone began to move off as instructed and Rose turned her piercing gaze to Aine. "Aine, I must see you,

Mabon and Aiden in my study, as soon as you have seen to your partners."

Shaken by the intensity of Rose's once kind eyes, Aine led Zephyr to her stall. She was horrified to see three long scratches on her neck. "Oh, Zephyr, you're hurt." She looked around in panic for a moment unsure what to do.

Mabon had been helping calm one of the younger pegasites when he saw Aine's pale face. "I'll get some ointment for that, the wuenta's claws are dirty and can cause infection."

"Ahhhh." Zephyr crooned with relief when Mabon returned and slathered her neck with the cool ointment. The filly regarded Aine, *"I tried to keep them from capturing you, mistress."*

With a sinking heart, Aine acknowledged the truth. The attack on the school had not been random. The focus of the attack had been to capture her.

Aiden led Dark Fire into the next stall and there was deep concern in Mabon's eyes as he said, "Phelan will walk Aine to Rose's study when you both are done here."

Aiden nodded.

Aine watched Mabon leave, her eyes troubled. Zephyr nudged her, *"I will be well and Phelan will see you safe."* Aine stroked Zephyr gently. Then she noticed Aiden grimace as he reached for a brush to clean Dark Fire. He had a long scratch on his arm and his shirt was torn and bloody.

Aine rushed to his side. "Oh, Aiden, you're hurt too!"

"It's not that bad. Jill will fix me up once I've seen to Dark Fire." Noting the shock and fear in Aine's eyes, he cupped her cheek with his good hand, "What about you, are you all right?"

Aine felt the warmth of his hand on her cheek and she looked up into his eyes unable to prevent the tears that filled her own. He pulled her into his arms murmuring softly as he held her close. "It's all right now Aine, no one was seriously hurt." He searched his pocket to find a clean handkerchief and handed it to her, waiting while she wiped her eyes.

"I was so worried about Zephyr, and I didn't know what to do for her." Aine's voice trembled.

"The ointment will help and I think she'll be fine. But tell you what," He gestured toward the front of the stable where an older man knelt to look at Peter's stallion's foot. "I'll ask John to keep an eye on Zephyr through the afternoon. He's the best at caring for pegasites. Will that help?"

Unsure of anything, Aine nodded. She followed Aiden to the others. Peter held his stallion's leg a crease of worry on his forehead. The older man finished wrapping the hoof and stood and wiped his face with his handkerchief. Peter was almost as disheveled as Aiden, his red tunic torn and dirty, but he had escaped injury.

The white stallion shifted and the older man patted his shoulder offering him a carrot. "That ought to do it. We'll keep him clean and quiet and he should be fine, Peter." John smiled, "He is strong and healthy, and he should heal quickly, right Tomah?"

Aine heard Tomah's reply, *"Please tell the healer thank you, it is much better."*

A look of profound relief on his face, Peter brushed his hair back. "Thanks, John. I'll check in again once I've seen to my pod.

He bowed slightly to Aine. "Tomah has told me that you are Zephyr's partner, Aine. I'm pleased to meet you."

Aine nodded and Peter shook her hand.

Aiden squeezed Peter's shoulder. "I'm glad Tomah will be all right, that was quite a bold move, my friend."

Peter grinned and glanced at his partner and a fleeting look of absolute adoration crossed his face. "Yes, he is a brave fellow isn't he?"

Peter threw his vest over his shoulder and nodded to Aiden. "While you're at it, you'd better have Jill tend that arm. Are any others in your pod injured?"

Aiden shook his head, "None, and yours?"

"No one injured, but Rika and Sadid were gone when I returned from patrol last night. Tomah says that she left for that mountain lake and Sadid said she was troubled."

"She *is* trouble, if you ask me," Aiden replied.

Peter took Tomah's reins, "Aine, it was nice to meet you, although I'm not sure I'd get into the habit of hanging out with this guy." Peter cocked his head indicating Aiden who chuckled.

"But she has no choice you know, I'm her senior trainer."

Peter's face straightened in mock sympathy but his grin grew. "Well you have my condolences then, Aine." He clasped arms with Aiden who winced slightly.

After he asked John to check Zephyr, Aiden told Aine that he'd meet her and the others once he'd cleaned up and had the healers tend his arm.

Aine checked on Zephyr once more and then, accompanied by Phelan, went straight to Rose's study. Mabon and Rose were in chairs near the fire and Rose motioned Aine to join them. A short while later Aiden came in followed by an elderly man who shuffled across the room with a tray of food and a large pot of tea.

"Thank you, Amos." Rose poured the tea.

"You are welcome, mistress." The old gentleman bowed slightly and closed the door quietly behind him.

Sipping the tea, Rose turned her piercing golden eyes to Aine and the others. "Merlin and the other raptors are searching the forest to ensure that the attackers do not return." She sighed and took another sip of tea. "I wish I had sent them for dawn surveillance as well."

"It would have made no difference," Mabon replied softly, "You know that."

Three sets of concerned eyes turned to Aine, and she shifted uncomfortably in her chair. "They attacked the school to find me, didn't they?" She looked down, already knowing the answer.

Rose said, "Yes Aine. Takkar does not give up easily and it is certain that he will return now that he knows you are here."

Mabon added, "Regrettably it is no longer safe for you to stay at the school."

Aine's teacup shook as she placed it back on the table and she clasped her hands in miserable silence.

Rose set her cup on the table, "Mabon believes that Takkar captured Zephyr before you arrived and that he has tried several times to find you, is that right?"

Aine nodded.

"Well, we aren't going to let him find her again!" Aiden growled a flush coloring his neck.

Rose cocked an eyebrow at Aiden and he apologized for his outburst. "I agree with Aiden. We cannot allow Takkar to succeed."

"How can we prevent it?" Aine felt a wave of defeat.

Rose sat back and everyone waited politely for her response. "We must find a way to hide you from him until you can be trained to protect yourself from his mind control."

Aine said, "It is my fault he found me here. If I hadn't flown off with Zephyr yesterday that man would not have seen us by the lake."

"That may not be how he found you, Aine." Mabon started, "It was inevitable to trace you to the school. Where else would one with the gifts come for training? Takkar is not stupid, he would know that."

Rose thought for a moment and turned to Mabon. "Could you return to the cave and hide her there?"

"He already found me there, and everything in that repository is so important," Aine objected.

"I doubt that he knew precisely where you were or he would have tried harder to find you then." Mabon reached over and patted her hand. "Your empathic signature is quite unique, but until today I still believe he has only found you by chance. The cave could be a short term solution, but I agree, we cannot risk Takkar finding it."

Rose nodded, "We must try something unexpected, something he cannot anticipate. The two of you could continue her training if we can think of somewhere she'll be safe."

Aiden's eyes lit up. "Of course! I've got it! We could disguise ourselves as gypsies. The tribes travel constantly this time of year so even if Takkar spies us, it wouldn't seem too unusual. There are always one or two wagons who are traders or tinkers off away from the tribes during the summer. The old wagon behind the stables would be perfect if we painted it."

Mabon raised his eyebrows at the younger man's exuberance. "Where, exactly, are we going?"

Aiden's face lit. "To my family, to the West Wind tribe."

Rose asked, "I thought that the tribes were more hesitant to offer sanctuary now. Do you think they would allow you to stay, especially if they learned that Takkar seeks Aine?"

Aiden's grin faded but a look of determination appeared in his midnight blue eyes. "With both Mabon and I speaking for her and especially with Mother's influence I think they would allow us to stay."

Mabon was cautious. "I'm not so sure that they would be inclined to offer sanctuary given the situation, but either way, we do need to leave the school. At least this way we'd be a moving target and more difficult to find."

Aiden's eyes sparkled. "It will work Mabon. I know it will. But you're right, even if it doesn't it will give us the chance to continue to train Aine and keep her hidden."

He smiled at Aine, "She's quick and very strong or she wouldn't even be here. She will probably know most of what she'll need to know by the time we reach the tribe."

Rose glanced at Aine, who didn't seem nearly as convinced. "And I suppose, since you are such a wonderful trainer she will progress as expected?"

Aiden laughed, "Naturally!"

Mabon chuckled, "Well, I'm glad to see that your ego hasn't been injured."

A tiny smile tugged at Aine's mouth and Aiden winked at her boldly.

Mabon said, "Well, it does have the virtue of being completely unexpected, and we certainly need that. I'm not sure I'm ready to go traipsing through the countryside masquerading as a gypsy, though."

Aiden grinned.

Merlin, Rose's owl, glided silently to his perch from the open window. *"The men with the hard sides have returned to their blackface cave, my mistress."*

The owl's empathic voice sounded like that of an old man, but his voice was affectionate toward Rose. *"The wings watch, as do the four paws in the forest."*

Rose stood and Merlin flew to her outstretched arm. "Thank you for your vigilance, go and feed, my friend."

The bird turned his head almost completely backward, his golden eyes the exact shade of Rose's and he stared directly at Aine, *"You must be wary of the hard side fools, little sister, but*

I think you have strength you've not yet tapped. In that you are like my mistress, and the evil one will not easily find you again. Fly free, little sister."

Aiden and Mabon regarded Rose and Aine in puzzlement, and Rose explained what Merlin had said to Aine. Almost as if he were talking to himself, Mabon mumbled, "You see, my dear, even our partners' wish you well." He nodded slowly, "And so you will be, and so you will be."

Mabon turned to Aiden. "How soon can we be ready to leave?"

"I'd say by sunset. I'll get Peter and Jared to help me paint the wagon, and we'll need to load it and set up a team." Aiden started for the door.

"Well, are we agreed then?" Both men looked at Aine.

Aine wasn't sure at all that she agreed. She'd had such high hopes of learning what she could here at the school. Mabon had thought that she would learn faster with the other students, but now, with a sinking feeling, she realized that her return home might be postponed indefinitely. She was almost afraid to ask how far away Aiden's family was and how many days it might take to travel there. She couldn't think how to reply to Mabon.

She had started the day so filled with hope and determined to learn. Even the fact that she had been unsuccessful in class had not caused undue concern because she had assumed that she would have the time she needed to attain her goal. Now she faced another setback. She nodded but didn't speak, looking away from the men.

Rose saw the disappointment in Aine's face, though both men missed it as they left the room. When the door closed behind them she turned to Aine. "Do you understand why you must leave Aine?"

Aine met Rose's look, her own face pale and drawn. "I'm not really sure what I understand right now, to be honest. I feel guilty for the attack and discouraged that I cannot stay and learn what I must. I am grateful that you want to help me, but I just wish I could go home."

"That is perfectly understandable." Rose walked with Aine to the door. "You need some time to get cleaned up and packed I'll send someone to your room to help you." Rose led Aine to the door, "Once you're ready, meet me here and we will see what we can accomplish in our limited time together."

As Aine walked away, she felt like her emotions were on overload. Torn from her home world, threatened by an unknown adversary and unsure of her abilities, she wished her sister, Carolinda was here right now.

CHAPTER FOURTEEN

A Friend Indeed

Back in her room once again, Aine removed her torn, dirty dress and wrapped up in a warm robe. Then she sat on her bed wishing that there was a piano here at the school. Whenever she had been troubled at home music had been her solace, but unless she started singing there seemed to be no option for that now. And the last thing in the world she felt like doing was singing.

Someone knocked on the door and she rose slowly to open it.

From somewhere behind two arms wrapped around an enormous collection of clothing in the most vivid hues of the rainbow came a cheerful but muffled voice, "Hi, I'm Jill."

Jill made her way into the room and spilled her assortment of dresses, scarves, blouses, skirts and shawls onto Aine's bed. Laughing, Jill said, "Among other things, I am the best seamstress at the S.E.D., and I am supposed to create the latest in gypsy fashions for your pleasure."

Eyes, the color of new spring leaves snapped with humor as Jill held out her hand to shake Aine's. Her blond hair cascaded well below her waist. Jill's forest green tunic was molded to her slender form and there were three golden leaves pinned high on her collar. Resting her hands on her hips, Jill smiled as she glanced at the crumpled dress Aine had left draped over the chair. "It's a shame you can't wear that dress, it's definitely your color although a bit worse for wear." She chuckled, "Don't worry though; I'll do my best not to make you look too...gypsy."

Jill sorted through the clothing, working quickly and efficiently. "You should have seen the colors that Aiden wore when he first arrived at the school. We'd never had a gypsy student before and we were eternally grateful when he was finally given his blue pod clothing. One of his outfits," Jill stopped and tapped her chin with one finger, her eyes raised, "it was purple, yellow and orange I think...anyway it made my eyes hurt. Peter and Brendan always accused Aiden of being color blind. And I'm not so sure they were wrong."

Aine smiled politely, amazed by the exuberance spilling from Jill. She felt herself relaxing.

Jill stopped sorting the clothes and shifted the pile to the end of the bed. "Rose told me about you; where you are from and everything about what's happened so far."

Aine looked down at her hands.

Jill sat on the space she'd cleared while Aine sat down on a chair to face her. "Look you don't know me, but I'd like to help. Do you want to talk?"

Aine hesitated, "I don't know."

Finally Aine met Jill's gaze, "I'm worried that going with Mabon and Aiden will put them at risk with Takkar too. But I don't know what else I can do. I wish I could stay here, but that's too dangerous as well."

Jill's brow rose, "So you think Mabon and Aiden can't handle the likes of Takkar's little playmates?" Jill reached over and touched Aine's hand. "They can, believe me. I've seen Mabon face Takkar and he had him running. I believe that Takkar is actually afraid of Mabon, as he should be."

"Really?" Aine said.

Jill continued, "Peter and I were just coming back from a recruiting trip and I was riding behind Peter on Tomah. When Jabari, my partner told me that Mabon and Phelan were nearby we decided to see what he was up to."

Jill held out the pendant she wore around her neck. It was crescent shaped and dark like a black crystal. "You know that Mabon finds and finishes most of the talismans we empaths wear don't you?"

Aine nodded.

"Mabon was searching for crystals in a cave near a waterfall. I waited outside with Jabari and Tomah and Peter went in to find him. Then I heard the sounds of a struggle from somewhere behind us. All three of our partners warned us that something was wrong and Phelan and Jabari raced off.

We ran to the field and found Takkar and a couple of his buddies trying to capture a young white pegasite filly. The lead stallion of the herd was fighting him but he'd thrown a rope around her neck and attached it to his saddle. When Jabari and Phelan got close, the herd scattered except for the stallion and another mare. Takkar's horse threw him and bolted off as did the other men.

"Takkar was furious, especially when he realized that it was Mabon's partner who thwarted his plans. Takkar tried to use the voice on Mabon and Mabon laughed at him."

Jill's eyes sparkled with glee. "Takkar mumbled a spell that prevented Peter and I from moving, but it seemed to have no effect on Mabon." Jill smiled, "Mabon was so calm, as if he had all the time in the world. He demanded that Takkar release us and the filly. Of course Takkar refused.

Mabon summoned about a hundred wolves who raced out of the forest and across the field toward us. Mabon offered him one more chance and Takkar took it and bolted off like a scared puppy. The spell he'd cast was broken and Phelan called off the wolves. We freed the filly and had a great time laughing about it."

Aine smiled, "Aiden told me that Takkar and Mabon are old enemies. So Mabon is stronger than Takkar?"

"I've absolutely no doubt of that," Jill answered.

Like a bright light in a dark room, Jill put Aine at ease telling her embarrassing things she and Aiden and Peter had experienced in their years at the school together. They sorted through the piles of clothing and folded what would go in the canvas traveling bag. "Well now, you're all ready to become a gypsy."

Aine looked away, her brow still knit with worry.

"What is it, Aine," Jill asked. "You can tell me."

Aine looked at Jill sitting patiently. Her calm acceptance reminded her of Carolinda. She needed a friend and here was someone who was offering to be just that.

Aine opened her heart and shared everything with Jill; traveling to Drayon, Takkar's threats, Mabon's belief in the prophecy and her feelings for Aiden as well as her own uncertainty.

"That's quite a story," Jill said. She took both of Aine's hands and looked into Aine's eyes. The blonde woman's pupils grew large and dark and they sat quietly for several moments, but strangely, Aine had no desire to pull away.

The timber of Jill's voice changed, "You are very strong, Aine. Once you put your mind to it, nothing will stop you from fulfilling your destiny. You will have the freedom to choose that destiny, and whatever you choose it will be the right choice. You already have many friends who will do all they can to help you. There are some you have not met yet, who will guide your path. But you must have faith in yourself. If you believe in yourself, there is no limit to what you will accomplish. Do not let fear of the unknown cripple you. Put your faith and trust in those who wish to love and protect you, for you are precious to them."

Jill's eyes changed back to normal.

Aine gasped, "What just happened?"

"Sometimes I can read into a person's empathic signature and I can see glimpses of their future. It's called a foretelling."

Aine blushed. "It was like you looked into my soul." Aine looked away for a moment, "Thank you, Jill."

"For what?"

"For listening," Aine said, with tears stinging her eyes. "I really needed a friend just now."

"You and I will be very good friends someday."

Aine brightened visibly, "I'd like that!"

"Now let's sort through this stuff and get packed.

Jill pulled out a long crimson cloak with a black lining and hood and draped it over Aine's shoulders.

"If I wear this, I'll look like Little Red Riding Hood." Aine frowned at her reflection in the mirror.

"Who's that?" Jill asked around a mouthful of pins and Aine told her the story of the little girl and the wolf.

"And, have you met any wolves you'd like to trick?" Jill quipped with a wicked gleam in her eye.

"Only one named Aiden." Aine laughed.

"I see, well I'm sure you can stay miles ahead of him, although he seems quite taken with you," Jill added, her eyes twinkling.

"He does?" Aine's eyes widened.

Jill spit the pins into her hand. "I had to patch up that cut on his arm. He bore it stoically, always the tough guy, you know. Heaven forbid that either he or Peter would admit to unmanly pain, yet he couldn't stop talking about you." Here she raised her eyes, looking at the ceiling, "Let's see, how did he put it? Totally over the edge. Yep, I think that's what he said."

"Interesting," Aine said, a sudden feeling of pleasure rushing through her veins.

"That a girl, keep him guessing!"

"Guessing?"

"Absolutely! Never let a man know you're interested. Stay cool, distant, and mysterious and he'll be eating out of your hand. It drives 'em crazy." Jill eyes had a mischievous glint. "Aiden is used to having girls fall in love with him so it's about time the tables were turned."

"Do you really think he's…?" Aine blushed.

Jill nodded, "Yep, I do. Aiden's a great guy. Now, don't you dare tell him I said that, and a good friend. He's also woefully short on humility!"

Aine smiled, "I did notice that."

Jill looked Aine over carefully. "You're right, the cloak is rather much, but it is reversible, so why don't you wear it with the black side out. Now that I know your size, it won't take long to adjust the rest of these things and get them packed."

The afternoon had fled by and Jill glanced up at the high windows as she laid a skirt and blouse on the chair. "Now, go ahead and put that on then we need to get you back to Rose."

When Aine was dressed, Jill opened the door and put her fingers to her lips and whistled. A black panther ran into the room and brushed his head against her hip. "Jabari, will you take this pack to the front entrance?"

"I will take it with ease, my mistress," the big cat replied as Jill tied the bundle to a harness on his back.

"Oh! He is absolutely amazing!" Aine exclaimed, itching to stroke his rich black coat.

"He is that." Jill tightened the straps on the bag. "The name Jabari means fearless warrior, also appropriate in his case."

Jabari sauntered down the hall in front of them. They reached Rose's office and Jill squeezed Aine's hand. "Good luck, my friend. Don't let the big bad wolf get you."

"I think I'll only let him get me, if I really want him to." Aine grinned back, feeling much better.

"Be careful all right?" Jill said, touching Aine's shoulder."

Aine thought she saw a shadow pass behind Jill's eyes, and then she brightened as if pushing it away. Aine nodded and turned to the door.

When she reached Rose's office, Rose stood and said, "You look like you've been a gypsy all your life, it becomes you, Aine."

"Thank you, Rose. It's a little unusual, but I like it." Aine folded the cloak with the bright red lining over one of the chairs.

"We'll eat and then I'll work with you for a while," Rose said.

After they had practiced for a while Rose smiled, "Something is blocking you from fully utilizing your talisman right now. It is quite normal for new empaths, and only a temporary setback." Rose gestured toward the adjoining room. "Your efforts have tired you. That, too, is normal for new students and it has been a stressful day. There is a small cot in the next room, go rest until Mabon and Aiden return."

Aine went to the room and covered herself with the red cloak, and immediately fell asleep. Sometime later a light touch on her shoulder awakened her.

Aiden stood next to the cot. It was dark in the room but his silhouette projected clearly by the light from the doorway behind him. Aine sat up, pushing the cloak off of her legs.

Mabon and Rose were bent over a table in the adjacent room, talking softly. Aiden folded the cloak over his arm and held out his hand to help her up.

Aiden took a step closer and looked into her eyes. The magnetic strength of their mutual feelings drew him nearer. He cupped her chin in one hand, and gently touched his lips to hers. They simultaneously felt a shock when their lips touched. Aine stepped back, the heat rising in her face.

Aiden cupped her cheek and whispered, "Aine, I know you are worried about leaving and having to delay your plans to go home yet again."

"How do you know that?"

Aiden smiled slightly, "I saw Jill on my way here and she told me to take care of you or I'd have to answer to her." He tilted his head. "No one argues with Jabari's partner when she gives an order."

Aine returned his smile thinking of Jill's panther. "You know it was interesting, I felt like I've known Jill forever, yet we just met. She told me that we would become very good friends someday."

"Jill is adept at foretelling and I've never known her to be wrong." Aiden shifted looking somewhat ill at ease. "Did she tell you anything else?"

Aine remembered the strangeness in Jill's voice and eyes and her words about believing in herself. She also remembered that Jill had said that she and Aiden would become much more than friends. The feel of Aiden's kiss lingered, but she remembered Jill's other advice and smiled mysteriously. "Of course she did."

Aiden looked at her expectantly the quirk of a smile on his lips as Aine gazed back guilelessly. "And, you're not going tell me are you?"

Aine grinned, "Well, a girl has to have some secrets."

Aiden laughed softly, "Well, let's see if you can keep this secret." He kissed her again. This time Aine's entire body thrummed like a string on a new violin. The heat burned in her cheeks. From the doorway's light Aine could see that Aiden's face was flushed as well. "Come with me," he said. He placed his hand on the small of her back and guided her toward the fireplace. She glanced at him wondering what he had in mind, and then he smiled widely with a mock bow.

That was when Aine got her first good look at the two "gypsies" that she would be traveling with.

Aiden wore dark green stockings with brown knee-length pants that molded tightly to his body. A bright yellow shirt with billowing sleeves was partially covered with a dark red leather vest that looked a bit too small for him.

Aine had to bite her lip to keep from giggling when she saw Mabon's outfit. His pants were dark fuchsia, his shirt light red and his vest boasted brilliant stripes of both. He had an outrageous orange bandana tied around his head and a large hoop earring in one ear. Looking up from the map he was studying he noticed Aine's smirk.

Mabon grumbled, "What I go through for you, young lady. Let's get going so I can cover this disaster with my traveling cloak. I'm not sure if I look more like a clown or a pirate."

Aiden pretended offense. "You mean you don't like the clothing we gypsies wear? I think I am highly insulted."

"Appropriate if one enjoys looking like a fool, at least in my case!" Mabon glowered. Glaring at Aiden he added, "I've never seen anyone in your tribe dressed in pink!"

"Well then, it will certainly distinguish you from the rest of us won't it?" Aiden countered.

Mabon frowned as they walked out to the courtyard a malicious look in his eye, "I seem to remember a lanky young gypsy boy, partnered to a skinny black pegasite colt who wore atrocious color combinations, until he was finally assigned to the blue pod and given school clothing. It's a wonder some of the big cats didn't bite you!"

He looked at Rose, "You've got the big cats locked up now haven't you?"

Rose suppressed a grin as they walked out the front door, Aiden snorted at Mabon's retort, and bowed again to Aine his grin still lighting his face. "You, however, look quite charming my lady." Flourishing another bow he added, "Your chariot awaits."

Mabon muttered as he climbed up into the driver's seat. "Ignore him Aine. He has absolutely no sense of propriety or respect for his elders!"

The wagon, now painted bright blue, sported yellow wheels and red trim. Hitched to the front, a striking pair of matched black and white horses shifted as Mabon picked up their lead reins to steady them.

Zephyr was tethered lightly behind the wagon and Dark Fire waited beside her. Horse blankets were wrapped around them hiding their wings. Aine was sure it wouldn't really fool anyone if they looked closely, but she supposed from a distance it would do.

Aiden's hands spanned her small waist, and he easily lifted her to Zephyr's back. His eyes twinkled, and there was a look of smug happiness in them. Nervously she looked away, and pulled her skirt down to cover her legs.

Zephyr danced happily on her tether, excited to be on a journey. Mabon clicked to the horses, and Aiden vaulted to Dark Fire's back as they started away from the school in the fading light of the day.

Rose raised her hand in farewell, "Be safe, all of you. I will send Merlin when I can, to share our news."

CHAPTER FIFTEEN

A Sign

They traveled long into the night and Aine had to shake herself awake several times to keep from falling off of Zephyr's back. The dark shadows beneath her eyes and the paleness of her face shone in the light of the full moon.

"Aine is exhausted," Aiden said, "Should we stop for the night?"

"I'll be fine if we could just rest a few minutes," Aine protested.

Mabon frowned, "It has been a long day and tired people make mistakes. If Takkar found you in this state, you might be more susceptible to him."

Aine shuddered at the thought. In truth, she was tired, but she had wanted to keep up and not complain.

They stopped at a tree-covered clearing and removed the pegasite's blankets so they could stretch their wings. Aiden fed and watered the horses.

Aine stifle another yawn as she leaned with her back against a tree.

"Rest a while longer and then you both will fly ahead to my cave," Mabon said.

"Isn't it dangerous to fly?" Aiden asked.

"Phelan and his pack have ranged ahead and he says the way is clear. If Zephyr flies above Dark Fire, he will obscure her lighter coloring from the ground. Besides, even if they are seen, Takkar has no one to my knowledge with a pegasite, so they could only watch."

When they were ready, Mabon gave Aiden a leather wrapped package. "This is the original scroll of the prophecy. Rose asked me to hide it at the repository after the attack. It would be a good idea for Aine to read it. I can answer any questions when I arrive. When you are done, lock it in the chest in the scroll room, you know the one."

Mabon's face grew serious. "I don't have to tell you how important it is to keep it safe. I have only read the original once; most people have only read copies."

Aiden nodded his understanding and placed the package in his pack.

Mabon turned to Aine. "I know you are still unsure about the prophecy, but I think you should read it for yourself, it might give you more insight into its meaning. Will you do that for me?"

Aine nodded.

Mabon regarded the young couple. "You both know to be careful and to pass above the forest unseen. You will have to rest at least once; perhaps the standing circle would be a good place. Do you remember where it is?"

Aiden nodded. "Yes, Dark Fire knows it too."

"The circle is about half way to my cave and there is fresh water and feed for the pegasites. Drink from the spring, it should refresh you both."

Aiden helped Aine to Zephyr's back and the pegasites rose silently to the sky. At first they flew directly above the trees as Mabon had suggested but when the forest gave way to open fields and rugged cliffs, they flew much higher next to each other. The pegasite's wing tips nearly touched and the cold wind stung Aine's cheeks. She wrapped the black cloak around her and hunkered down on Zephyr's back.

As they flew she glanced at Aiden surreptitiously. She knew that the attraction between them was more than just a crush. Jill had said, "Things happen for a reason." She wondered if Aiden was tied to this prophecy in some way too. Reading the prophecy would help her gain the clarity she needed, or at least Mabon thought so. Perhaps she'd read it tonight.

Aiden, silhouetted against the sky, looked like he had been born riding Dark Fire. His cloak flew back in the breeze and his legs were wrapped tightly against Dark Fire's sides. Aine's eyes moved up to his torso to his profile. With his hair blowing back, and his arms resting easily on Dark Fire's neck both the stallion and his rider were impressive.

"You like Dark Fire's rider don't you, my mistress?" Zephyr's tone was secretive as if she were whispering.

"Of course I do." Aine patted the filly's neck.

"I like the stallion, too. He is the strongest stallion I have seen since leaving the wild herd," Zephyr stated. *"Perhaps I will allow him to mate me when my time comes."*

"Allow him?"

"Certainly, though I am yet a filly, I have seen the mating flights. Stallions can be quite demanding, but it is the mare that chooses."

"Interesting," Aine replied.

Zephyr added smugly, *"I think that you will choose the dark rider for your mate one day too. You watch him even when he does not see you. He is in your thoughts most of the time and your body longs for him as well."*

Aine felt a blush grow on her face. She had no idea that her thoughts were so open to Zephyr. *"Well, let's just keep that to ourselves for now."*

Zephyr agreed. *"Of course! A filly must never show a stallion that she wants him before he claims her. The stronger the desire, the stronger the mating."*

Aine laughed aloud and Aiden turned to smile at her.

Aine's tiredness faded. It was heaven to soar over the tops of the trees and enjoy the freedom of flight with Zephyr. Their other flights had been during stressful situations like escaping captors and attacks.

Soon Dark Fire soared to the ground and Zephyr back-winged to settle next to him. Vaulting from Dark Fire's back, Aiden reached up to lift Aine from Zephyr's back.

Aiden took Aine's hand. "The standing circle is not far and there is water and good grass for the pegasites. There is a tiny spring nearby, it's quite refreshing. Let's go there first."

The spring was nearly hidden in a side path and Aiden knelt and filled his water skin and handed it to Aine. She lifted the skin and squirted the liquid into her mouth. It was very cold and tasted almost sweet with a slight lemony tang. Moments after drinking it she felt invigorated and smiled as she handed the container to Aiden. "That's wonderful, I've never tasted water like that before."

Aiden smiled and drank as well, wiping his mouth with the back of his hand. "The spring is sacred to the forest people in this area. My mother always thought it had restorative qualities as well."

They followed a path that led to huge stones that stood like dark sentinels in the center of a tree-lined meadow. Aine could just barely see their outline against the dark sky. Some of the towering rock formations were an inverted U like giant doorways and others stood in pairs. One stone lay prone in the center. Aiden spread his cloak and they shared some food.

Aine saw something twinkling at the edge of her vision, but the light disappeared when she tried to look directly at the spot. "Are those fireflies, Aiden?"

"Fireflies?" He sounded puzzled.

"Something twinkled like a bug we have at home that glows and blinks on and off, but when I looked to see what it was, it disappeared."

Aiden stared intently past the large stone that lay in the center of the group of stones. He was rewarded when he saw the sparkle too. His face was lit only by starlight but Aine heard the excitement in his voice. "I think we are about to see something wonderful, I had forgotten that tonight is the first full moon of summer." Aiden whispered in her ear, "The first full moon of the summer is a special celebration for the pixies. I've heard of it, but I have never seen it."

More twinkles began to appear and as they got closer, Aine could see that they were actually tiny fairy-like creatures, much like the one that had greeted her and Mabon at the school. An ethereal tinkling music filled the night air, and the little creatures began to spin and dance with bursts of golden light. It was magical to watch and reminded Aine of fireworks, only in fairy form, suffused with lively sprightly melodies.

The amber hint of moonlight outlined the horizon beyond the stone formations. As the moon rose, it flooded the stones with the clarity of mid day and Aine gasped with delight. The moon's huge orange orb was ten times the size of any moon she had ever seen on her world, almost mis-shapen as it arose over the doorway of stones opposite them and filled the opening with brilliant light.

"It's amazing!" Aine whispered. As she grasped Aiden's hand in excitement, unconscious of anything but the scene before them.

The pixies danced and spun around the stones and they

heard a longing sound to their music.

"Aine, can you hear them? They are calling you." Aiden whispered, "I think they want you to go to them."

"Really?" Aine breathed.

"Yes, I'm sure of it," Aiden whispered excitedly. He helped her to her feet and she took a few steps toward the tiny dancers. As she moved closer, the silver music filled her mind and she closed her eyes feeling a strange sensation, as if a thousand butterflies were touching her. When she opened them again the tiny beings surrounded her, touching her hair and skin. She was entirely outlined by the silver glow from the pixies and the moonlight. They circled around her touching her and illuminating her face and body. They began to sing a haunting melody in their high chiming voices:

> "She will light our world and way,
> Without her, darkness has its sway,
> Blessed by the fairies of the summer's night,
> She becomes our guiding light.
>
> Lady of the moon, Lady of the moon.
> Come and bless us all.
> Lady of the moon, Lady of the moon.
> Listen to our call.
>
> Kiss her lips, and touch her hair
> She is pure, beyond compare.
> Though she comes from afar,
> She will be our evening star.
>
> Lady of the moon, Lady of the moon.
> Come and keep us all.
> Lady of the moon, Lady of the moon.
> Listen to our call.

She will soar on silver wings,
In her lover's arms she sings,
Sister, lover, mother dear.
Bring your tender loving here.

Lady of the moon, Lady of the moon.
Come and save us all.
Lady of the moon, Lady of the moon.
Never shall you fall."

Touching her with their gossamer wings and lilting voices they paid homage to Aine. She closed her eyes and swayed with the tune.

This was the prophecy in another form, and these tiny creatures filled with light touched Aine with their song.

At long last, the song diminished into a distant melody as one by one, each pixie flew off. Finally Aine stood alone in the moonlight, completely still. The song and the touch of the tiny creatures had changed her in some inexorable way. She felt light and free as if she too could fly and she opened her eyes and looked at Aiden in wonder.

He walked slowly to her. There was a glow about her as if she were covered in a residual light from the moon and the touch of the pixies.

"Oh Aiden. Did you see?"

"Yes." He stood in front of her. "It was the most incredible thing I have ever seen." He touched her cheek softly, his voice soft with wonder. "You are glowing you know."

Aine smiled shyly.

He brushed her hair with his hand and she looked up into his eyes. The moon was bright on his face and he asked, "Did you hear the words of the song they sang?"

Aine remembered the words and the smile faded from her face as she nodded. "It has something to do with the prophecy doesn't it?"

"My Grandmother always thought so; she sang it to me when I was a young boy." He moved closer and pulled her into a hug murmuring, "It was the most beautiful thing I have ever seen."

Aine stepped back so that she could see his face. "Aiden?"

"Yes," he whispered.

"Kiss me."

He smiled and bent his head to her and pulled her closer. His lips were warm and inviting and Aine felt a rush of butterflies in her stomach that gave way to a warm sensation. She felt herself grow dizzy.

Afterwards, Aiden took her hand and led her down the path. "Let's call our partners and be on our way, all right?"

"Sure." Aine agreed still spinning from the kiss.

CHAPTER SIXTEEN

The Prophecy

As they walked, Aine asked Aiden to repeat the words to the song the pixies sang for her. In some way she could still feel their delicate touch and she couldn't stop replaying it in her mind. Why had they touched her that way, what did the words mean? There were so many questions and she needed answers.

Aine decided to read the prophecy tonight as soon as they arrived at Mabon's cave. The pixie touch and the song were a catalyst for her and she knew she'd never rest until she tried to understand the true meaning of the prophecy. Aside from being intensely curious about it, she was also tired of being afraid of its meaning. If she really had come to Drayon for a reason, it was time she truly understood what it was, and what her options were.

Soon they reached the field by the cave and they fed and watered the pegasites and put them in the stable. Aiden opened the cave and Aine stayed with Zephyr a bit longer. Just touching her partner calmed her, and strengthened her resolve to find some answers to some of her questions.

Aine joined Aiden inside. He had built the fire and set the kettle on for tea. As he turned to face her, Aine felt attuned to him, as if a charged current coursed through her veins. She reached up to push the stray hair from his forehead and he pulled her into his arms, his warm full lips tasting hers once again.

He smiled and motioned for her to sit next to him and poured their tea. "I added one of my mother's famous restoratives to the tea," he said. "It won't prevent you from sleeping, but it will relax and refresh you."

"I think it already has," Aine smiled as she sipped the tea.

"Maybe, it's my delightful company," he winked.

Reluctant to spoil the comfortable feelings between them she hesitated, and then took a deep breath, "Aiden, I want to read the prophecy tonight."

Aiden frowned, "Why tonight? I don't think Mabon meant for you to read it immediately, we could wait until tomorrow."

"I don't think I will sleep until I read it," she insisted.

"You have been thinking about it ever since the pixies touched you, haven't you?"

She nodded. "Yes." Noting the crease between his eyes she said, "You think I'm the woman of the prophecy don't you?"

He waited for a moment before answering, "I think you might be, but it's hard to know for sure."

"That's just it, Aiden. Even if it is only a possibility, I need to know everything I can about it. Can you see why?"

"Sure I can." With a sigh he rose and retrieved the leather package and handed it to Aine, his face troubled.

"What is it, Aiden?"

He sighed, "The prophecy is difficult to understand in the best of times, and with you being so tired, it might not be the best time to try and figure it out."

She looked into his eyes and saw the concern there, and something else. Aine realized that Aiden was trying to protect her, just as he had promised Mabon that he would. Yet she had to find a way to make him understand how she felt.

She looked down and sighed. Then, after a long pause she said, "I'm tired of being afraid, I'm tired of Takkar trying to find me, and most of all I'm tired of not having any control over my life. Maybe, if I understand more about this prophecy, I will find a way to change all of that. Does that make sense?" Her eyes entreated.

He took her hand in his and raised it to his lips, kissing the back gently. "Yes, I suppose it does. I would probably want to read it too, if I were you."

Aine nodded and removed the scroll from the sheath unrolling it in front of them.

Aiden said, "I've read transcriptions of the prophecy scroll but have never seen the original." He noted the fragile parchment and the fading ink. "This scroll is very old, from before the time of my great-great grandfather. Legend has it that the prophecy was written by one of the first empaths who was also adept in foretelling. No one knows why he wrote it and it is unclear whether it is a vision or a true foretelling."

Aine tilted her head in question, "What's the difference?"

"Visions or dreams tell of events that *might* happen, while a foretelling is what *will* happen. But from what Mabon has said, prophecies can be unclear and may not unfold as you think they might."

Aine shifted so she could meet his eyes. "Do you believe the prophecy is a true foretelling?"

"Yes I do." She could see the reluctance in his eyes.

"Aiden, when I first found the crystal ball at home, it was as if it wanted something from me, and I had to see it through. I feel the same way now about this prophecy. I need to know what it means, it is very important."

"You're a brave and beautiful lady." He smiled and touched her cheek. "And I love how you blush when I compliment you."

His smile faded, "Just remember what Mabon said about prophecies being fluid? There are many possible interpretations."

She nodded and turned to the parchment. The words were written in a text resembling old English script with flourishes and fancy capital letters. The paper was golden-white and while some words were faint, most were easy enough to read. Taking a breath, she read aloud:

Through a portal in the days yet to come shall she arrive; untried, and a novice in experience yet a chalice of power exceeding all others. Demands, desire or coercion cannot achieve what her heart's true freedom will.

Aine remembered Mabon being emphatic that it was her choice whether to fulfill a role in the prophecy. That was comforting. She read the words again nodding her head slowly in agreement. She was definitely a novice in all of this, and she had come through a portal. For a moment her heart thudded. Could it be? She bit her lip and then read on.

She will face a malevolent one who will hold our realm in thrall. His obsession seeks the ultimate path of ascendance toward the dominion over all.

That was exactly as Mabon had explained it. He had not said so but she was quite sure that he thought Takkar was this malevolent one. If Takkar believed she was the woman of the prophecy (as he clearly did), that had to be why he was so obsessed with finding her.

So too will come her champion. Of royal blood and ancient lineage he shall know despair when she rests in peril both near and far away. He must give of his very soul to prove his love.

Mabon had not said anything about a champion, Aine wondered what that meant, but she felt a pang of fear at the words "rest in peril." What could near and far away mean? Aiden was right, it was obscure in its meaning. She felt herself tense but she forced herself to continue reading.

While the days will be dark, there is still hope. A charm of ultimate power lies hidden in the dark domain. It will be found, by one whose redemption is death.

If the woman and her champion prevail, the world will be free. If she fails or submits, the malevolent one will become an inexorable force in our world and beyond.

Aine rested the scroll on her lap. A sense of foreboding entered her heart at the words malevolent one seeks to bind her.

"That's strange," Aiden said. "I don't remember the mention of a charm before. I can't have forgotten it." He turned the parchment over and looked at every part of it. "Why wouldn't I remember it? I'm not sure what that means, but it does sound hopeful, don't you think?"

Aine didn't reply. She re-read the first part again. "Mabon thinks that Takkar is the malevolent one, do you?"

Aiden hesitated, "Yes, I believe he is."

"Aiden, what do you think it means 'She shall rest in peril'?"

"If you are the woman of the prophecy, it could mean that you will return to your home," he answered clearly troubled by that idea.

"Yes, I thought that too, but why would that be perilous. I wonder what it means, both near and far away?" Aine's brow furrowed.

Aiden shrugged, "I just don't know, Aine. We will have to ask Mabon when he arrives."

Glancing at the scroll a slow smile grew on his face. "The next part is good though, I like the idea of a champion." But his face fell. "Yet this part about knowing despair worries me. The thought of Takkar trying to bind or capture you makes me both furious and terrified."

Aiden's fear was contagious. Aine shuddered as she recalled her response to Takkar, especially in the pool in this very cave. If it hadn't been for Zephyr stopping her, Takkar might have found her even then.

As she focused on the scroll again the words lifted off the page and danced before her eyes flaming as if they were made of fire. Her body stiffened and the room swirled around her.

The fire in front of them grew to a wild red vortex and the heat of it seared her thoughts. Unable to take her eyes off the blaze, she saw a vision of a young man writing at a table as it formed within the flames. He scribbled frantically as if he must complete his task or die. When he finished he sat very still, tearing his eyes from the parchment. He looked outward from the flames, directly into Aine's eyes. There was a look of pain and profound sorrow on his face and ever so softly she heard his heartfelt cry, *"Forgive me."*

Aine violently shook her head trying to dispel the vision. She shouted at the man, her voice torn with sudden fury. "I want no part of this." Aine pressed her temples with her palms dropping the scroll. "Leave me alone!"

Aiden grasped her arm and she pulled away. "Aine, what is it? What do you see?"

Deaf to him, beyond words or comfort, she only saw the agonized face of the prophet. She was pulled into the maelstrom of the vision. She tried to fight it, but it was too powerful. She had to get away from it, she jumped up and ran away but the man in her vision followed her, reaching and grasping. She had to escape.

From the stable Zephyr cried, *"What is it, my mistress? Are you hurt? Should we flee? Answer me!"* Zephyr grew more frantic and repeatedly struck the stable door with her hooves finally shaking the latch. She rushed from the stable and threw herself against the door to Mabon's cave.

Dark Fire tried to block the filly and whinnied loudly with a stallion's demand to obey, but like her mistress, Zephyr was beyond hearing. Dark Fire's empathic voice was strained with fear. *"Help them, my master, the filly is broadcasting and I cannot contain her. You must stop them!"*

Aiden grabbed Aine, gripping her shoulders hard. He shook her once gently and then harder, but she didn't even register that he held her. "Aine, look at me!"

Firmer this time, he spoke his command, "Aine, look at me."

She looked at him with empty horror in her eyes. Someone was holding her, preventing her escape. She had to get away. She screamed and pulled away trying to break free. "Let me go!"

Aiden let go and Aine stumbled away.

Zephyr continued to throw herself against the door over and over. It was a measure of Aine's irrational blind terror that she didn't hear her partner.

Aiden grabbed Aine's arms and dragged her to the door, kicking it open. She fought him, frantically trying to free herself still unaware that it was Aiden who held her.

The cool night air hit her face as Aiden dug his hands hard into her arms. Pain flashed across her face.

"Aine!" Aiden shouted and shook her so hard that she bit her lip and blood welled. "Listen to me! Stop this! You must stop Zephyr. She is broadcasting her fears far beyond this place. If Takkar finds us, if he finds this place, Aine! Listen to me! Please hear me!"

The face of the demon holding her changed back to that of the sad man who had asked her forgiveness and from a very great distance Aine heard Zephyr and Aiden calling to her. She tried to listen through the throbbing of her heart, but she couldn't seem to slow it down. Then she finally recognized Aiden's anguished face and the vision of the prophet faded.

Sanity returned to her eyes and she heard Zephyr's frantic cries. *"Zephyr!"* In a voice hoarse from screaming, she begged, "Let me go to her, Aiden. Please, let me go."

Aiden released her and Aine lurched a few steps and then ran to Zephyr. The filly tried to wrap Aine in her wings in her instinct to shelter her.

"Oh, Zephyr, I'm so sorry. I am safe, we are safe." Aine wrapped both of her arms around Zephyr's neck. *"I never meant to frighten you or hurt you. Settle down, settle down. Please Zephyr…"* Aine pressed her face to the filly's sweaty neck, switching to the mental communication. *"Oh, Zephyr, it was a vision, only a vision. It wasn't real. It's gone."*

Dark Fire reared magnificently behind them. His massive black wings spread and he held the pose radiating power. Aine heard his shouted command to the filly, *"Stop or we will be found. Listen to your mistress, Zephyr!"*

Zephyr flipped her wings to her back lowering her head in submission to the dominant stallion of the herd. She shuddered and then stood still as Aine stroked her neck. Very softly, Zephyr said, *"I am here and you are here, mistress. We are safe as you said. It seemed like you were no longer here, and I was so afraid. There was someone between us and you could not hear my call. I thought we had lost you, mistress. And I could do nothing to help you."*

"Oh, Zephyr, there was someone, I think it was the man who wrote the prophecy. Somehow I could see him, and nothing else. Are you all right now?"

"I am well," Zephyr replied.

Drawing comfort from their bond, eventually they both calmed. Finally, Aine stepped back and Dark Fire moved to lay his neck over Zephyr's. The filly's shivers subsided as the stallion nuzzled her.

Dark Fire looked toward the stable. *"She is quiet now, little sister. I will watch over her until morning."*

"Thank you, Dark Fire, I am sorry." Aine swallowed profound shame at her loss of emotional control, and Dark Fire felt those emotions. *"My master loves you, and he will protect you. Do not be afraid. All will be well. Nothing can defeat the love we share."* Dark Fire's gentle confidence assured Aine and tears formed in her eyes at his words. She reached over to pat his neck.

Aiden leaned against the doorway waiting; his face unreadable in the light flowing from the open door. Aine walked slowly toward him and he closed the door behind them, keeping his expression carefully neutral.

He stood quietly and Aine gazed into his eyes, seeing the warmth and concern. "Oh Aiden, I am so sorry." Her voice faded. "Please, Aiden, hold me."

In two strides he wrapped her in his embrace. Stroking her back, he murmured, "It's all right now, Aine." Aiden rested his chin on the top of her head and then kissed her brow.

Lifting her chin so that she looked into his eyes he wiped her tears away with his handkerchief. "Let me warm up the tea. I know you won't sleep until we talk this out, so tell me everything. Tell me what happened if you can. I am here, Aine. I will always be here for you." Aiden's midnight blue eyes caressed her and he waited with infinite patience.

CHAPTER SEVENTEEN

Revelations

The next night low angled moonlight cast a soft glow on the path beside the wagon as Mabon drove it from between the thick pines near the cave. Aiden and Aine had just finished feeding Dark Fire and Zephyr when Phelan ran into the clearing.

Mabon backed the wagon up and unhitched the horses. "You look better Aine, more rested. What kind of adventures have you two had since we parted?"

"Well I learned how to translocate an object," Aine volunteered and grasped her talisman and moved one of the packs from the ground to inside the door.

Mabon chuckled, "Well, well, you have been busy."

Aiden helped Mabon pull a dark tarp over the wagon to hide the bright gypsy colors. "I'll stable the horses."

Once inside Mabon filled the kettle for tea. "It usually takes students several weeks to learn translocation. You must be very pleased at your progress. Tell me, how you learned so quickly?"

Aine blushed.

Mabon handed her a mug, his eyebrows raised in query.

Aine sipped her tea. "I was still blocked and getting nowhere all morning, but then we went to the repository and Aiden…" She paused as the color grew in her face. "He kissed me, and then it happened," Aine blurted.

Mabon smiled, "I see." Then he noted the paleness of Aine's face.

Aine told him how she'd seen the vision of the prophet when she had read the scroll of the prophecy. She spoke very softly as she explained how she had reacted.

"What frightened you so, Aine?" Mabon asked.

"I don't know. The prophet didn't seem to be a threat. In fact he asked my forgiveness."

Mabon sat back. "I have heard of an illumining spell attached to certain documents of power. It is as if the one who has been chosen to read them can also see the original author. A document of power like the prophecy might have that effect."

Aiden came in then and made his way to the fire. He sat down to warm his hands. "The horses are settled, but the gelding has some damage on his left rear hoof. I cleaned it and wrapped it, but I don't think he should travel tomorrow night. He could use a day's rest to heal."

Mabon nodded. "That's about as long as we can risk staying here."

Just then they heard something scratching the window and they saw the silhouette of a great horned owl in the glass. Aine ran to open the door and Merlin flew in and landed by the fireplace. *"My lady mistress sends greetings, little sister, first protector and champion mate. She hopes you are well."* His round golden eyes blinked and it seemed as if the light in the room dimmed for a second.

Merlin's proper demeanor seemed to imply a formal response. Aine nodded slightly as she said, "Please tell your mistress that we are well and thank her for her consideration."

"Did Merlin bring news from the school?" Mabon asked turning to Phelan who had followed the owl into the room.

"Sadid and his partner have been missing since before the attack. Another student and his partner have disappeared as well. There was no sign to show how it happened. We have found deer, game, birds and rabbits torn but not consumed and other small animals in similar condition around the lake," Phelan's voice had a disgusted tone.

Mabon leaned forward, his dark eyes intent on the bird, "Who, besides Rika, is missing?"

"Tikat and his partner are gone. They were on patrol the evening you left, and did not return. Search efforts have been unsuccessful."

Aine explained to Aiden what the Owl was saying.

"It smells of the evil one," Phelan growled.

Mabon's face was strained as he rose and extended his arm. The owl vaulted to it, resting his talons on the padded sleeve of Mabon's gypsy cloak. *"Please tell your lady mistress to be watchful; it is possible that our enemy has infiltrated the school."*

Then Merlin turned his piercing gaze to Aine, *"Be not afraid and accept the protection of the champion. You are to be his mate, and you should put your trust in him. You are strong now and grow more in your power every day. Fly free and see clearly, little sister. Tell the silver one to fly like the wind whose name she bears."* As he finished he blinked once and then launched himself from Mabon's arm through the door and was gone. Aine sat quietly considering what he had said.

Aiden's brow furrowed, "How could Andy and Tikat have disappeared? And I'm surprised that Rika is still missing. It's not the first time she's taken off in a huff when something didn't go her way, but never for this long."

Mabon's voice was tinged with sadness. "This is not the first time someone has disappeared from the school."

"Really?" Aine asked.

He sighed, "Shortly after we were promoted to senior trainers, Rose and I were sent to collect some new students. While we were gone, three pairs from the school went missing." Mabon looked to Aiden. "Andy was in your pod wasn't he Aiden, what was his special skill?"

Aiden pushed the stray lock of hair from his forehead. He was clearly worried and his voice was tight. "Andy was in Peter's pod, but he was quite talented for one so young, and I worked with him often. Andy's special skill is to find things that are missing. In fact, there is no better pair for that than he and Tikat. They once found a silver button that had come off Jill's cloak in a very thick grassy meadow near the lake. What Andy couldn't find through his empathic sense, Tikat could find with his remarkable raptor vision."

"That could be why Takkar took him," Mabon replied.

"Do you think that he has Rika too?" Aine asked

"It's possible," Mabon sighed.

Aine asked, "Did you find the three that were missing?"

Mabon's eyes were desolate, "We searched for almost a week before we found two of the students who had gone missing. They had lost their empathic bond and there was no trace of their partners. It was as if their minds had been wiped clean and there was not even a residual of their empathic abilities. They left the school but did not survive the year, or so we were told."

Mabon continued, "Losing a partner is like losing a family member, especially if they are separated without explanation. Like any major loss, support from others with the empathic bond helps. We didn't know that then and allowed them to leave the school when we shouldn't have.

"Only one of the animal partners was ever found, and he died shortly after we found him. His partner, a young woman named Deidre, was never found."

Aiden put his arm around Aine. He had heard Mabon's story from others, but never from Mabon.

"Deidre was a beautiful young woman, with long black hair and violet eyes. She was serious, quiet and a talented multi-lingual. We were…" Mabon's voice thickened and trailed off. He swallowed hard. Phelan rose and laid his head in Mabon's lap. Mabon petted him absently.

They listened to the crackle of the fire while Mabon continued, "Deidre's partner was a handsome chocolate-colored pegasite named Mocha. He was found deep in the forest, almost dead. All he could tell Phelan before he died was that he no longer heard his mistress but he knew she was still alive. They had been captured by someone from the Dark Castle and then Mocha had been dragged away and staked to the trees. His wings had been clipped so that he would never fly again." Slow tears brimmed in Mabon's eyes. "Just before he died, Mocha told me that Deidre was with child.

"We tried desperately to breach the castle walls, but despite the rumors of a secret passage we never found it. Two of my friends were killed in the attempt and finally Rose and Serat convinced me that it was too dangerous to continue."

Mabon bowed his head. Aine could see tears dropping to his hands as they rested in his lap. "It took me a very long time to accept it. I could no longer remain at the school where the memories of her were everywhere."

He swallowed several times before continuing. "About a year later, Phelan and I came to a circle of quivering birch trees deep in the forest. We found Deidre entombed within an impenetrable crystal dome. She was as beautiful in her final resting, as she was in life."

Mabon looked up his face filled with anguish. They barely heard his whisper, "She was my love...and my wife."

Aine's throat closed with emotion and Aiden held her hand tightly. The three of them sat lost in their own thoughts for a long time, watching the fire as it died in the hearth.

Finally, Mabon stirred from his quiet melancholy, "Well, it has been a long day and long past time for sleeping, I'll get some more wood for the fire, while you check on the pegasites, Aiden."

Mabon rose and Aine hugged him. There seemed to be no words sufficient to either of them.

Aine said, "I'm going to bathe before I go to bed." Aine was quick about her bath and walked quietly through the passage to return to her room when she overheard Aiden and Mabon, "...of the prophecy. I'm convinced of it, and I also believe that I am the champion."

Mabon replied, "I have always thought that you were the champion, Aiden. The pixies truly sang the song and touched her?"

"Yes. It was the most beautiful thing I have ever seen."

Mabon spoke softly, "I wish I had seen it too. It is yet another sign that Aine is the woman of the prophecy."

There was a pause, then Aiden blurted, "Mabon, I don't know how it happened, but from the first moment I met Aine in the garden at the school, I have loved her. I cannot stop thinking of her and I would do almost anything to keep her safe."

There was a trace of humor in Mabon's voice, "So you are smitten at last my young friend." Then his voice changed and he sounded more serious, "Nevertheless, you must control your passions. Aine is not like the girls you have known in your tribe or the school. While she is of the age to be mated in your tribe, she is not ready for that. Aine comes from a different world, from a family where she has been protected and loved. She is barely past childhood there, and still quite innocent. It is our job to teach and protect her."

Now there was an element of steely command in his voice, "We must all remember that the decision to stay or leave this world is her choice, alone. She must be free to choose her destiny, and you must be careful not to push her, Aiden. No matter how much you might want to."

Aiden whispered, "I will be careful Mabon. I have restrained myself, believe me I have." Aiden sighed, "But, I have never felt this way about anyone." There was another pause. "I cannot promise not to love her."

Mabon's voice was stern, "We all love Aine and we are all committed to helping her, even if it means she chooses to leave us and never return to Drayon. You must accept that. That is the only way she can be free to choose what her heart tells her to."

As she stood listening in the hall, Aine's initial euphoria at Aiden's declaration faded when she thought what it would be like to leave him and return home. Could she give in to her growing feelings for him, and then leave him, perhaps forever? The conflict tore at her heart. How could she ever choose between Zephyr, and Aiden and the others she had grown to love here, and the love of her family? And what about the prophecy, if she really was the woman foretold how could she ever challenge someone with powers like Takkar's?

She stood in the cool hallway until she had control of her emotions and then made some noise. "Goodnight, gentlemen."

Aiden's eyes were glowing as he smiled at her from his seat by the fire and both men bid her goodnight.

As she pulled the covers up she felt the cold touch of Phelan's nose and she reached out to scratch behind his ears.

"Rest well, little sister; I will stay at your side. My pack hunts nearby and nothing can elude them."

"Thank you, Phelan." She quickly began to drift off.

CHAPTER EIGHTEEN

The Three Gypsies

By the following evening, the gelding's hoof had healed enough for them to set out on their journey. Initially clear and cool the weather changed to a continuous rain a few days later. Though Aine was fairly dry in the waterproof cape and hood, the pegasites were miserable under their heavy wet blankets. At one point the wagon was nearly mired in deep muddy ruts and it became too dangerous to travel at night.

They found an abandoned homestead and decided to wait out the rain. Only one of the original buildings remained intact, but Mabon was able to back the wagon into it obscuring their presence. He and Aiden built a fire and put the horses and pegasites in the rickety barn where they could stretch their sodden wings and dry out.

Aine stood in the doorway of the cabin staring at the storm. Aiden joined her. "I've never seen you look lovelier," he said. She turned when she heard his approach and smiled.

Without hesitation he took her in his arms and kissed her. He stepped back, held her hands and looked deeply into her eyes. "Aine, I love you," he said.

Her eyes darkened slightly and color rose on her face. The tension between them was tangible. "I love you, too," she finally replied.

"You do?" He sighed. "Really?"

She laughed and then he pulled her into his arms and kissed her again. When they stepped back she smiled, "Of course, I love you. I don't let just anyone go around kissing me until my toes curl!"

Aiden glanced at her feet, and Aine burst out laughing again. "I was using a figure of speech," she said.

Aine took his hand, "I've never felt this way about anyone before, and sometimes when you kiss me, I think I'd do anything at all to keep you kissing me." She looked away, then back to meet his eyes. "You know, at some point I have to go home. And when I do, what will that mean to you?"

Aiden looked like his heart sank. It took him a moment to reply. "I don't know. I guess I would hope that you would come back. With your ability as a traveler, you could." He looked at Aine and saw the conflict in her eyes.

"It's tearing you apart isn't it?"

She nodded.

Aiden wrapped his arms around her kissing the top of her head. "Look, no one knows what will happen. You could stay, you could go, you could come back. No one knows. I think we should stop worrying about it and make the most of the time we have together." He tickled her lightly and she blinked rapidly to control her emotions.

"You've still got a lot to learn about being an empath, and our main goal is to keep you safe with my family while you do it."

CHAPTER NINETEEN

The Lady of the Wood

The next morning, Mabon caught a nice stringer of fish and Aine offered to cook them. "Dad and I used to cook trout right at our campfire; I just need to find some herbs to flavor them."

Mabon said, "Phelan is out hunting, do you want me to go with you?"

"No, I'll stay nearby."

As she searched along the edge of the woods she thought about her conversation with Aiden. In some ways it was a relief to admit her feelings.

She wanted to go home, but she wanted to learn more about being an empath as well. She was convinced; as Mabon was that the disappearances from the school had been orchestrated by Takkar. There was no doubt that Takkar wanted to find her and was willing to do almost anything to accomplish his goal.

Aine had grown to love Aiden. She had also developed a deep respect and fondness for Mabon. And, the bond between her and Zephyr was the most amazing thing she had ever experienced. Yet, despite the vision of the prophet and the other clues that she might be the woman of the prophecy, she was still reluctant to believe she was really the one foretold.

Having filled her basket with the herbs she sought, she sat down on a log in the sunlight just to think. Since leaving the school she had rarely been alone, and always Zephyr or one of the other empathic animals maintained a light touch in her mind. Tentatively she reached out to Zephyr and sensed that she was sleeping, so she broke off her contact.

The raven fluttered to the railing on the turret and Takkar rushed to greet it. The bird flicked his wings as if to fly off but was drawn back by the bowl of fresh meat Takkar held.

"What have you seen?" he asked the bird.

The bird's bright black eyes met Takkar's and although the raven didn't speak, Takkar could see the images in the bird's eyes of a dark-haired man leading a horse from the village by the red river.

Takkar's spies had been watching all of the villages ever since Aine had vanished from the school. Takkar touched the bird's mind gently and saw how it had flown off when the man had thrown a knife at it. The horse was black and white; definitely not a pegasite, and his hopes faded, but the bird interrupted his thoughts with another vision. The man had gazed after the bird and Takkar saw a pair of dark blue eyes. A slow grin grew on his face. He had not seen Aiden since he was younger, but Takkar had no doubt it was him.

His excitement grew. The bird had sensed empathic ability in the man and if, as he suspected, Aine was with him, he would have her at last. All he needed was the slightest touch of her signature. Startled by Takkar's strong emotions the bird bolted off but Takkar laughed aloud at his good fortune. He returned to his room and grabbed a vial of his special elixir and raced up the stairs two at a time to the highest tower.

The process of summoning required a calm, focused mind. The elixir would enhance his powers and he found it difficult to contain his excitement at the thought of touching her signature at last. Gulping the liquid he waited for its effect as the searing heat of the sun burned his sweat-drenched body. Closing his eyes he began the intricate mental steps to summon. Like a bird of prey he felt his inner vision rise and soar.

His empathic vision took him to the village near where the bird had seen Aiden. He sensed two untrained empathic signatures but not the one he sought. Tracing along the paths leading away from the village Takkar worried that too much time had elapsed.

Summoning anyone typically took time, but summoning her was especially elusive. It was as if she unconsciously obscured his thoughts. But this time he would find her, this time he would not fail.

Skimming over the forest beyond the village he saw the giant tree and then felt the sudden surge of an unshielded aura. It was Aine! Takkar traced her with his mind as a hound scents a rabbit. Opening his eyes he hovered above the thick forest. He sensed four other empathic patterns, although those of the humans were muted. Ignoring the others he extended his reach following her unique signature until he found her sitting alone on a log.

Her head was tilted back and her eyes were closed, her face lifted to the sun. Her rich lips begged for a kiss and he had all he could do to control his natural urges. She was incredibly lovely and he felt the rush of desire and fulfillment of the hunt. She had shielded herself but not well enough. Such was his power to summon.

She had changed, he sensed it immediately. She was much stronger than when he had last touched her. But not enough, he hoped, to resist him this time. Filled with joy at the thought of having her to himself at last, he cascaded toward her, when a white hot pain lanced his mind, physically dashing him to the hard hot stones of the tower.

"You will not!" The voice commanded as he tried to lift his head to move away from the power piercing his mind.

"Never again!" Another, more familiar one agreed.

His heart throbbed, it was impossible. He knew that voice. He tried to open his eyes but he was blind to anything but the mind that commanded him. He gasped with fear. No one had been able to control him this way, not since childhood.

"Be gone," the first voice demanded and the burning heat of the sun filled his mind. The summoning dissolved and he wondered if he would die. He almost wished he could, just to relieve the agony, and then he faded to unconsciousness.

Enjoying the warmth of the sun on her face Aine felt a sudden chilling sensation along her spine and a burning in her head. She gasped and clenched her head, but just as quickly as it had come, the sensation was gone. A shiver of unease filled her body, "Aiden!" she called out. He should have been able to hear her. She'd heard his cheery whistle just before she'd felt that strange sensation.

"*Zephyr?*" The filly had never failed to respond to her telepathic calls, but there was no reply now.

At the edge of her vision she saw sparkling lights. It reminded her of the lights she'd seen in the loft when she first found the crystal ball. She followed them with her vision, and in the path in front of her stood a woman surrounded by an unusual nimbus. Aine took a step backward and looked around to find a path of escape.

The woman nodded, *"I did not mean to startle you. Are you well?"*

Aine regarded the woman hesitantly. *"I didn't know people could talk to each other telepathically."*

The hint of a smile touched the woman's lips, *"Not many can, but I knew that you could."* The woman continued quickly, *"You are open to me and your thoughts and your speech are as one."*

Aine retreated again, speaking aloud this time, "What do you want? Who are you?"

The woman also spoke aloud, "I am here to help you, Aine."

Aine scanned the path to see if she could run. *"No way, lady, I'm not letting you in! How do you know my name?"* Quickly, Aine blocked telepathic access by filling her mind with the music of Bach invention. Concentrating on the exact replication of every note, every dynamic, the shading of expression even the fingerings she filled her mind with it. Without a doubt if she'd had a piano available she would have thrilled Mr. Miller with a perfect performance.

The woman smiled broadly and stepped closer. "Excellent, Aine! That was a flawless response."

"Who are you?" Aine demanded, unable to keep the musical image in her mind indefinitely. She tried to call Zephyr again with no response. "What have you done? Why can't I hear Zephyr? What was that strange feeling?" Aine crossed her arms, feeling the hot blush of anger climbing up her neck.

"You were being summoned by Takkar. We had to prevent him so we have blocked all empathic signatures except mine."

"Who is we?" Aine spit. Then her vision blurred and she saw a shimmering image of Lula appear in front of her and for a moment she wondered if she was transferring back to her home world. A rush of excitement engulfed her.

"Aine, listen to me. Takkar was nearly upon you this time. We had to protect you. I have asked this guardian to watch out for you, she is my friend and guards you in my place. She is also here to guide you. There are things you must learn from her. If you trust me, you can trust her. Search your heart, what do you feel?"

The vision faded and Aine watched the woman warily feeling suddenly bereft. She wanted to reach our and pull Lula back.

The other woman spoke softly, "Do not be afraid, Aine. Lula's words are true, she is a sister guardian incapable of deceit. Touch me with your gifts, you will know the truth."

Aine hesitated for a moment and then crossed to the woman. She reached out and touched the woman's temples gently. With the touch, Aine felt immersed in the aura of the woman. It was like looking into someone's soul, incredibly pure and untainted.

Instinctively Aine closed her eyes using her empathic abilities and felt no barrier between them. A vibrant yellow glow permeated Aine's perception and it carried her deep into the woman's being. For several moments they were merged as if they were one being. She felt the kindness and patience of the other one and a tingle of excitement. Aine stumbled back releasing her touch and sat down abruptly.

Quickly, the woman knelt on the ground before her. "Stay still for a moment, it will pass." The woman's deep violet-blue eyes were lit with concern.

"What happened?"

"When you touched me we melded. It is a similar process to bonding with your empathic partner, but one that is relatively rare and requires significant training. You also used a form of healing to reach deeper. That gift is something we thought lost long ago." The woman smiled and pushed her long black hair back from her face. Then she met Aine's eyes, her voice full of wonder, "Will you come with me now?"

The strange yellow light had indeed felt warm and inviting and Aine was stunned to learn that it had emanated from her and not the woman. In that brief touch she had seen that this woman was indeed here for a reason and that she could trust and believe her. In that split second of melding, Aine had also felt the protective barrier the woman had surrounded them with. She knew without question that she would be safe with her.

She stood, "Yes, I will come."

She followed her, walking briskly and they came to a small cottage in a tightly intertwined grove of trees. The entrance was woven of bark and flowers. Inside small lights illuminated the hut. A dark violet cloth covered a round shape on a table. The woman removed it, uncovering a beautiful crystal ball that was larger than the one in Lula's cabin.

"This is like the crystal ball that brought you to our world, isn't it?" She turned to Aine, her empathic voice like music in Aine's head.

"Yes."

They sat at the table and the woman reached to touch the ball with her finger tips. Colors began to swirl inside of it followed by images that formed rapidly one after the other. Aine saw a desert landscape with flying dragon-like beasts, then a forested world followed quickly by that of a bustling city where flying vehicles zipped from one place to another. Panoramas of an infinite variety flashed, changing from scene to scene like a flashing slide show of people, animals and landscapes.

Aine stared, entranced. "What are all of these places?"

"These are some of the worlds connected by the Celestial Band. I wanted you to see them so you could see some of the infinite variety that exists in our universe."

Aine met the woman's eyes. "And each world has a guardian?

The woman nodded, "Yes, except for worlds that have no sentient life forms."

"Is that why Lula wanted me to come with you?"

"Initially, that was the plan, but it became necessary for us to intercept Takkar's summoning to keep you safe."

"Did Takkar see me?"

The woman's eyes darkened, "Yes, but he only saw you for a second, and he has been dealt with."

Aine felt a chill on her spine and the thought of Takkar, "By 'us,' do you mean Lula?"

"Yes, as I explained, Lula and I worked in tandem. You have learned enough of your powers to move to the next level and only a guardian can teach you what you must learn now."

The woman smiled, "I have already learned much from you as well. That was a wonderful protection you wove with the music in your mind, and your innate ability to heal is quite amazing. Have you ever used music as a block before?"

Aine relaxed a bit, "I tried it once when Aiden was teaching me to hide my empathic signature."

The woman nodded slightly, "It was quite effective."

Aine shrugged, "Well, it's probably not something I could do for very long, Bach is incredibly complex."

"I see." The woman removed her hands from the crystal

and the interior reverted to a blend of colors swirling, but not forming any images.

"Aine, you have powers that you have not begun to tap yet. It is my role to help you develop them and to help prepare you for the role you may choose to play in the future."

"My role in the future...you mean the prophecy?"

"Yes. Let me explain."

Quite sure there was no other option, Aine nodded.

"You and I share many talents. I am a portal guardian and I am also multi-lingual. I keep watch over the gateways and portals between our worlds." She nodded at the dormant crystal ball.

"Time for Mabon and Aiden and your partners has been temporarily slowed preventing empathic communication so that no one can interrupt us except another guardian. That is one of the abilities of a portal guardian, to adjust time if needed.

"You have come to Drayon for two reasons. To learn about the prophecy and to discover and become competent with your empathic gifts." The guardian reached to touch Aine's hand. "Before you can choose your destiny, you must develop your abilities and expand your knowledge so that you can make an informed choice."

Aine shook her head, "If that's the case, why couldn't Lula tell me about it before I came?"

"Would you have believed her if she had?"

Aine shrugged, "Probably not."

"I suspect that you are a skeptic, not easily convinced of something without proof."

Aine nodded smiling slightly.

"Your coming has been foretold and I saw you when you first arrived on Drayon."

That was a surprise. Aine wanted to ask how she'd seen her, but before she could the woman added, "Your affections for Zephyr, Aiden and Mabon," the woman's face softened just for an instant, a flash of emotion in her eyes, then it was gone, "will give you the strength to make the right choice regarding your destiny."

Aine blurted, "I don't really want to be the woman of the prophecy. Everyone says that I will return when I am ready, well, I'm ready now!"

"When we say it will happen when you are ready, we mean that you must be able to use your gifts to protect yourself completely. Until that happens, it would not be safe for you to try to return. If you were to open a conduit to your world, without knowing how to protect that pathway, it is possible that Takkar could follow you there."

That got Aine's attention. She didn't want to even think about Takkar following her home.

"What about Aiden and Mabon? What is their role?"

"The First Protectors have always protected those of the champion's line and both he and the champion have roles almost as important as that of the woman foretold. It is our hope that you will learn to trust and love them as they do you, for they are essential to the fulfillment of the prophecy as well."

"I do trust them, and I love them, too," Aine said. Somehow she felt better after saying that, and the woman's eyes warmed with her gentle smile.

"That is good. You will find that trust and love hold great power, young Aine."

"I don't really want to be powerful though."

The woman smiled. "That, my child, is your greatest strength. Now, let me teach you something important that you have not yet completely grasped. I want to teach you how to block others from finding you. It will be different from what you have learned from Mabon and Aiden, but it could save your life."

The woman showed Aine how to use her talisman differently. She discovered that it was like translocating an object but the effect was the opposite. It built a protective layer around her empathic signature.

The guardian encouraged Aine to use the same tactic of mentally picturing music while projecting an image of emptiness and Aine was pleased that she grasped the concept quickly.

Testing it, the guardian tried to touch Aine empathically, but was unable to do so until Aine released her talisman and opened the contact.

They practiced for a bit longer and Aine grew weary. The guardian's dark eyes were kind and the muted sparkles that surrounded her had faded significantly as well.

Trying to focus again, Aine asked, "When will I be able to return home?"

"I do not know, exactly." The woman's eyes seemed sad, "You miss your family very much don't you?"

Aine swallowed a lump of longing in her throat and nodded.

The guardian took Aine's hand, her touch felt warm and comforting.

"I understand the pain of being separated from your family only too well." The sparkles surrounding her faded even more. "Would it ease your mind to see your family through my crystal? I can show you that they are well and still unaware that you are here."

"You can? Oh, yes, show me!" Aine cried.

"Who you would like to see?" The guardian touched the

crystal ball with one hand and Aine's hand with her other and the color within swirled, once again.

Aine thought of her father and Carolinda and immediately, a scene began to form in the crystal ball. Dad and Carolinda were in the garden talking about Latin names for flowers. Dad arched his back to stretch like he always did after leaning over his plants for too long. Carolinda stood, hands on hips, her freckled cheeks lit with pink and the sunlight blazed in her rich curly brown hair. Aine smiled as Dad teased Carolinda about her recall and her sister laughed as their father pulled her sister into a happy hug.

Tears formed in Aine's eyes and the image of them dissolved in the mist of the crystal ball. They seemed so very far away.

The guardian rose and covered the ball with the cloth and placed her hand on Aine's shoulder. "Showing you was not meant to hurt you, it is meant to comfort you, Aine. What you just witnessed happened the afternoon before you came to Drayon. Right now they are not even aware that you've gone. They won't miss you for a long time, and Lula will protect you in your world by slowing time there."

The guardian rose and moved toward the doorway motioning for Aine to follow. As they left the small dwelling the sparkles surrounding the guardian brightened. Aine had the sense that their time together was drawing to a close and her mind raced trying to think what else she should know. "You said that I am free to choose. How will I choose?"

"I don't think anyone can know how you will choose and you must learn more of our world first. We do not know why you are or are not given the choice to fulfill the prophecy. We just know that it is essential that you make the choice freely."

"What if I choose to return home and not to fulfill the prophecy? What will happen to everyone here?" Aine's voice quavered.

"The prophecy says that the woman must choose to aid us, or we will be lost. I suspect that means that the evil one will gain dominion over this world. But that is actually why you must be given the freedom of choice, for once your decision is made, whatever it is, it will be final."

Aine had not known that.

"Aine, you would not have been able to travel to us if you were incapable of fulfilling the prophecy. Once you learn more of your own powers, you will find that you are very strong, and you will do what is right. Whatever decision you make will be the right one. But it will be a long time before you must make that decision. Just like your ability to travel back to your home, you will only choose when you are ready to."

Aine grew solemn. She was tired of everyone telling her it would be a "long time." She was ready now.

"Now, my dear, our time has grown short and you must return to the time just before you met me. Do not fear, young Aine, we will meet again."

The guardian then faded and disappeared a few lingering sparkles dissipating in the shadows. Aine stood alone in the woods near the camp, the bag of herbs lay scattered at her feet. Aiden's happy whistle was clear once again.

Aine ran to the camp and the two men looked up alarmed as she rushed into the site. Her words tumbled, "Mabon, Aiden…it was, she was…you have to come!"

Mabon rose, his face alarmed. "What is it?"

She forced herself to take a deep breath and then she told them about the Lady of the Woods and everything that she had learned.

"Mabon, she knew you and Aiden and Phelan too."

She paused, not wanting to hurt him but she had to tell him, "I think she may have been Deidre."

The color drained from Mabon's face and he grasped Aine's arms. "Why do you think that, Aine? Deidre is dead, I saw her in that coffin with my own eyes."

"I don't know what you saw, Mabon, but this woman looked exactly as you described Deidre. I really think it was her." Aine watched the intensity grow in Mabon's eyes.

"Where did you see her last, Aine? Please it's very important!"

"Come, I'll show you."

Phelan jumped to his feet with a growl, his hackles raised, and rushed stiff legged to Mabon's side.

Aine took them to the place where she had first seen the woman and they searched through the woods trying to find the hut. Even with Phelan's nose they could find no trace of her. Mabon's face turned sorrowful as he sat down on the same log where Aine had encountered the guardian.

"Mabon, she was here. You must believe me."

"I don't doubt you Aine, but she is certainly gone now."

Mabon's grey eyes grew bleak. "From your description, I think it was Deidre, too. First he took her and now he's tried to take you!" The stick Mabon was holding snapped in his hand and he threw the pieces violently away, his face suffused with fury.

Aine had never seen him look like this and he frightened her.

"I thought she was dead when I saw her in that crystal casket, now I wonder if it was another of Takkar's vile tricks. He would have delighted in causing me that kind of pain. He would be thrilled to have me think she was dead when she really wasn't." Then he sighed, "But why would she not come to me if she was free of him and alive?"

Aine knelt quickly at Mabon's feet taking his hands in hers. "Listen to me, Mabon. The woman I saw today was not dead. She is as real as you or me." She squeezed his hand harder as if to show him. "She held my hand and I felt her just as I feel yours. If it is Deidre, she'll find you again. I know she will! She told me she would see me again. She said she was a portal guardian. Maybe she just has to find the right time, or the right place in order to return for good."

Mabon's eyes lost some of their despair and the color returned to his face. Aine was heartened to see it.

Aiden leaned forward, "She said she was sent to help Aine. Perhaps she isn't able to really show herself until whatever is supposed to happen, actually does."

Mabon sighed, "I hope you are right, both of you. What I wouldn't give to see her again."

"She told me she would see me again, Mabon. And when she does, perhaps it will be her chance to come back to you, for good." Aine said as Mabon rose and they walked quietly back to the camp.

CHAPTER TWENTY

Rika's Return

Takkar smirked at Rika as she entered the room in her simple shepherdess dress. Her eyes were hopeful. "Do you think it will work?" she said.

"It's much too rustic for my tastes, but I think it will suffice." His eyes held hers. "Remember the plan, Rika. You must be contrite and sorry for your absence and most of all, very convincing."

"I will be. I promise." Rika answered eagerly unable to tear her eyes from the compulsion in his. His smile never extended to his eyes, and he never lost eye contact with her. She took a step forward, waiting for the inevitable invitation, but he made no effort to touch her.

She whispered, "I will miss you so very much."

"Yes, you will, but make sure that you remember everything, you must not fail."

Turning from her he took a box filled with the silver twists of paper from his desk. "If you are careful this will last for several weeks. Take one packet a day from now on." His dark eyes bored into hers, "I wouldn't want you to run out before you return." He knew that she was now addicted to the restorative and between his mastery of compulsion and this powerful drug, it was impossible for her to resist him.

"Thank you," Rika said.

Takkar strode to the window. "They have brought Sadid from the stable, are you ready?"

Rika joined him at the window, happy to see her handsome pegasite again. "I am."

Takkar continued, his voice smooth but demanding, "See that your partner keeps his thoughts to himself as well."

"He will. I'm sure he will be happy to get back to the school." Her voice faded, "I will miss you, Master."

Takkar laughed, "Of course you will, just don't disappoint me."

She knelt and kissed his hand and then ran off. In the courtyard below she leapt to Sadid's back waving at Takkar as they rose to the sky.

He turned back to the room and poured a drink. "Care to join me?" He directed his gaze at the bank of mirrors along one wall.

The seam on one of the mirrors parted where a beautiful woman with long black hair and eyes like midnight emerged. She nearly spilled from the tight black blouse. Jeweled bangles jingled on her ankles beneath a multi-colored skirt.

"That was interesting." Her voice was like velvet caressing his ears. "She does not bore you?"

Takkar chuckled, "Not at all, Ravyn. Rika can be quite creative when she is properly motivated."

"What of Rose? She may see right through her, I'm not sure that girl can be truly convincing, no matter how well you've motivated her." Ravyn poured a glass of wine and drank.

Takkar's fingers encircled hers on the glass. "Perhaps, if she were at the school that might be the case, Rose is quite perceptive after all. But I made sure to send Rika back when Rose is at the council meeting in Kierst."

Ravyn laughed. "Well then, you've thought of everything, haven't you?" Her smile faded, "Now don't you think it is time you returned my book." Her dark eyes commanded his and he threw back his head and laughed. "Ah, Ravyn, you never give up do you? I will be happy to return it to you as soon as you've completed your task as well."

Ravyn's eyes spit fire. "Don't even think that you can evade returning it to me. I can be quite creative as well, but you would be wise to enjoy me as a lover, rather than your enemy."

Takkar chuckled and licked his lips. "Oh I have every intention of returning it to you, and I plan to remain one of your dearest friends, my lovely Ravyn. Remember, I've seen what happens to the lovers you spurn."

His finger traced the line of her jaw and down her plunging neckline. "Now, I think we should enjoy the rest of the morning, don't you."

Ravyn licked her lips and laughed.

CHAPTER TWENTY-ONE

The West Wind Tribe

Tall pines and the craggy rocks of the foothills came into view as the wagon lumbered along the rocky trail.

"I think we are close," Aiden said with excitement in his voice. "I know a couple of places where they might be. After it is dark tonight, I'll fly ahead with Dark Fire and look for them."

Despite Aiden's enthusiasm about finding his family, Aine grew more and more nervous about it. Aiden had explained how the tribe's elders questioned people requesting sanctuary and she wondered how they could convince them. What if they refused sanctuary once they knew Takkar sought her? Could she blame them?

Dark Fire's black wings and powerful body faded to invisibility as he and Aiden rose to the night sky. Aine's jitters must have become apparent because Mabon invited her to come play her flute by the fire.

"Are you ready to finally stop our travels," Mabon asked while puffing on his pipe.

"I suppose so," she sighed.

Mabon put his pipe down. "Are you nervous about meeting the tribe and Aiden's family?"

A slight smile tugged her lips, "Is it that obvious?"

Mabon chuckled. "Perhaps not to Aiden, but I can certainly understand your feelings."

Aine faced him. "What is his family like, Mabon?"

Mabon leaned back, the firelight dancing on his face. "Zahra is the shaman of the tribe, second only to the elders. Her support in our request will be necessary."

Phelan walked into the campfire and settled by Mabon's feet. "Do you remember when Phelan showed us his mate, Noir and the pups."

"Yes."

"Zahra is like that she-wolf; always focused on protecting the tribe, just as Noir protects her pups and the pack. Aiden's sense of responsibility is a lot like hers. Zahra and her son are quite passionate people, and dedicated to friends and family.

"Aiden's father, Daved, is older than his wife. He is more easy-going, but I've seen him in a fight and would want him on my side."

Mabon chuckled. "The last time I saw Aiden's sister, Maia, was about two years ago. She's always been precocious and strong willed, but I think you'll like her."

Aine sighed. "What will we do if they refuse sanctuary, Mabon?"

Mabon reached over and took her hand, "I don't think they will, dear, or I never would have come this far to find them."

Aine's face relaxed. "Really?"

"Of course. We'll find a way to convince them, I'm not without skills at convincing people," he smiled.

Aiden returned a short time later to say he'd found them. He thought they could reach them midday tomorrow.

Searching through her things the following morning, Aine found a deep violet dress that Jill had packed. The soft material had stayed wrinkle free even after being packed in the trunk for so long. She brushed her long hair, leaving it flowing down her back. Aiden's smile of appreciation when she stepped down from the wagon helped to relieve her jangled nerves.

Aiden vaulted to Dark Fire's back and the black stallion reared fanning his magnificent wings. Zephyr twirled and said, *"I think he feels his master's excitement."* Aine smiled watching them. Everyone was more than ready to end their long journey.

After traveling until mid-afternoon, they reached a narrow trail at the edge of a clear lake. Phelan raised his hackles and growled low in his throat and both pegasites ruffled their wings.

Mabon pulled the wagon to a halt and called Phelan to his side. Moments later a group of young men and women rode out from the thick bushes. Dressed in clothing of vivid blues, oranges, yellows, reds and greens, they sat on their horses with the confidence of long years of riding. The men were tall and fit, well muscled and wearing only pants and colorful vests. The women were barefooted with jangles on their arms and ankles with low cut blouses and full skirts.

Aiden and Dark Fire moved forward and the stallion reared and spread his wings magnificently. Aine felt butterflies in her stomach as a young man astride a tall golden palomino met them. He leaned forward to clasp arms with Aiden. His blond hair matched that of his mount.

"It's a shame that the tribe could find no one more experienced to serve as a sentry, Neil," Aiden teased. "Or are you out this far to hunt?"

Neil was a photographic negative of Aiden. Where Aiden's hair was black, Neil's was golden, and his eyes were a deep brown to Aiden's startling blue. Aiden was lithe and supple with the build of a natural athlete, and his friend appeared broader through the shoulders and upper arms. Observing their similar facial structure, Aine wondered if they were related.

Her question was answered with his laughing reply. "I haven't seen any game, cousin, but I certainly, see a beautiful woman."

Neil rode to the wagon and bowed his head slightly touching his heart and lips. "Be welcome, First Protector. I am most pleased to offer you the hospitality of the tribe."

Mabon returned the gesture and replied formally, "Thank you for your welcome, Neil. Might I introduce my companion? This is Aine."

Neil moved his horse closer and held his hand out in greeting. Aine leaned forward thinking to shake it but he surprised her by grasping hers, raising it to his lips, and kissing her palm, all the while looking intently at her with his rich brown eyes. "I am pleased to welcome you, Aine. Your beauty will brighten our days."

Aine had no idea what to say and pulled her hand back to her lap a deep pink coloring her cheeks.

Aiden chuckled. "That's enough flirting, Neil." He grinned and added, "Pay no attention to him, Aine, Neil is a notorious heart breaker and my cousin to boot!"

Neil returned the laugh. "Ah, but at least I am more reputable than this wild gypsy rider!" Neil tilted his head and nodded to Dark Fire. "I am surprised that a steed this magnificent still chooses someone as crazy as you, Aiden! How are you Dark Fire?"

Through Aiden Dark Fire replied, *"I am well, as is my master."* Then aside to Zephyr, Dark Fire added, *"These two play at each other like colts, yet they are as brothers."*

The corner of Aine's mouth turned up at the friendly banter between the two men. Zephyr fluttered her wings slightly and Neil's eyes widened as he noticed her for the first time. "And who have we here?"

Mabon explained, "This is Zephyr, Aine's partner."

Neil touched his heart and bowed. "She is as beautiful as her mistress."

Aine felt his eyes on her again but she did not return his gaze.

A tinge of awe entered Neil's tone. "I can't wait to see her aloft; she must be beautiful and as fleet as the wind."

"She is that," Aiden agreed as he greeted the rest of the riders and introduced those that he knew to Aine. They surrounded the wagon and Neil led them past the lake to a narrow road. Soon they approached a large camp where wagons of every color were drawn into circles. A troop of children raced to them giggling and shouting.

"Aiden has come!"

"Be welcome, First Protector."

The children skipped alongside the wagon showing no fear of Phelan who trotted easily with his wolf grin on his face and long tongue lolling from his mouth.

Two little boys prodded a third and he approached the wagon as it drew to a stop. The child looked a bit nervous and he stared up at Mabon. "Welcome, First Protector," he said.

Mabon took a bag from the wagon. "Thank you for your welcome, youngling." Mabon touched his heart and lips in greeting. "Perhaps you would share this with the others." He held out the bag of rock candy and the child climbed nimbly up to him.

"Thank you!" The boy grinned and jumped down to run off with the other urchins racing to follow.

Mabon set the brake and climbed down and Aine followed him. Aiden jumped from Dark Fire's back and the black stallion flapped his wings inciting the remaining children to shout with glee. Zephyr followed suit and the children darted closer to touch the pair. Both pegasites regarded the children calmly.

A little girl looked up at Dark Fire with wonder. "Will you let him fly, Aiden?" In answer both pegasites lifted to the sky, flying the short distance to the edge of the meadow just outside the camp and the children exhaled with awe.

A number of adults came forward at the sound of the children and a tall exotic woman moved from the center of the group toward them. Aiden's face lit with pleasure.

Dressed in deep reds with a black shawl trimmed in red, she wore golden earrings and bracelets that jingled as she moved. Her hair was long and dark like Aiden's and bound in an intricate braid that fell to her hips. He had the look of her in his face, high cheek bones strong nose and chin, but her eyes were very different, dark brown and piercing. Carrying herself with dignity, she drank in the sight of Aiden with her eyes.

Aine knew without asking that this was Zahra, Aiden's mother. There was an air of self-assurance about her and an unconscious mantle of leadership and protection. Seeing her, she agreed with Mabon about her resemblance to Phelan's mate. Aiden bowed his head and touched his heart and his lips with his right hand. "Greetings, Mother. Are you well?"

The woman responded with the same gesture, her voice flowed like warm honey. "I am well, my son, welcome."

They placed their hands on each other's shoulders and touched foreheads, closing their eyes for several moments.

When Aiden stepped back moisture glistened in his eyes. He gestured toward Mabon, "Mother, I am sure you remember Mabon."

Her eyes smiled in greeting, "You are always welcome, First Protector."

Mabon moved to her making the same gesture of heart to lips as Aiden had. He grasped Zahra's outstretched hands. "You are as beautiful and gracious as always, Zahra. Thank you for your welcome."

As Mabon greeted Aiden's mother, another man wended through the group of people. When he reached Aiden they grasped arms and then he pulled Aiden into a strong embrace. His hair was dark brown and although he was not as tall as Aiden, Aine noted the same full generous mouth and sparkling blue eyes she had grown to love in Aiden.

"Ah, you would not turn my lady's head would you, First Protector?" He smiled at Mabon.

"She sees no one else but you, my friend." Mabon clasped arms with the man.

Aiden wrapped Aine's hand on his arm and led her to his parents unaware that her knees were knocking so hard that she was afraid she would fall if he let go. Bowing slightly he said, "Mother, Father, I would like to introduce you to Aine. She is from a land far away and also an empath from the school." Then he squeezed Aine's hand adding, "I pray that someday she might choose me as her life mate."

Aine's eyes widened in shock but she controlled her gasp as Aiden's parents returned his bow. Zahra touched her forehead and then Aine's with two fingers. "Be welcome, Aine. As my son's chosen, I pray you will become as a daughter to us."

Out of her depth, Aine bowed her head mumbling, "Thank you."

Others gathered to welcome them. Daved and Mabon went to pull the wagon into their circle. Aine soon lost track of everyone's names and saw Mabon and Daved return just as a girl her own age bolted past people and horses and flung herself into Aiden's arms squealing with joy. Aiden swung her around and around and kissed her soundly on both cheeks.

Aine realized that this was Aiden's sister, Maia. Her hair was dark brown like her father's and her dark eyes, so like her mother's, glowed with lively excitement. Shorter than Aine, she chattered with infectious joy and didn't wait for introductions but rushed to Aine and gave her a hug. "Be welcome, sister friend." Her voice, breathless with excitement had the same musical timbre as her mother's. "I can't wait to hear all about you."

Zahra tried and failed to look sternly at her daughter, her mouth quirking with humor. "Maia, you have the manners of a child, please greet the First Protector too."

Maia ran to Mabon and kissed both of his cheeks. "It is good to see you again, Mabon! Be welcome."

Mabon chuckled as he regarded Maia, "And I suppose you are driving the young men crazy as you seek a life mate?"

Maia twirled once and giggled, "I'm doing the best I can! Can I show Aine around and introduce her to some of my friends?"

Aine was a bit overwhelmed with Maia's exuberance but Mabon smiled with encouragement. "Of course, please do." Maia grabbed Aine's hand and pulled her in a half run to various wagons throughout the camp. Aiden followed more slowly, joining Neil and some of the other young men who waved and smiled at the girls as they hurried past. Maia chattered incessantly and flitted from group to group like a hungry honey bee.

"So tell me everything. Where are you from? How did you meet Aiden? I saw your partner when she flew off with

Dark Fire. She is incredible. What's it like to be an empath? I think it's wonderful that Aiden has chosen an empath to be his life mate. That will bode well for your children." Maia giggled.

Though Maia was nosy and talkative, Aine liked her immediately. "I am from far away, and I met Aiden at the school."

"Has he kissed you yet? Are you in love? How long have you known him? You must tell me everything," Maia prodded.

Aine's cheeks grew red. Maia burst out laughing.

"Ah, so he has kissed you and it looks like you liked it. I shall have to ask him about it, too. I would never have imagined my brother falling in love so quickly, but then he's never been one to hold back when he wants something."

They were both surprised when Neil sauntered up from behind them. "Hello, ladies."

Aine nodded and Maia said, "Hello."

"Aine, I have come to ask if you and the First Protector would like to join my family for dinner this evening. I wish to know you better." His handsome face reddened, "Aiden tells me that you are quite a musician, and I would be happy to play my guitar with you."

Aine wasn't quite sure how to answer and she secretly blessed her mother for instilling manners for situations like this. "Thank you for your invitation, Neil, but I must check with Mabon first, he may have made other plans and I must abide by his wishes."

"Certainly," Neil agreed. "If not this evening, perhaps another night?" he asked hopefully.

Aine didn't want to lead him on, and wasn't sure how to answer. Maia, however, had no such inhibitions and retorted bluntly, "Don't you think you should be careful about making plans with Aiden's intended?" Maia's eyes snapped.

Neil ignored Maia's tone. "They are not intended yet. His declaration for her simply means that he is willing. Until she chooses, she is as free as any woman."

He turned to Aine, a lock of his light blond hair falling across his forehead exactly as Aiden's did. "I will await your decision about this evening." Neil nodded and bowed to Aine, and walked back toward the camp.

Maia crossed her arms in front of her and cocked her head. "Neil might really be interested in you, Aine. He isn't usually quite so formal around girls. It might be fun to see someone give my brother a challenge where ladies are concerned for a change. Of course, those two have always been best friends and fierce competitors. Like a couple of dogs always fighting over the same bone when there are ten other bones lying around."

"Well, Neil might be very nice, but I don't plan on being anyone's bone!" Aine said.

Maia roared with laughter and hugged Aine impulsively, "Then I will teach you the Hakan dance so you can make your wishes known whenever you like."

Uncomfortable with the talk of life mates and dances Aine said, "I'm not sure I'm ready for that yet." She stood and brushed her skirt. "I really should check on Zephyr."

Maia jumped up bubbling with excitement. "Can I come with you?" She walked briskly around the circled wagons never waiting for Aine's answer. "They may be near our horses, let me show you."

As they walked through the busy camp Aine smiled to see Maia sway her hips just a little more provocatively as they passed some of the young men. Zephyr and Dark Fire were at the edge of the horse corral and Maia's eyes widened with excitement. "Oh, she is the most beautiful pegasite I've ever seen. Is she as fast as she looks? Do you think I could ride her sometime?"

Maia's questions were fired one after the other in her enthusiasm, and Aine laughed. "I'm sure you could."

Zephyr nudged Maia, and she ran to a closed box at the horse shelter and grabbed carrots for the pegasites who greedily consumed them. *"This filly will need a strong stallion to keep her with the herd,"* Zephyr tossed her head as she spoke to Aine.

Aine agreed with Zephyr, Maia would need a strong man. "She likes you, Maia," Aine said.

Maia touched one of Zephyr's wings. "Of course she does, especially when I give her treats." Maia laughed as Zephyr crowded in front of Dark Fire and sniffed her hands. "You are so lucky, Aine. I would give anything to be an empath with a partner like Zephyr!"

Aine barely heard Dark Fire's thought it was said so quietly. *"I think she is an empath, but Tomah will know for sure."*

Assured that the pegasites were fine, Aine returned to her wagon and Maia ran off to her friends. Mabon was sorting through some items in one of his chests.

Aine helped him and started pulling Aiden's clothing from the cupboard. "Mabon, Neil invited us to join his family for dinner, but I really don't want to go, at least not tonight. Is that all right with you?"

Mabon kept his eyes on the task at hand. "Why is that?"

"He seems very nice, it's just that…" Aine hesitated. "I think he is interested in me, and I don't want to lead him on. But I don't want to seem impolite either."

Mabon regarded her with his kind gray eyes. "I will tell Neil that I have already accepted an invitation to join Aiden's family for dinner tonight, since in truth I have. Will that help?"

Aine nodded. "Thanks, Mabon."

Mabon smiled. "You can't really blame Neil for being interested in you, my dear. You are an attractive young lady and I wouldn't be surprised to see several of the young men interested." He noted the crease between her brows. "Are you ready to consider a more formal status with Aiden?"

She answered honestly, "No, I'm not ready for that."

"I understand. It is one thing to think you love someone and quite another to make a lifetime commitment."

Aine nodded and sighed. "I'm not sure Aiden understands that though."

Mabon chuckled. "He can be a bit impatient."

"I do love Aiden, Mabon," Aine said earnestly.

"And, he loves you too, dear, but you both must temper the passion with wisdom. There will be plenty of time for passion, and even more time for a life of love if that is what is to be."

CHAPTER TWENTY-TWO

Request for Sanctuary

"It is good to see the First Protector again," Zahra said as she folded the clothes Aiden had brought.

The men were outside repairing a wagon wheel, which left Aine alone for a few minutes with Aiden's mother.

"Why is Mabon called the First Protector?" Aine asked.

"Mabon was a fairly young man when he was given that role. He is of an age with Daved and knew my family when he was still a student at the school. Ever since the prophecy came to be, there has been a protector who would prepare the men in my family for the possibility of becoming the champion, for it is of our line that the champion will be chosen. That person is always called the First Protector."

Aine tried and failed to keep the concern out of her voice. "Does that mean that Aiden is the champion of the prophecy?"

Zahra's dark eyes met Aine's. "Does that possibility concern you, Aine?"

"It does," Aine hesitated, "Mabon thinks that I am the woman of the prophecy."

"Do you think that you are the woman, Aine?" Zahra's eyes were suddenly more intense.

"I honestly don't know. I met someone on the way here who made me think that I might be." She forced herself to meet Zahra's eyes. "I don't think I could save even one person let alone a whole world. I don't want to see Aiden in danger because of me."

The men had finished with the wagon and were walking toward Aine and Zahra. Aiden's smile was bright and his eyes merry as he got closer.

Zahra smiled. "Perhaps you shouldn't think about the prophecy for a while." Then she chuckled. "Aiden obviously loves you, I can see that in his eyes when he looks at you."

Aine smiled too. "Probably anyone can see that."

"He has chosen you, but he cannot make your choice for you. Since he has invited your claim, we will keep you close to us and you will be considered as one of our family if the elders permit you to stay. Meanwhile, you are an honored guest."

After dinner, people gathered at a huge bonfire. Log benches covered in brightly decorated blankets were set in a circle around the fire, and the older people sat on the logs while children raced in and out among the gathering adults.

Daved carried his violin and joined another man who carried a guitar. Maia ran ahead to join her friends and Mabon and Zahra followed deep in conversation.

Aiden squeezed Aine's hand as they followed the others, his eyes sparkling. "You're really going to enjoy this, Aine. The tribe gathers for evenfire whenever they wish to celebrate a special occasion. There are stories, music, and the best gypsy dancing you'll ever see."

She paused to watch as Zephyr leapt from the ground beyond the camp with Dark Fire just a blink behind her. Phelan bounded across the path and melted into the forest.

Dark Fire's smug baritone voice said, *"She is a wily creature and I will let her think she has out flown me, but I shall make sure she is safe."*

Sharing the happiness of his partner, Aiden pulled Aine into the shadows by a wagon and kissed her then they laughed and raced hand in hand to join the others. The music had already started with wild spirited instruments including drums, guitars, and tambourines; and, of course, Daved's violin. There was a thrumming beat from the small hand drums and younger men and women twirled in intricate dances. Even the children joined, laughing and collapsing into heaps when they tired.

Maia was often the center of attention spinning faster and faster, until a young man lifted her twirling high above his head and then threw her to the arms of another young man. Everyone watching laughed when she planted a quick kiss on his cheek and danced away.

Aiden clasped arms with a man named Meklush who was visiting from the Northern tribe. "Meklush is one of the best dancers in all the tribes. I think only my sister can keep up with him."

A younger boy ran to Aiden's side and whispered in his ear. Aiden nodded to a couple of older men and said, "One of the colts has gotten out and they need some help catching him. Stay and enjoy yourself, Aine, we won't be long." He squeezed her hand and started around the circle of people while Aine watched the dancers.

After a couple more dances Maia, now breathless but still tingling with energy, joined her. She laughed and grabbed Meklush's hand, "Come on Meklush! Let's dance the Metuska! Join us Aine, you'll love it!"

"Oh, no, I'm enjoying just watching," Aine said quickly.

Maia ignored her and grabbed Aine's hand pulling her to the center of the circle. "I'll get the other girls, Meklush, you get the boys," she said.

Meklush grinned and bowed, "As you wish, Maia."

Maia giggled, "Now that's how a man ought to behave."

Aine laughed nervously, "Maia, really, I'd much rather watch, I'm not a good dancer."

Maia tapped her toe resting her hands on her hips, her eyes snapping with vitality. "Well then, you'll have to learn won't you? If you're going to live with gypsies, you have to dance."

Aine sighed and looked at Meklush who shrugged. When they had gathered the other dancers, Meklush and Maia walked everyone through the moves slowly without any music. His ebony hair and eyes complimented Maia's rich beauty and their movements were incredibly graceful.

The young man who stood opposite Aine introduced himself as Ciro. There was a reddish cast to his hair, and every time he made a mistake he blushed furiously. Once the dance started, the dancers changed partners often as the music got faster and faster. Tired by their exertions some of the dancers bowed out, leaving three couples. Maia and Neil, Meklush and a pretty girl named Eris, and Aine and Ciro.

Aine was paired with Meklush after the first set and realized that Maia was right, he was a wonderful dancer and a good teacher. She followed his lead as they wrapped their arms around each other's waists, their heads turned sideways with their faces very close.

As the music got faster they whirled faster and faster until Aine felt dizzy. Meklush lifted her easily and turned her and she watched his feet intently. Soon she memorized the intricate footwork and started to really enjoy herself. Meklush kept her close in his arms and his friendly smile and his rich chuckle when she made a mistake was infectious.

When the music changed again, she was paired with Neil who danced almost as well as Meklush. Neil lifted her with only one arm, twirling her and she grasped his shoulder in alarm but laughed when he set her down easily. At the end of the dance all of the dancers stopped, frozen in place. Chests heaving from their exertions, Neil's lips were just inches from hers and he made no effort to move away.

Neil was a handsome man, and Aine felt a surge of attraction at the way his blond hair fell rakishly across his forehead and his muscular arms held her close. He held her just a moment longer than the other dancers, and suddenly realizing that people were watching Aine stepped back with her heart beating wildly.

Neil bowed and kissed her palm. "Thank you, Aine that was wonderful." His face held a worshipful look and Aine looked away feeling suddenly guilty.

She turned and saw that Aiden had rejoined the circle of people but his eyes were dark with emotion as he stared at his cousin's face. Then, ignoring Neil completely, Aiden smiled and walked to her and wrapped his arm tightly around her waist, leading her from the circle of dancers.

"Come, Aine, let me get you some cider, dancing is thirsty work." Obviously struggling to control his feelings, his voice was light. "Did you enjoy the dance?"

Aine didn't look at him. The last time she'd seen that dark look of anger in his eyes had been when she'd first met him and told him of her vision of Takkar. For a moment she felt overcome by Aiden's strong feelings, and even a bit angry at her lingering sense of guilt. In truth, she had enjoyed the dance, but now that momentary happiness disappeared.

"Yes, I did." She murmured softly, "Meklush is a good teacher."

Aine pulled away slightly and Aiden dropped the arm encircling her waist. Again his voice was light as if he had no concerns, but Aine knew he was trying very hard to cover his true feelings. "You're very good, especially for the first time." Aiden leaned down and whispered in her ear, "Maybe next time I can dance with you." He kissed her lightly on her cheek.

"Maybe," Aine replied.

She and Aiden chatted with some of the people standing at the edge of the circle as they sipped their cider. Every time Aine looked, Neil's eyes were on her. She tried to ignore him although once, when he caught her looking back, he raised his drink to her in a toast. Aine felt the heat on her face, unsure whether it was embarrassment or annoyance.

The music stopped and Zahra made her way to the center of the circle. Aiden whispered, "As shaman, my mother is the one to welcome newcomers. This is when you will be formally introduced and when she has finished, Mabon will request sanctuary. Then the elders will answer his request."

Aine took a shaky breath at Aiden's explanation having completely forgotten about the request for sanctuary.

"You mean, right here? In front of everybody?" she said.

Aiden patted her hand and gave a reassuring smile.

Zahra held up her hand and everyone quieted and waited. Glancing around the circle, she bowed her head to the older men and women seated on the logs closest to the fire.

"This evenfire we celebrate the homecoming of family, old friends, and welcome a new one." Zahra's dark eyes met Aiden's. "Son of my heart, it is with joy that I bless your return to our family and tribe." Aiden squeezed Aine's hand briefly and walked to his mother. They repeated the greeting they had made when he arrived, resting their hands on each other's shoulders, touching foreheads. This time when they raised their eyes it was Zahra's that glistened.

Daved joined them and at Zahra's nod he touched his heart and lips nodding to Mabon. "Be welcome, First Protector. Your presence gladdens our hearts."

Mabon joined them repeating the gesture, "I am warmed by your fire and your welcome, my friend. I would also seek your acceptance for Aine, who is my ward." Everyone turned to look at Aine and she swallowed nervously unsure what she was supposed to do.

Maia squeezed in next to her and whispered, "Come on Aine, it's all right." Maia walked with her to the center with the others and Aine grasped Aiden's hand holding tightly as if her life depended on it. Maia gave Aine's other hand a squeeze.

Mabon turned to face the elders, bowing low and showing great reverence. "People of the West Wind Tribe, I thank you for welcoming me once again into your midst." A natural speaker, Mabon paused and gazed around the circle of faces. Some people seemed vaguely interested, and others more distant. Aine noted the indefinable undercurrent of tension in the group.

Mabon said, "Aine is from a land far away and has not been with us long. She is partner to the silver pegasite that came with us." The people began to warm to him, nodding in recognition having seen Zephyr earlier.

Mabon took a deep breath. "I request the gift of sanctuary for Aine and myself." He paused, "But before you grant it, you must know that the Lost One seeks her."

A low murmur rumbled among the people but they quieted as Zahra raised her hand.

Mabon focused on the elders seated at the front of the gathering. "Takkar seeks Aine to steal the power of her gifts. He has attempted to summon her, first in her homeland, again at The School for Empathic Discovery, and once more on our way here."

The grumbling grew louder and Mabon waited for it to die down. "As First Protector it is my duty to keep all empaths from danger. I am also honor bound to protect those of the champion's line." Mabon's eyes rested briefly on Aiden and several of the elders murmured to each other.

"As senior trainer at the school, it is also Aiden's responsibility to see Aine, who is a member of his pod safe. While we seek the safety of the tribe, we do not wish to risk endangerment for you."

Aiden stepped forward and bowed to the elders as well. "May I continue, First Protector?"

Nodding, Mabon moved behind Aine and placed his hand on her left shoulder. Aiden looked at Aine and then back at the elders, a ghost of a smile touching his lips.

"I brought Aine to the West Wind Tribe for two reasons. First, and most important, so that she would be safe from the Lost One. The second reason is more personal." Aiden paused to take a deep breath and then he turned to face Aine, his dark blue gaze filled with hope and love, "My hope is that someday she will consent to become my life mate."

There was such hope and passion in his eyes that Aine felt her heart jump. Their eyes locked and suddenly nothing else seemed important. *"You really mean it, don't you?"* Aine spoke telepathically and Aiden's eyes widened with surprise. He nodded never looking away and took her hand. When they touched he whispered telepathically, *"With all of my heart."*

There was a sudden loud clatter of a staff banging against hollow log and Aine started and dropped Aiden's hand. The people who had been mumbling and whispering since Aiden's announcement were instantly silent and Aine could hear her heart pounding in her ears.

The elder rattled the staff was ancient and the dark intelligent eyes bored into Aine's. She had the feeling that the elder easily read her thoughts and Aine could not, for the life of her, determine whether it was an old man or an old woman.

Another elder rose and pointed at Aine. "If the Lost One seeks this woman, we must ensure that she cannot draw him to us, or that she is not in league with him. She must be tested."

A tinge of fear shot up Aine's spine. What did they mean by tested? She had expected to be questioned, but she didn't like the sound of this. Both Aiden and Mabon were focused on the elder who was still seated.

The old one's lips curled into a ghost of a smile and stood slowly. The dark eyes focused on Aine for a moment and then on Zahra, "Prepare her and bring her to the council tent."

Zahra bowed low, "Thank you for your concern and protection, honored one. I will bring Aine."

Not knowing quite what to do, Aine followed Zahra's example and bowed deeply as well. Zahra and Mabon smiled and Aiden beamed with pride.

Aine was surprised when the old one crossed to her and took her hands. The old bones were fragile but the grip was strong and Aine saw a wisp of kindness in the dark eyes. As they touched, Aine understood that the elder was a woman. Her eyes grew wide with surprise when the old gypsy spoke to her telepathically. *"I am Jodal, the eldest. Do not be afraid, child, the council will hear your story but all will be well."*

Aine felt like a heavy burden had been lifted from her shoulders and she bowed again. The elder straightened and Daved stepped forward to assist her on her way.

As they walked to her wagon, Zahra explained what was to come. "Since Takkar seeks you, it is not surprising that the elders wish to question you in more depth."

"How will they test me?" Aine asked nervously.

"Each time is different, so it is difficult to know for sure, but you need have no fear. Your gesture of respect toward the elder was perfect and they will see your honest heart, just as I do."

Once inside the wagon Zahra found a white robe hemmed with elaborate gold designs for Aine to wear. "Strangers, who come before the council of elders, must be robed in the garb of the family that sponsors them." Removing her clothes, Aine slipped the robe on feeling its silken fabric fall from her shoulders to her ankles. The thin, translucent material clung to her making her feel nearly naked.

"I will brush your hair so that it hangs freely and mark your cheeks with a special design unique to our family. It will show our wish that you become one with us."

Zahra changed into a robe similar to Aine's, but of a deep crimson color with silver decoration. Zahra painted golden shimmering designs on Aine's cheeks. Then Zahra fastened a headband with a similar design around Aine's forehead and a wide golden belt cinched tightly around her waist. Aine looked in the mirror and stifled a nervous giggle at her strange appearance.

As they stepped down from the wagon Zahra said, "The council of elders must be convinced that you are not one of Takkar's followers. They will ask you many questions, some of them quite personal, but you must answer honestly for they will know if you do not."

"Can I ask you or anyone for help if I don't know how to answer a question?" Aine worried.

"You may ask questions, but we may not be allowed to answer them. Just be yourself, Aine, once they are sure that you are not a threat, all will be well."

Great butterflies spun in Aine's stomach as the flaps of the council tent were pulled aside. Light from candles and lanterns bathed the interior a golden glow. A pleasant citrus scent rose from a brazier and kettle set in the corner. Seven elders sat on two tiers of benches and other leaders of the tribe stood behind the elders. Mabon, Aiden and Daved, also dressed in white robes, knelt on the rich rugs in front of the elders.

Zahra led Aine to stand in front of the elders and her face warmed as she walked past Aiden. She risked a peek at him relieved at his smile of encouragement.

Aine stood quietly as an old woman rose and came forward. She took Aine's face in her boney hand and peered into her eyes, silent for what seemed like an hour. Aine tried to relax and not fidget. The woman touched the designs on Aine's cheeks and turned away. Suddenly she turned again and thrust her face close to Aine's staring into her eyes. Caught off guard, Aine flinched back. The old woman's penetrating gaze never left Aine. "Have you been with a man, young Aine?"

Well this was certainly a great start. Aine swallowed and whispered, "No."

As the old woman continued to stare, Aine had visions of bolting from the tent and running as far and as fast as she could. Finally, to her relief, the old woman returned to her seat.

The next elder was an old man. He also peered at Aine's eyes just as the first woman had and Aine prayed that he would not get any closer. He gazed at her fiercely and grasped both of her hands, placing her palms on his chest. "Do you have more than one empathic partner?"

"No sir." Aine controlled her urge to pull away from him, yet continued to meet his gaze.

Suddenly, he shouted, "She hides the truth."

Aine jerked away from him but he stalked closer glaring into her face as he bellowed, "Do not lie! Tell the truth, do you have more than one empathic partner?"

Nothing had ever infuriated Aine more than being falsely accused of something, and she met his glare, eye to eye. Her face burned with anger and her green eyes were sparking. Her voice was low, but firm, "No sir, I have only one empathic partner." *And if you keep this up, I'm going to jump on her back and get the hell out of here!* She added silently.

The old man pulled a knife from his waist and brandished it in front of her. "She hides!"

Aiden shot to his feet and pulled Aine behind him. Mabon and Zahra rose as well and everyone froze.

Aiden's voice was tight. "She speaks the truth, elder. Aine has only one partner."

The old man turned toward the others and smirked. "She hides and he is blind to her. I sense the residuals of two pegasites, a wolf, and even a man."

Mabon bowed deeply to the old man, taking his time to show great respect. Speaking mildly, he was the voice of reason as he addressed them, "I was not aware that the tribe had a spirit finder."

Aiden, suddenly looked deeply embarrassed, knelt and touched his forehead to the floor.

Confused, Aine looked to Mabon for an explanation. Mabon nodded to her, his look offering confidence and support. "Aine speaks the truth when she says that her only empathic partner is Zephyr."

The elders mumbled among themselves and Jodal pounded her staff on the floor and commanded, "Silence! Let the First Protector speak." The other elders immediately touched their hearts and lips and Aine heard one of them murmur, "Forgive, Dear One."

Mabon continued, "The residuals you feel indicate Aine's multi-lingual abilities, which allow her to communicate with every empath." Seeing that, the man who had accused Aine looked confused and a bit angry. Mabon continued, "As you know, the ability to commune with empaths other than one's partner is extremely rare." Turning to Aine with a question in his eyes, Mabon said, "I am not sure what you sense when you say she has spoken this way to a man."

Aine explained, "I spoke telepathically to Aiden earlier. That is the first time I have communicated so with a man, but I learned the technique from another empath."

Aine boldly met her accuser's glare and time seemed to stop. Aine knew if the old man doubted her that she, Mabon and Aiden would have to leave. She bowed her head to wait for his response.

Still staring at her as if to glean the truth of her words the old man walked around her three times. Then he took her chin in his hand and stared into her eyes.

Unable to remain silent any longer Aine met his look clearly. "I have been taught to respect my elders and would never tell an untruth to them. You may not believe me and you may tell us to leave, but you will be wrong. To tell the truth is never wrong and I will never believe otherwise."

The old man's eyes opened wide and for just a moment he wavered, and then a slow smile relaxed his face. "She speaks the truth." He turned and shuffled back to his place with the others.

Just then they heard shouting from the camp.

"Please! I must see the Shaman. Please!" It was a woman's voice urgent and terrified.

Zahra went to the tent flap and opened it. "What is it?"

The man who had been guarding the door stepped aside. A young woman with a small girl in her arms stood outside. The child's face and chest were bleeding as if she'd been raked with knives. Tears streamed down the mother's face. "Please, Shaman. Please help."

"Lay her by the fire," Zahra ordered. She glanced quickly at Aiden, "Get my things." He raced from the tent.

They laid the child on a blanket by the fire and a woman knelt next to Zahra tearing strips from a blanket. Zahra wrapped them tightly around the child but almost as soon as she did, the cloth was saturated with blood.

Aiden returned with Zahra's basket and she worked quickly trying to staunch the wounds. Zahra looked at the mother who knelt trembling. "She has lost much blood, if I cannot stop the bleeding, she will die. I dare not give her anything for the pain as she is too weak."

The woman began to sob. "Oh, no, please…"

Aine watched them with her heart in her throat. To lose a child had to be the most terrible thing that any mother could experience. The scene before her faded and once again she saw the lady of the wood. She remembered how she had touched her with healing and suddenly she knew what to do.

Wending around the others, she knelt next to Zahra.

"Please, let me try to help."

What can you…" Zahra's voice faded as Aine reached forward to touch the child.

The minute her hands rested on the child's head a brilliant yellow glow surrounded them. Aine felt the tiny heart, thrusting the blood from the grievous wounds and extended her empathic touch within the small body. The pain was excruciating and Aine gasped and nearly retreated, but she forced herself to stay with the child. Following the path of the blood, she absorbed every gash.

Aiden was horrified to see the deep slices appear on Aine's body exactly in the same places as they were on the child's body. Her white robe was soon sopped with blood from her wounds. She swayed and he lurched forward to kneel behind her and hold her up. After a moment the wounds began to fade from Aine's body. Zahra uncovered the child's chest and found clear unblemished skin, as new as the day she was born. Likewise Aine's sympathetic wounds had faded as well.

The child's eyes fluttered open and she whimpered, "Mamma?" Aine sighed and leaned back against Aiden.

Tears streaming down the mother's face she held the little girl to her, kissing and soothing her. The young mother looked at Aine and murmured, "Thank you, blessed one."

More than one person in the tent had tears in their eyes. People helped the young mother lift the child but the little girl reached for Aine, "I saw your heart, holding mine. Are you my angel?"

Unable to speak for a moment Aine hesitated, and then she took the child's hand. "No, little one, I am just your friend."

The child sighed and closed her eyes in sleep.

Aine sat feeling weak and Aiden wrapped a shawl around her, covering the blood on her robe.

"Are you all right?" His brow creased with worry.

Aine smiled and raised her hand to touch his cheek and caress the fear from his eyes. "I'm fine. A little thirsty, but I'm fine."

Zahra had anticipated that and gave her a cup of wine with something mixed in. Everyone except the elders filed out the door. Zahra settled next to Aine. "Your help came at great risk and pain to yourself."

Tears filled Aine's eyes, "I could not bear the thought of a child so young being so hurt. I had to help her." The tears overflowed. "She looked so much like my little sister; I just couldn't imagine losing her."

Jodal came to join them and Aine stood as the elder touched her heart and lips and bowed very low before Aine. She was much shorter than Aine and she reached up to hold Aine's face in her hands. *"I have seen you in my dreams, young one. You are a gift to our world, one we shall cherish, and one we shall protect. Even before your healing of the child, I could see the truth of your testimony."*

Jodal spoke aloud to the others, "The words of the prophecy say, *'With this woman shall rest our fate.'* Thus it will be our honor, and our duty to offer sanctuary for you and do all that we can to keep you safe." Jodal touched her heart and her lips. "Be welcome, young Aine."

Each of the elders moved to touch Aine saying softly, "Be welcome. It is our honor to protect you." They shuffled slowly from the tent.

Aine swayed on her feet feeling as if everyone were far away. Aiden lifted her into his arms and carried her from the tent. He kissed her brow lightly, worry filled his eyes. "Are you sure you are all right?"

"Yes," she answered softly. "Just a little overwhelmed and very tired."

Daved who was walking next to them said, "Not surprising. Jodal is a very powerful elder. And what you did for that child was amazing."

Aiden took her to her wagon, and she couldn't wait to change out of the bloody robe, and bathe. Once cleaned up she dressed, feeling restless with her thoughts racing. Stepping from her wagon she saw the family seated around the fire nearby. Aiden rose quickly to join her.

"I'm too restless to sleep so I'm going to see Zephyr."

There was a crease of worry between Aiden's brows, "Do you want me to go with you?"

Aine shook her head, "I'm fine Aiden. I won't be long."

Phelan appeared from nowhere and walked silently next to her. It seemed that Mabon was leaving nothing to chance. Deep in thought she headed slowly toward the corral.

"Hello, Aine. How did things go with the Elders?" Neil stepped into the path, jolting her from her reverie. She stared at him blankly, as if seeing him for the first time.

"I asked if everything went well with the Elders."

"Oh, yes," she said. "They granted us sanctuary." Aine made a move to pass around him.

"May I walk with you?" His face was hopeful.

Aine felt annoyed. She needed to be alone with Zephyr and had no desire to be polite. Looking past him she frowned, unable to spot Zephyr in the corral or in the meadow beyond.

Neil waited for her response. Her impatience surged. "Neil, you're aware that Aiden and I—.

Before she could finish, he stepped forward and touched her arm. "When we danced I thought…" His voice trailed off.

Aine moved back shaking his hand from her arm. "I don't know what you thought, Neil, but right now I just want to find my partner and be alone with her."

He took one more step closer to her. "Aine…I…"

Her adrenalin percolating into anger, Aine turned and walked away from him.

CHAPTER TWENTY-THREE

Choices

As Aine stormed back to camp, Mabon stumbled out of his wagon, his face pale and drawn.

"Mabon! What is it?" Aiden asked.

Mabon sat down hard on a stool, "It's Jill. She and Jabari have been taken."

Aine's hands flew to her mouth, "Oh, no not Jill!"

"Impossible!" Aiden gasped.

"Rose and I have been in contact using my communication crystal. She told me that Rika returned to the school about a week after we left with a story about flying off and getting sick and rescued by a peasant family. Later she almost died from an overdose of something, but they couldn't get her to tell them what it was. Then despite her condition she snuck out to the stables and flew off on Sadid.

"Jill was on patrol that same night. She was waiting for Jared to pick her up, but when he got there, there was no sign of her or Jabari. A few days later a note wrapped in a strand of long blond hair was nailed to the front door."

"I have the blonde woman and her panther. Give me Aine or they will die." - Takkar

Aine's throat filled with fury.

"The school has all but closed down. They've taken the younger students to the garrison at Lorrit. They are crowded there but safe. Rose, Peter and the other senior trainers have stayed on at the school so that it appears to be occupied. They are working on a plan to rescue Jill and Andy."

Aine choked back tears. How many others would be hurt or even killed until Takkar accomplished his goal. If he learned that she was here with the West Wind Tribe, they would be next. Valiant though the men and women of the tribe might be in the defense of their homes and families, they would be no match for the Wuenta and Takkar's brutal men.

"Should I go back to the school?" Aiden asked.

"No, we need you here more than they do," Mabon said.

"We must tell the Elders." Aiden rose, "We will need to move camp immediately and set up a regular night watch."

Mabon glanced at Aine. "I saw Zahra and some of the others by the healing tent, can you go and tell her?"

"Yes, of course," Aine agreed, as the two men started for the council tent.

Watching them go, Aine shivered, wanting to bury her face in her hands or tear her hair out, she wasn't sure which. She felt responsible for Jill's capture as surely as if she'd been there and she knew that Takkar would make good on his threats to kill his captives if they didn't surrender her to him. She walked quickly to find Zahra and told her what Mabon had said about moving the camp. Then she started for the meadow to find Zephyr.

Zephyr was at the far side of the meadow grazing and they had just started walking back toward the gypsy encampment when Aine saw Neil walking toward her.

When he reached her, he smiled and held out a bouquet of wild flowers. "These are for you, Aine."

Aine almost wanted to laugh. His timing was either impeccable or atrocious and she tended to think it was the latter rather than the former.

"Well, you certainly are persistent," Aine said as she reluctantly took the flowers and inhaled their lovely scent.

"Think of them as a peace offering," he said. "I was out of line earlier and I feel bad about my advances."

They stood in silence watching Zephyr move past them to graze in the tall grass.

"She's a beautiful filly, Aine. How long have you been Zephyr's partner?"

"Not long," Aine answered as she struggled to think of a way to get him to leave.

"Do you need anything for Zephyr? I have lots of supplies, brushes and special feed."

"I don't think so. Daved has given us everything she needs. But, thank you."

Zephyr came to Aine and greedily reached for the bouquet of flowers, her lips extended. Both Neil and Aine laughed, breaking the tension between them.

"Let me put them up here until you're ready to leave." Neil placed the flowers in the fork of a tree and they continued to watch the filly as she grazed nearby.

Aine's smile quickly faded when a strange feeling filled her mind. As if under a spell, she turned to Neil and smiled seductively and reached up to stroke his upper arm.

"Your arms are so strong, Neil. I loved how they held me when we danced." Her voice now low and husky unlike her own.

Neil stood absolutely still with his mouth gaping wearing a confused look.

Aine was suddenly consumed with an overwhelming desire for Neil. She looked up into his face and ran her moist tongue over her lips in invitation. Neil stared at her in disbelief as she thrust her body against him. Her look was haunting and demanding and she wrapped her fingers in his hair and pulled his head to hers. She kissed him hard pressing her body to his. She groaned and murmured against his lips, "I need you, please. I need you now," she begged.

Neil opened his eyes surprised by Aine's uncontrolled hunger, and for a second he swore her eyes turned dark and her hair was now long and black.

In an instant, Zephyr's body crashed between them and roughly pushed Neil out of the way. Aine's face slackened and she collapsed into unconsciousness. Neil caught her and lowered her carefully to the ground. Her face was drained of all color and she was limp and very cold to the touch. Neil chaffed her hands and then sighed with relief when Aine's eyes fluttered open. Zephyr kept trying to nudge him out of the way but she settled when Aine reached up and touched her, their inner communication evident in Aine's eyes.

She sat up shakily with her face still pale. A sheen of sweat formed on her brow.

"Aine, what happened? Are you all right?" Neil took one of her hands, his eyes filled with concern.

"I'm fine," Aine lied as she pulled her hands away from him.

"Should I go and get Mabon or Zahra?" Neil watched her pale face earnestly.

"I'm fine, really. I just fainted, I think," she said pulling herself up from the ground.

"Zephyr, I'm all right, but please help me. I need him to go, can you figure out a way to make him leave?"

"Yes, but are you sure you do not need him? I felt something very strange before you fell, it was as if there was someone between us." Zephyr pushed her body abruptly between them. Neil stroked Zephyr's back, watching Aine over the filly's shoulder.

Finally Aine gathered the courage to meet his eyes. His cheeks glowed with embarrassment.

"What happened, Neil?"

"You don't remember?"

"No."

"You kissed me, Aine." His voice was soft.

Her blank eyes were filled with misery and despair.

He frowned, "You really don't remember?"

"No Neil. I don't. I need to be alone now?"

"I will leave, but I don't understand what happened. You certainly acted like you wanted me." Then he looked away color rising from his neck to his cheeks. "Aine, you didn't act like yourself and almost as soon as we kissed, you collapsed."

"I'm sorry, Neil." Aine turned away unable to meet his eyes. She took a deep breath and went to the tree to get the flowers. Keeping her voice cool she said, "Thank you for the flowers, Neil, and thank you for your concern." She looked up at him with her now clear eyes. "Something just came over me. I wasn't myself. I didn't mean to lead you on."

Quickly she added, "But, I need you to go. I'll be all right, Zephyr is here with me. Please take the flowers, if I accept these, you will think that I am encouraging your affection, so please take them." Aine saw the disappointment in his face and her own colored with guilt.

Neil did not look away, but he did not reach to take the flowers from her either. "Please keep them, Aine. Consider them a welcome gift and nothing more." Neil's confusion was written on his face, and then he said softly, "Maybe Zephyr would like them for dessert?"

Aine tried, but couldn't smile. She looked down at the flowers and back up at Neil. "I don't think they'd be very good for her and…" Aine stepped back closing her eyes trying to keep her voice from shaking, "…I wouldn't want Aiden to misunderstand."

Neil looked past her, a look of dismay and chagrin flashed across his features as Aiden sauntered toward them stopping just behind Aine.

Aine had sensed him before she saw him. She wasn't sure how much Aiden had seen or heard of their exchange.

"What could I possibly misunderstand?" Aiden drawled. "I wonder what could be misunderstood by giving such lovely flowers to my girl."

Though there was a stiff smile on his face, Aine could tell that Aiden was holding in strong emotion. Standing casually, his fists were tight, and he seemed poised for action.

Neil had the grace to blush. "They are merely a welcome gift," he said, and turned and walked away.

Aiden turned to Aine, his face unreadable, but she could see the pain in his eyes. Aine looked away from him wishing, for the first time since she had known him that he would leave her alone too, yet she could feel Aiden's emotions as if they were a part of the very air they breathed. She was suddenly weary of the conflict between the two men. She couldn't seem to think clearly and she was desperately afraid that somehow, if she didn't get control of herself, Takkar would. What just happened to her had been incredibly powerful, enough so that she had responded to the unspoken demand in his eyes thinking that Neil was Takkar. She had made no effort to diffuse it or protect herself. How stupid!

Aine looked up at Aiden with dull, lifeless eyes. She couldn't begin to think what to say to him so she simply stared at him.

Aiden pushed the stray hair from his forehead. He took the flowers from her hand and laid them at her feet. Putting his hands on her shoulders, he rested his forehead against hers.

"Aine, I do not know what happened between you and Neil. But it scared me. There was something there with him, but it wasn't you." He forced himself to relax his grip on her shoulders and spoke from his heart. *"You are everything to me; I have given you my heart and would give you my soul if I could. I cannot imagine what I would do if you choose someone else. I want you in every way you can imagine. I want you to share my life, bear our children and I want to grow old forever with you in laughter and love. I cannot imagine life without you. I am not a patient man, Aine, I have tried hard not to push, not to demand, but I don't want to lose you. Oh, Aine, I love you so!"*

Somewhere deep inside her heart, Aine was thrilled at his words, but that part of her was hidden and unreachable right now. It was as if a solid insurmountable wall had been built around her.

"Aiden, I have to go." Blindly, she stumbled away and Zephyr followed her down the path.

Mabon and Daved were packing up the wagon when Aine returned. When she brushed past them, he knew that something was wrong. Mabon stepped into the wagon and sat down opposite Aine. Her normal friendly face was closed with pain. Her eyes were dull and her demeanor was closed as if she had wrapped herself in a cloak of protection.

"What is it, Aine? What has happened?" he asked.

She didn't look at him, "I don't feel well. I'd like to lie down for a while."

He reached over and patted her hand. "All right, I'll wake you when dinner is ready."

Aine spoke few words during dinner and ate almost nothing. As the sun dropped below the trees she excused herself and went to see Zephyr.

Aine placed her cheek against Zephyr's neck. *"What is it that troubles you so, my mistress? What happened this afternoon?"*

"Oh, Zephyr, I had another vision of Takkar. I could feel him calling me. It was so powerful and for a moment I thought that Neil was Takkar and I kissed him. Then it was gone and there was no way to explain it to Neil. Aiden saw us. I didn't mean it. I couldn't help it!

"Takkar is never going to give up. He is going to hurt or kill people until he finds me. Maybe if I go away where he can't find me, he'll let Jill go. There would be no reason for him to keep her if I was gone."

Zephyr lowered her head, as Aine continued to pour out her heart. *"Aiden just told me how much he loves me. I'm sure he thinks that he is losing me. I do love him. But, I miss my home so much. I just can't stand this anymore. I don't want to be the woman of the prophecy. I just want to go home."*

Aine sighed and closed her eyes. She felt the touch of Zephyr's love and the pegasite's sadness too. *"It's different in my home world, Zephyr. There are no empaths there and no evil one. I'm safe there. He can't hurt me there. It's where I belong."* She let the tears flow down her face.

Zephyr's soft whiskers tickled Aine's cheek. *"What do you wish to do?"* The silver pegasite tossed her head and her white mane settled around her neck.

Aine brushed it back. *"I'm almost afraid to tell you, Zephyr, because it means that I must leave you."*

"I know that you will leave me. I have known from that day by the lake." Zephyr looked directly into Aine's eyes, her warm brown gaze showed the honesty of her thoughts. *"I do not want to lose you but if you must return to your family I will help you. I would rather live without you forever, than see you unhappy. I believe that you will return to us and I will wait for you."*

Hot tears flowed freely down Aine's face. *"I don't want to leave you either. I just have to try to get back. I love Aiden, but I will only hurt him more when I do leave. Everyone here wants something from me and I have nothing to give anyone. All I've brought is trouble and I have to get away, I have to."*

"We can go tonight, my mistress, meet me here when everything is quiet." The sadness in Zephyr's mental tone broke Aine's heart.

"I'm sorry Zephyr, I wish…" Aine hesitated.

The silver pegasite lifted her wing in the ancient gesture of protection among her kind, and Aine was comforted as she was wrapped closely to Zephyr's body.

"Perhaps if you can go back to your home world and take sometime there with your herd, you will regain your strength and your confidence. Whatever happens, I will always be here for you. That will never change."

As Aine thought about what Zephyr was willing to do for her, she realized the depth of the bond they shared. *"Thank you Zephyr, for understanding. I will find you when I am ready."*

Aine returned to the wagon and changed into her jeans and sweater. Wrapped in her black cloak she laid down on her bed feeling numb. She closed her eyes and tried to rest.

Outside she could hear the fire snap and crackle, and the strong scent of pine from the forest beyond filled the air as the cool damp of the evening arose. People were packing their wagons as the tribe would move on in the morning.

CHAPTER TWENTY-FOUR

Escape

A sickle moon drifted between murky clouds when Aine awoke and looked out of her wagon. She silently chastised herself for sleeping so long. Mabon snored on the other bed and she breathed a sigh of relief. He would not still be asleep if dawn was nigh, Aine knew he had agreed to take the morning watch.

She reached for Zephyr with her thoughts.

"I wait by the stream, my mistress," Zephyr replied.

Aine wrapped herself in the dark cloak, and stepped down from the wagon. She moved carefully past the sentries posted around the camp. Throwing her dark cloak over Zephyr's back, they walked into the forest. When Aine couldn't see any of the campfires she bounded to Zephyr's back, and in seconds they were high above the trees flying silently through the night.

Aine had decided to make her attempt near the whirlpool and Zephyr's strong wings beat steadily through the remainder of the night.

When they landed, Zephyr tossed her head indicating a stand of trees opposite them. *"The whirlpool is just through those trees and down the bank. The cave where you found me is on the other side of the stream."*

When they reached the steep slope, Aine touched Zephyr's neck and the filly turned her luminous eyes toward Aine. "I know you didn't want to come here again, Zephyr. You must leave as soon as I do. I do not want you to be captured again."

"It is you who must be careful, my mistress. I sense danger."

Aine strained to see around the clearing. The pale moon was not bright and she breathed softly, listening. There was only the faint rustle of wind in the pines and the distant trickle of the water from the stream.

Aine threw her arms around Zephyr's neck and held her, biting her lip to keep from crying. She had to do this, she had to be strong. Her heart broke as she tore free and stumbled down the steep bank leading to the whirlpool. Pausing once to look back up the slope, she saw the outline of Zephyr's body through the trees. Torn with indecision she hesitated. The thought of leaving Zephyr and Mabon, and most of all Aiden, clogged her brain but she forced herself to move on.

Her feet sank into the thick, wet leaves and she tripped and slipped toward the rush of the water below finally grasping a sapling just above the whirlpool. Gasping to catch her breath she prayed aloud, "Please God. Help me to do the right thing."

Settling next to the whirling water, Aine pushed her wavering thoughts away and knelt on her folded cloak. Pulling her talisman out from under her sweater, she glanced back up the hill one last time, but Zephyr was lost to view.

Gripping her pendant so hard that it cut into her palm she focused only on the sound of the water as it fell to the whirlpool below. For just a brief moment she felt a tingling sensation in her hand and that familiar hum and sense of movement and then it was lost. She tried again but the tingling sensation disappeared and the smell of the cold water and undergrowth intruded.

She closed her eyes shutting out everything, forcing her mind on her task. Her concentration grew focused and she became deaf and blind to anything but her goal. She sensed something, remote, just out of reach. Again and again she reached out with her empathic abilities to the world so far away, to home and safety. Chilled by the dampness she shifted and wrapped her cloak around her and tried again.

Deep in her trance, Aine was shocked when a sweaty hand covered her mouth and another, equally strong, pulled her arms behind her.

"*Run, mistress, run!*" She heard Zephyr's shout a moment too late.

Pulled roughly to her feet Aine kicked hard, trying to pull free. The man's hand loosened from around her mouth and she screamed. She saw the silver flash of Zephyr bolting to the sky through the trees and she was thankful that the filly had escaped.

The man dragged her up the slope and she kicked and thrashed only managing to connect once with his shins. He pulled her tighter dragging her to the edge of the trees by the clearing.

Zephyr hovered above them in the thin moonlight and the man pulled the cloak like a shroud around her. Her arms were pinned between the cloak and his body and she couldn't get her leg free to kick him. He laughed when she threw her head back hard, trying to hit him in the jaw but only connected with his chest.

Aine gagged at the sour smell of wine on his breath and she felt the hard handle of his knife as it dug into her side.

His rock hard arm felt like a steel belt across her chest and she grew dizzy just trying to breathe.

A horse pounded across the field and skidded to a halt in front of her. Silhouetted by the first glow of daylight against the sky behind him a tall man jumped from the heaving horse and strode to her. "Tie her hands behind her."

Aine shuddered, recognizing Takkar's voice.

Aine heard Zephyr cry empathically to Dark Fire telling him where they were…

"Fly away Zephyr."

Zephyr dove toward them trying to strike the men with her hooves.

"Shoot the filly if she comes again," Takkar said roughly and stepped closer to Aine.

She jerked her head back when he reached out to touch her lips. A satisfied smile grew on his face and he cupped her cheek in his hand. "You might wish to tell her to stay away, or we will kill her."

Aine called frantically to Zephyr, *"Fly away Zephyr, they will kill you! Please!"*

Takkar smiled and bowed, "We meet at last, my bride."

"How did you find me?" She asked sullenly.

"Oh, that." He laughed the sound of it grating on her ears. "Just a little trick from a friend of mine. She seems to have inspired some discord back at that filthy gypsy camp." He traced her jaw again with his finger and she clamped her teeth together to keep from screaming. "You have a marvelously strong aura."

So that was it, Aine thought. *It had not been Takkar after all who had placed that vision in Aine's mind. Whoever had done it had lost control when Aine fainted.* "Well, you might want to have a discussion with your assistant. Her attempt failed!"

"She is a novice compared to me!" Takkar boasted and grabbed Aine and kissed her hard. Aine twisted to the side and stumbled away from him. She felt a buzzing in her ears, much like a swarm of mosquitoes. At first it irritated her, and then it seemed intensely calming and compelling. She closed her eyes and pictured the Bach invention.

Takkar frowned when he realized she was resisting him.

"What is this? What has Mabon taught you?"

The fury in his voice would have frightened Aine if she had heard him, but only the music filled her mind.

He turned to his men, "Hold the horse. Once I'm up bring her to me."

The man pulled Aine against his body his arm wrapped around her chest. Takkar kicked him and drew his knife. "Do not touch her any more than you must or I will roast you over a slow fire and feed you to my dogs. She is mine and none of you will even look at her until I say so."

Aine's head lolled in a near faint and the man holding her loosened his arm in fear of Takkar. She let her head fall until she could see his hand and then she bit him, hard. Cursing he released his grip and she spun and kicked a solid blow to the groin. With her captor doubled over in pain, she sprinted to the safety of the dark forest dropping her cloak to the ground behind her. The rope on her hands was loose and she pulled one hand free as she ran.

"Fly Zephyr! Fly away!"

"I will not leave you!" Zephyr shouted.

"Stop!" Takkar shouted in her mind, the power of compulsion nearly overwhelming her. Aine stubbornly pictured the music again and sped up the tempo to match her race to the forest beyond them. She forced herself to run as fast as she could, the manic music throbbing in her mind.

Takkar's men were already stumbling toward her when a dark shadow dropped from the sky and neatly kicked one man in the head. He crumpled to the ground.

Aiden flew from Dark Fire's back a sword in his hand. Two of Takkar's men engaged him and he knocked both to the ground where they lay without moving.

Takkar had grabbed his horse and started to turn but Dark Fire landed in front of the frantic animal and reared trumpeting loudly. The horse threw Takkar, but he came to his feet with a sword in his hand as well.

"So you're not going to run away like a scared child, Takkar? What's wrong, no women to abuse?" Aiden taunted as both men circled each other slowly.

Takkar laughed, "Like I would be frightened of a filthy gypsy whelp. I cannot imagine for the life of me what she possibly sees in you, dear cousin."

Aiden lunged and the blades met with a spark and a loud ring. Takkar had a longer reach but he was not nearly as nimble as the younger man. Soon they both were breathing hard, fighting defensively.

Aiden watched him carefully waiting to discover a weakness. He was grateful to Peter for the hours they had spent practicing with swords at school. Then he saw how Takkar lowered his sword arm, just before he struck. The next time he did, Aiden sliced Takkar's forearm and Takkar hissed.

Tripping through the thick undergrowth that whipped her face and arms Aine didn't see the conflict behind her. One of the men still pursued her and he spat clipped curses as he blundered after her. Slapped savagely by the rebound of branches and briars, she was blinded by tears of pain as she ran. Something white flashed in the sky through the trees and she saw Zephyr evade two arrows as they whizzed past her.

"Zephyr go! They will kill you!"

"*Stay near the edge of the trees until you reach those boulders ahead. I will be there and we will fly.*" Zephyr flew off ahead.

Aine kept the clearing on her left as she caught glimpses of Zephyr ahead of her. She no longer heard the snap of the brush and the curses of the man who chased her and a wild surge of hope filled her as she plunged into a thicket to avoid detection. She sensed rather than saw that Zephyr was not far ahead.

She stopped for a moment her throat aching as she gasped for breath then lurched back into motion. The man blundered out of the thicket behind her.

"*Zephyr, he is too close. Fly past the rocks, I'll find you on the other side.*"

Wishing she still had the dark cloak to hide herself she ran swiftly along the narrow passage between a huge rock outcropping and the trees. Stumbling in the darkness with a painful stitch in her side, she sped toward a copse of pines ahead.

Scuttling through the thicket as quietly as possible she looked over her shoulder to see where her pursuer was. She never saw the root that tripped her, and she fell hard to the ground twisting her ankle.

The man heard her fall and started toward her. Aine pulled the loose debris and leaves over her to hide her bright sweater in the growing light of day. Her ankle throbbed painfully and she knew she would not be able to run fast enough if he found her again.

Meanwhile, Takkar's sword sliced wildly catching Aiden's forehead. Aiden had a hard time seeing clearly through the blood in his eyes and soon he heard other men approaching. He was now fighting three of them.

Takkar backed away and mounted his horse. "Finish him. I'm going for the girl."

Then, Dark Fire was there. He flew like an arrow toward Takkar and his horse and Takkar brandished his sword wildly shouting, "Kill the black demon, now!" Deftly, Dark Fire evaded the thrust of the sword swinging to the side. The powerful back hoof kicked the sword hand and the bones in Takkar's arm snapped releasing the sword from his hand. Takkar screamed in fury and pain. Holding his damaged arm against his chest, he turned for the woods and galloped away.

Dark Fire flew in twice more, downing men until Aiden fought the last man. When Dark Fire dropped to the ground and reared once more, the man dropped his sword and ran after the others.

The man searching for her stopped so close that Aine could hear his rasping breath and smell the stink of his sweaty body. He turned at the sound of screams from the fighting behind. Torn between his goal and the action behind, he hesitated and then moved to the open space beyond the copse to get a view of the fight. Takkar's men shouted to retreat. He looked once more at the brush where she hid and then he ran off toward them.

After the woods went silent, Aine crawled out to the edge of the copse. The sun traced the trees in orange light and she could make out three shapes on the ground, one moaning in pain.

Aine could not see either of the fighters clearly, but they seemed equally matched. They were just starting to tire when a huge dark shadow came at them from above, clipping the larger man in the side of his head with a hoof. He folded on himself and fell like a tree to the ground. It was only then that she realized that the other man fighting was Aiden.

Desperate to control her ragged breathing she heard Zephyr's triumphant shout, "*They flee!*"

Takkar astride his horse screamed from the edge of the clearing, beyond Aiden, "I will have her, cousin. You cannot prevent me. She will be mine! It is only a matter of time."

Aiden faced the woods where the sound of retreating hoof beats echoed and shouted, "She will never be yours, Takkar. Never!"

Zephyr landed in front of Aine and she limped over to grasp the filly's neck. Moments later Dark Fire landed next to them and Aiden slid from Dark Fire's back. There was a deep black slash on his forehead dripping into his eyes and a stain darkened his shirt but he paid no attention to his injuries and ran to Aine.

Aiden pulled her into his arms and held her so tightly that she could barely breathe. Then he kissed her soundly and shook her shoulders, his face torn and bruised and filled with anguish. "Did he hurt you?"

Aine shook her head, unable for the moment to speak.

"Why, Aine. What are you doing here?"

Dark Fire interrupted, *"We cannot stay here. They rouse, we must flee!"*

Aiden glanced back to see that one man was crawling around tapping the ground clearly trying to find his weapon. Only two had fled with Takkar but the other three had started running toward them.

Aiden pulled his cloak from Dark Fire's back and wrapped it around Aine, lifting her to Zephyr's back. Then he raced to Dark Fire and with one powerful down stroke, the pegasites vaulted to the sky as an arrow whizzed past them.

The fully risen sun streamed over the bright meadow where they landed, miles away from the whirlpool. Aine slid off Zephyr's back and fell to her hands and knees when she tried to put her weight on her sore ankle.

Aiden jumped from Dark Fire's back and raced to help her up. "He did hurt you! I should have killed him!"

Aine held onto Aiden's shoulders. "No, I tripped while I was running and twisted my ankle. I'll be all right."

"Let me see." Aiden picked her up and carried her to a broad rock. The warmth of the sun on the surface felt wonderful. He knelt in front of her to look at her ankle, gently removing her shoe and sock. He circled it with his hands and she winced.

"It's twisted and bruised, but I don't think it's broken." A trickle of blood from the cut on his forehead dripped down catching in his eyebrow. He absently wiped it with the back of his hand.

"Get some water and a rag," she ordered.

He looked up in surprise but tore a swatch of cloth from the lining of his cloak and wetted it with his water flask. He handed the wet rag to her thinking she meant to wrap her ankle with it to reduce the swelling.

"Take off your shirt, you're bleeding," she said.

He pulled the shirt over his head, grimacing in pain at the wound in his shoulder. His shirt caught in the dried blood and the movement reopened his wound. The flow of blood snaked down his side and back.

Aine dabbed the gash with the cool cloth and then pressed it hard until the bleeding slowed. She tore another long strip of cloth from his cloak and bound it tightly around his chest, staunching the flow of blood. She bit down on her bottom lip as she worked, cleaning the cuts on his forehead and several others that his torn shirt had hidden. She wrapped another strip from the cloak around his head to stop that wound from breaking open again and when she was finished she picked up the water flask and drank and handed it to Aiden.

"Let me try to heal you," Aine said.

"No, I will be fine and I don't want you to be too weak to ride," he said.

As he tilted his head back to drink, she noticed how beautiful his body was in the golden blaze of the new sun, even though it was torn and beaten. His long black hair lay tangled and curled around his face, and the red headband against his darkly tanned skin made him look like a handsome Indian. He lowered the flask and met her eyes with the midnight blue of his own.

"I think we can rest here for a few minutes, and then we must be on our way. We'll need to get back to the tribe and warn them." He lifted the shirt to put it back on and he inhaled sharply at the pain and she leaned down to help him.

Aiden rinsed the cloth and wiped her face where the branches and brambles had scratched her. As he finished, Aine grasped his face in her hands and joined her lips to his. Aiden leaned in and responded with a deep kiss of his own, his good arm pulling her closer.

She asked him how they had known to come and was surprised when Dark Fire tossed his head, *"I make it a point to know where the fillies of my herd are."*

Aiden chuckled at Dark Fire's response and Aine's mouth quirked. He shifted to sit in front of her, leaning against the rock. "When you and Zephyr left the camp, Dark Fire alerted me. Mabon suspected that you would come here and we were almost here when Zephyr called."

Aiden reached down and touched her talisman as he gazed deeply into her eyes, "You were trying to go home, weren't you?"

Aine nodded. Emotion filled her throat and tears stung her eyes, she looked away. "But it didn't work. So I guess you're stuck with me."

Aiden drew in a deep breath there was determination in his eyes. "Do you want to try it again, now? I'll go with you. I can watch while you try and keep you safe."

"It won't work, at least not now," Aine replied simply. "Takkar could still be lurking around the whirlpool. If we went back it could endanger us all." Aine brushed back his hair as it fell across the band she'd tied on his head. "Like everyone has told me, I'm just not ready yet. I have to trust that when the time is right, I will be able to go home."

Aiden's eyes met hers with honesty. "I know staying is not what you wanted, but I'm glad it didn't work. I can't even think what I would have done if you had been seriously hurt."

"You really would have gone back and helped me to try again wouldn't you?" Aine gazed at him, her eyes filled with wonder.

"Yes, if that is what you wanted to do."

"We all would, little sister," Dark Fire added.

Tears of joy filled her eyes at the love and dedication that Aiden and Dark Fire shared. Her heart was as light as a butterfly and she gave herself completely to the feeling.

Aiden's indigo gaze met hers and she let the powerful love she felt for Aiden show at last. Her love for this man had started that day by the lake, when he had protected her the first time, but she had been too afraid to allow it to grow. Now she owed this man her life, but she owed him even more than that.

"Aiden, I have to tell you why."

"No you don't." He looked away embarrassed then he sighed and took her hand.

"Yes, I do." Aine spoke softly, "I've been torn all along between my desire to go home and…" she hesitated and then looked at him, the love shining from her eyes, "…how I feel about my purpose here. I've been unprepared for Takkar before and he almost had me several times. But when I saw him today, I realized that I could defy him. I was strong enough to resist his compulsions at last."

Aine blushed, "At least long enough to get away from him.But it won't happen again. I know that now. I will never be his, Aiden. No matter what he tries to do, he will not succeed."

Her smile shone as bright as the sun and she dismissed Takkar from her thoughts. She touched Aiden's cheek lightly with her two fingers, letting the clear honest intensity of her eyes meet his. "In my world there is a saying 'If you love something set it free. If it returns, it is yours, if it does not, it never was.'"

A look of wonder grew on his face.

"I will always return to you, Aiden. Always, my love."

It was at that moment that Aine decided she would dance the Hakan dance for him. He loved her, and she certainly loved him. He had risked his life to rescue her and was willing to help her get home if that was her true desire. To be willing to help someone you love, and risk losing them forever to do it, was the ultimate gift. She would never again turn away from that kind of love. And the thought of a commitment to Aiden filled her with hope for the future. Their future.

Aiden pulled her to her feet and looked down into her eyes. His smile grew as wide as hers and he kissed her very gently.

"I am very tired, and awfully hungry, can we go now?" Zephyr pleaded. Aine laughed and hugged her filly's neck. "Take us home my friends." The two pegasites lifted them to the morning sky.

CHARACTERS

Aine (Aw-nay)—Seventeen-year-old girl from the small village of Riverdale in our world. Empathic partner to Zephyr, a silver and white pegasite filly. She is the woman foretold in the prophecy to save Drayon.

Aiden (Aay-den)—Twenty-one-year-old man, gypsy heritage and empathic partner to Dark Fire (black pegasite stallion).Blue Pod Senior Trainer, foretold of the prophecy to champion Aine in fight against the evil one Drayon.

Andy—Empathic partner to Tikat a hawk (male) red pod later orange pod.

Brendan—Orange Pod Senior Trainer, partner Shadow, a dark gray pegasite stallion.

Blair—Chancellor of Kierst, the largest city on Drayon.

Caldor—Grand Duke of the stony river city of Dorash.

Carolinda (Care-o-lin-dah)—Aine's older sister in Riverdale (recessive empath).

Conval—Wolf partner to Lara (indigo pod).

Dad—Aine's father (full empath).

Dancer—Pegasite filly, appaloosa markings, partner to Micah. Violet pod leader.

Daved (Dah-veed)—Aiden's father (recessive empath).

Dark Fire—Black pegasite stallion, partner to Aiden mate to Zephyr.

Deidre (Dee-ear-drah)—A portal guardian on Drayon, Mabon's wife, former empathic partner to Mocha, a chocolate-colored pegasite stallion.

Danae (Da-nay)—Aine's best friend in Riverdale.

Dorash—The second largest city on Drayon.

Drayon—Another world home of the prophecy as well as empathic animals and people who can hear them speak telepathically.

Dunla (Doon-lah)—Phelan's mother all black female wolf mated to Filtiarn.

Empath—A person who is able to communicate telepathically with their partner animal on Drayon. Most people with this ability can only hear one animal and that one is bonded to them in a special link. People are either full empaths or recessives (carry the ability to bear empathic children).

Faye—A pixie (fairy-like) creature, lives at the S.E.D.

Filtiarn (fil-tea-arn)—Wolf partner to Serant and previous director of the SED, also Phelan's father.

Garson—Lula's mentor on Krialla the training world for guardians.

Ghanda—White pegasite mare, partner to Jared (green pod), twin to Tomah, a white stallion.

Gilded—One of the first pegasites, partner to a river nymph.

Hakan Dance—A very sensual dance young gypsy girls perform to indicate desire for a certain man. If the man accepts her request they are betrothed and commit to become lifemates.

Istas—Female wolf pup empath, offspring of Phelan and Noir, partner to Kira.

Jenna—Aine's younger sister 9 years old, also a full empath.

Jessie—Aine's neighbor in Riverdale.

Jill—Empath, Green Pod Senior Trainer, partner a black panther Jabari (Jab-a-ree) also a seer.

Jodal—The eldest of the elders in the gypsy camp full empath.

Jared—Blue pod empathic partner is a pegasite mare named Ghanda.

Kierst—The largest city on Drayon.

Krialla (kree-al-la)—Training world for Lula and other guardians.

Lula (loo-lah)—Primary guardian for Aine's world and Drayon. Alien empath, partner a goat named Priscilla. Aine's mentor in Riverdale.

Larimore (Lair-ih-more)—A prison on Drayon.

Lara (Lah-rah)—Woman empath Indigo Pod Senior Trainer, wolf partner Conval (male).

Mabon (Mah-bahn)—Also known as the First Protector, empathic leader of the same generation as Rose. Partner to Phelan, alpha male wolf. Takkar's arch enemy.

Mother—Carolinda, Aine and Jenna's mother (recessive empath).

Maia (May-ah)—Aiden's sister full empath.

Meklush (Meek-loosh)—A man, gypsy of the Northern tribe.

Micah (My-kah)—Female Healer from the S.E.D, also Violet Pot Senior Trainer, partner to Dancer, an Appaloosa filly, husband Brendan (orange pod).

Multi-lingual—An empath that is able to hear all of the other empathic animal partners. At this time there are only two known multi-linguals, Aine and Deidre.

Nora (Nor-ah)—Aine's mother.

Noir (No-war)—A she-wolf alpha female, mate to Phelan, mother of Istas.

Neil—Aiden's best friend and cousin (recessive empath).

Merlin—An owl, Rose's partner.

Pegasite (Peg-ah-site)—Flying horses descended from the original Pegasus. Indigenous only to Drayon.

Priscilla—A goat, Lula's empathic partner.

Penny—Aine's Irish Setter in Riverdale.

Phelan (Fay-lan)—Mabon's partner, an alpha male wolf, mate to Noir, father of Istas.

Peter—Red Pod Senior Trainer, empathic partner white pegasite Tomah, also Rose's son.

Pods—Training groups at the S. E. D. Colors are those of the rainbow: red, orange, yellow, green, blue, indigo, violet. Each pod has a senior trainer who reports to Rose, the school's administrator.

Ravyn—Female sorceress who taught Takkar how to use compulsion.

Rose—Empath who runs the School for Empathic Discovery (partner Merlin an owl).

Rika (Rick-ah)—Female student (red pod) from the S.E.D. in league with Takkar. Partner Sadid, a brown pegasite stallion.

Runik—Takkar's father (full empath, never bonded).

Sperrinal Swamps—Swampy area with deadly quick sand and whirlpools.

S.E.D.—School for Empathic Discovery. Training place for empathic partners on Drayon.

Serant (See-rahnt)—Director of the S.E.D. before Rose.

Sadid (Sah-deed)—Rika's pegasite partner, a bay color stallion.

Tanya (Than-yah)—Takkar's mother, full empath, never bonded.

Takkar (Tak-kar)—Empath also known as the evil one or the last one. Seeks to use compulsion to control his world and others.

Turat (Too-rat)—One of Takkar's followers (male).

Tran (Trahn)—A village blacksmith friend to Aiden's tribe father of Kirt and Kira.

Wuenta (Woo-ehn-tah)—Reptilian beast-like creatures that Takkar's defenders use in battle.

Zephyr (Zeff-er)—Silver pegasite filly, Aine's empathic partner.

Zahra (Zah-rah)—Aiden's mother, a shaman or healer to the tribe (full empath, never bonded).

About the Author

Cheryl Jackson Poules

 Cheryl's initial foray into creative writing began in fifth grade when she became the organizer and editor of her school newspaper, *The Editorial Star.* She continued creative writing through high school where her first published article was an interview of Robert Kennedy. She has published several short stories and poems in local papers and media.

The setting of the Empaths of Drayon is a small town in western New York where she grew up. Cheryl is a music teacher in Colorado where she lives with her husband and two Aussie mix dogs. This is Cheryl's first novel, and she is busy working on the next two books in the Crystal Traveler Series.

www.ingramcontent.com/pod-product-compliance
Lightning Source LLC
Chambersburg PA
CBHW030656260626
47157CB00007B/2676

* 9 7 8 0 9 8 3 6 1 4 4 0 1 *